HOSTAGE

ANNIKA MARTIN & SKYE WARREN

**I never knew when he'd come to me. Only that he
would.**

I'd never even kissed a boy the night I met Stone.
The night I saw him kill. The night he spared my life.
That was only the beginning.

He turns up in my car again and again, dangerous
and full of raw power. "Drive," he tells me, and I have no
choice. He's a criminal with burning green eyes, invading
my life and my dreams.

The police say he's dangerously obsessed with me,
but I'm the one who can't stop thinking about him.
Maybe it's wrong to let him touch me. Maybe it's wrong
to touch him back. Maybe these twisted dates need to
stop. Except he feels like the only real thing in my world
of designer labels and mansions.

So I drive us under threat, until it's hard to remember I don't want to be there.

Until it's too late to turn back.

CHAPTER ONE

~BROOKE~

I SMILE WIDE for the cameras from the *Franklin City Herald-Star*. The shots that get into the newspaper tomorrow will show a lucky girl surrounded by her friends and her adoring parents, daughter of one of the most powerful families in all of Franklin City, at her sweet-sixteen ball. If you're looking at them online, you might enlarge them and see the pale pink embroidered roses around the sleeves and bodice of the white cocktail-length Givenchy gown I'm wearing.

What you won't see is the blood in the water.

My dad always says you can't let them smell blood. If the world is sharks, this whole party is about swimming past them, around them. Fooling them into believing you're okay.

The pictures will never show that I've eaten two strawberries today because otherwise I won't fit into the gown my mom bought from a consignment store. It's a size too small, but it was cheap and this season. I told her it wasn't a problem. I'd make it fit. People have to think it's new.

Last year's gown is blood in the water.

The cameras will never pick up that the smile on my father's face is pure desperation. People see our family name—Carson—on cranes all over the city. Why would he be anything but happy?

They can never know that the great Carson Development empire is crumbling, little by little, and that this party is a lifeline. Or that I've hardly gotten any sleep over the past few nights because I keep having nightmares where I forgot to confirm the flowers or update the RSVP count for the caterers or get the DJ deposit in, and the party is deemed a disaster.

My mom couldn't do much of the planning—she's been working double shifts at a bakery in the next town to pay for this. Nobody can know that.

Nobody can know that this party is an elaborate charade.

Every member of Franklin City's upper-crust elite throws their daughter a sweet-sixteen party. It's our version of the debutante ball. Not to do it means you're not one of the group. People do business with their kind.

Tomorrow morning, as people click to the *Herald-Star* on their phones or tablets and sip their coffee and flip through the pictures, they'll see my mother smiling proudly, her slender arm draped around my shoulders.

What they won't see is the tiny, burning little spot

on the back of my arm where she pinched me to remind me of my posture. They won't see how ashamed I felt that I'd forgotten again. Because I'm so tired. Because I'm trying so hard.

The cameras won't pick up that she just whispered, through her bared teeth, *Try to look like you care at least a little, Brooke.*

They won't get that her words are a punch in my chest, because I know I'm not what she needs. I know that I'm letting my parents down in a million little ways.

But I'm trying; I really am. They can't see how I feel like curling up in a corner and dying. Because I love them, and I know they love me even though I'm not the popular size-two daughter with perfect skin and manners that they need right now.

So yeah.

Nobody can ever know that my glorious smile is actually cracking me in half. I know how to smile like nothing's wrong. It's a great talent of mine.

I am one of the lucky ones in Franklin City—I know that. A lot of people south of downtown went to bed hungry tonight, and I'm surrounded by mounds of foie gras and lobster, most of which will be thrown out. Not only do I feel guilty about my sweet-sixteen party, but I feel guilty for feeling guilty.

I suck in a breath through gritted teeth, still smiling for all I'm worth.

Halfway there.

My vision is almost blurring, but I smile and say hello to one of the investors my dad is courting for this big outdoor mall deal he's putting together. I try to remember the details. He's been to our house. We let him use our vacation home before we secretly sold it.

The investor asks me about my schoolwork, and we're having a good conversation—at least I think we are until I look over and see my mother's ashen face, her mouth a tight line under her powdered nose.

My heart starts pounding like crazy because I don't know what I'm doing wrong, and I'm so hungry and exhausted that I'm suddenly fumbling my words and saying *uh* and *um*, and we've practiced how many hours on that? He wishes me luck with exams and leaves.

Mom grips my arm tight enough to make the skin white. I hold my breath, wondering where I screwed up. Afraid to know but needing to. "You called him Mr. Kimball," she hisses.

"But that's…" I'm about to say that's his name when I realize it isn't—Mr. Kimball is one of his rivals. They drilled me on everybody's names right before the party, but I'm not thinking straight. My throat feels thick. "He didn't—"

"Correct you?" Her gaze shoots after him. *He's too polite.* She doesn't have to say it.

"Should I—"

"No!" she says. Meaning, *don't go after him, don't apologize.* Meaning, *the damage is done.*

She wouldn't say it, though. Not here and not like that. Somehow that makes it worse.

Why are the things parents don't say the most painful?

Right then the Shaffer twins come up. They're beautiful and good at everything. They were my friends in tennis camp, but teens smell blood in the water way faster than adults. Enthusiastic greetings turn to frozen smiles and awkward excuses to leave.

Leaving before the dinner—not a good sign.

Slowly but surely, I'm ruining this. There's so much more at stake here than a party. There's my dad's company. My mother's social standing. I can feel her eyes on me as I smile and thank them for coming.

It's then that it happens—this feeling like my chest is expanding, filling with stuffed-down sobs that won't be contained any longer. My eyes are hot, and I'm sure my face is red as a cherry. I mumble something about going to the bathroom.

Mom squeezes my shoulder. "Take your time, honey," she whispers.

And I know she says this partly because she needs me to calm down and stop ruining things, and partly because she loves me and, really, this is hard on all of us, which gives the sobs even more power. They feel like fists, pounding up from inside my chest and throat. So I'm walking through my party crying, but lucky for me, I know how to smile so brightly that it makes people not notice the shine of my eyes.

I see a trio of neighbors from Mom's bridge club heading into the bathroom. No going there, then. I pass it by and push through the next door, a swinging door, which leads to the food-staging area.

Some of the caterers look at me funny. I manage a wave. "Looking good out there. Maybe another round of canapés on the far side." I keep walking, a wild girl in a gorgeous, secondhand dress, cheeks burning, chest feeling like it might explode with undetonated sobs.

I push through another swinging door, heading into the kitchen. Stainless steel counters display the delicious food I can't eat. Curious pairs of eyes monitor my progress. I keep going, heading for a red exit sign.

I burst out the door. I shut it behind me.

A sob escapes, and then another and another. I stand there, full-on sobbing.

I sound pathetic.

I'm a Givenchy-wrapped crazy person in the lonely service parking lot of the Franklin City Starlight Ballroom.

Even now, even crying, I'm thinking about appearances. About family and duty. I cry strategically, avoiding mascara stains on the dress. I stay standing, because if I sit, I might pop a seam. This isn't my dress. This doesn't even feel like my party. *Appearances.*

A moth flies into my updo, and I bat it out. Then another flies in. Suddenly I'm doing this whole ridiculous sobbing dance. It's the light above the door, attracting bugs. "Shit!" I stumble, sobbing, slapping my hair, into the shadows between catering vans.

No more strategy, no more duty.

My hair is utterly ruined and maybe even has dead moths in it. At least it matches my mascara-smeared eyes. I have to laugh-sob at that. I'm a mess.

It actually makes me feel a little better. So stupid.

I have to get back. Fix my face. Retwist my hair into a simple bun. *Just one more minute*, I tell myself.

It's bad that I'm gone, but it would be even worse to go back like this. I open the bejeweled clutch that hangs from my wrist and check my phone through bleary eyes. Twenty minutes until seating for dinner.

I start to pull myself together, and that's when I hear the footsteps. They're loud—somebody running from far off, way down the alley, maybe, running toward where I'm standing. My pulse pounds.

I'm not even supposed to be back here.

I swipe at my cheeks, determined to stay silent as a mouse until they pass.

Another set of footsteps sounds out. The first is drawing nearer.

Being chased? I pull deeper into the shadows to the sound of gravel churning, crunching. They're close now—just a few feet away, behind the van.

Close enough that I hear loud breathing. A grunt of surprise. I stiffen. Suddenly there are loud *thwaps* and *thwocks* and guttural groans of pain. Hair rises on the back of my neck.

I've never heard these kinds of sounds before, but the animal instinct in me recognizes them as deep and real and serious. Life-and-death serious. There was figurative blood in the water inside that party, but out here, the blood is real.

More *thwaps*. I'm holding my breath, shocked and horrified. Can this be happening? Someone is being hurt, really hurt. This isn't about canapés. It's not about appearances.

A man—the attacker, I think—is gritting out questions. Something about a cop—"You fucking tell me…gimme a name…" Something else—foreman or Dorman. "…working for Dorman…frame my friend…gonna pay…"

The man is crying and begging. "I don't know…don't know…please."

A crunch of gravel. The voices get more distinct: "That's right, you beg me. You beg me for your fucking life."

Oh God. I have to do something. I have to.

I clutch my bag, creeping to the van window, and I catch sight of them—it's one guy hitting the other one. Beating him. The one being hit is older—gray hair. He looks faintly familiar. Was he at the party? Or in the kitchen? Is he being robbed?

Maybe I should help. I could go out there. I could…

Then I see the attacker's face, wild with fury.

I freeze.

He's a savage god with green eyes and a shaggy black crown. He's so far gone in anger, he seems more animal than human. He kneels on top of the older man, smashing his face over and over.

With shaking hands, I punch in my phone unlock code. I need to call somebody. I need to save this man. Except I keep getting the code wrong, and the hitting goes on, and I know deep down that he's dying, that he doesn't have the twenty or ten or even five minutes it would take for help to arrive.

It's him or me. It's stand here and let a man die, or do something—for once in my life, do something that's not wearing a dress and smiling and getting it all wrong.

So I run out there. I watch myself do it, like a movie almost. "Stop it," I yell.

The attacker just keeps on, a dark storm, all fists and fury. My presence means nothing to him. My words don't touch him. It's as if I'm yelling at thunder.

My heart beats out of my chest. I've risked everything, come out in the open, but it's not enough. I stamp my foot to get his attention, crushing gravel beneath my mother's Louboutins.

"The cops are coming," I say.

The man stills and looks up. It's a shock when it happens, even though I've been trying to get him to see me. His eyes seem to blaze into my chest, hot and bright.

Breathless, I back away.

He stands, leaving the man in a groaning, whimpering heap.

I retreat slowly, showing him my phone, as though that might protect me. "Cops are coming," I say again. A lie. I couldn't punch in the code.

He's coming at me, expression unreadable. He's a few years older than I am—late twenties, maybe.

My back hits something hard. The van.

He keeps coming. I try to spin and run, but he grabs my arm and slams me back into the van. "Where do you think you're going, little girl?"

I stare up at him, panting.

His warm breath is a feather on my nose; the heat in his eyes invades me. He grabs my hair and tilts my head back, forcing me to stare into his face, as if he's trying to read my eyes.

A moment later, he looks up at the night sky. He seems almost wolfish, and I'm conscious, suddenly, of my bare neck so close to his snarling mouth. I wonder if he's staring at the moon. It's like he's going to howl or something.

Then I get it. He's listening for sirens.

"You're a little fucking liar."

"No," I whisper.

He studies my eyes. Can he tell? I don't think so. At least he's not so sure. "Fuck," he says. He loops an arm around my neck, and he's fumbling in his pocket. I gasp when he pulls out something shiny—a knife or piece of metal or something. He jams it against the passenger-side window of the van, down into the door part, jamming and thrusting; then he pulls it up and jerks open the door. The alarm blares into the night.

"Get in there."

He doesn't wait for me to move; he shoves me in and shuts the door. Then he goes around and pulls open the hood.

Should I try to run? Could I, in these heels?

The alarm stills. He slams the hood, grabs the half-dead guy, and drags him over behind the van. I hear the door open, feel the thump as he throws the man in.

My throat is tight. *Why did I try to help? Why did I leave my party?* I put my hand on the door handle.

"Don't do it if you want to live," he growls, getting into the driver's seat. There's no way he can see my hand. It's like he knows. "You want to live, you do not move." He rips something out of the steering column. He works calmly, like a machine. Alarms and witnesses and murders, he doesn't care. And I can't help but be amazed, because I was out here crying because I called somebody the wrong name. This guy, he's cold as ice.

The van starts up. He peels out backward. He rams it into drive, and we're off.

"Show me your phone."

I hold it up. My hand is trembling. This feels surreal. Maybe it's a dream.

He grabs my wrist—hard. No dream. "Fire it up."

"Ow," I say.

He lets me go. I hit the button, and the thing lights up. There's red around my wrist. It's the other man's blood.

"You can't just kill him," I say, voice shaking.

My iPhone lights his face from below, illuminating the curves of his thick lips. I can see the quiver of the nostrils that form the base of his chunky nose, the thick lashes that line his huge green eyes. He looks like the devil—the devil as a primitive young thug, seething with hate.

And then he smiles. His smile is like nothing I've ever seen. As if he has so much hate and anger in him that it flipped over to a kind of evil beauty.

Again he speaks. "Fire. It. Up."

Again I try to punch in my code. We're stopped at a light, and he's watching. I get it this time.

"Recents," he growls. "And if you even touch that door, I'll snap your little neck."

I stare down at my phone. He'll know I'm lying if I show him. He'll kill me if I don't. I hit recents and turn the screen to him. He grabs it and looks at the call history, showing no 911 calls, then up at me, his devil face red in the light. "Thought so." He shoves it in his pocket. The light turns green, and he speeds off.

I glance back at the unmoving shadow in the back of the van. "You can't just kill that guy."

"He's already dead," he says.

"I can hear him breathing. Drop him at a hospital. You've proved your point."

He turns to me. His wild fury has mass. Weight. It forces the breath from my lungs. "You think I've proved my point?"

There's this buzzing in my ears. Everything feels unreal, or maybe it's all too real. I try to say something, but my mouth is dry.

He doesn't even have tattoos like regular bad guys. He has some sort of design etched into his right forearm—crude scars that seem to form an *X*. When I dare to look a little more closely, I see that it's crossed weapons of some kind.

His voice is a rumble, as if it's surging up from an underworld of pure hate. "I could shove a meat hook in his belly and hoist him up and rip his teeth out one by one with pliers, and then cut off his balls and make him chew them with his toothless bloody mouth, and that wouldn't even begin to prove my point. Got it?"

I just gape at him.

"He wants to save himself, he'll give me a name."

"Whose name?"

"How about you stop worrying about him and start worrying about yourself?" He turns back to the road and keeps driving, staying exactly at the speed limit.

My heart pounds like mad. The man back there is making a horrible sound. The sound of a man crying out of a crushed face.

"Shut up!" he calls back.

I look out the window. A calm comes over me. "Are you going to kill me, too?"

"So far, you haven't shown you can follow orders very well, have you?"

"I won't tell on you," I blurt out.

He snorts.

We're heading west, out of the city. The party seems like a million years ago. They'll be sitting down for dinner now. Wondering where I am. Will they think I left?

The man's face is in shadows. Streetlamps flash over his face as the van moves along, revealing a nose carved out of granite and a strong jaw. I wouldn't call him handsome. He's too rough-hewn for that, like someone forgot to sand over the angles.

"Please—"

"Be quiet." His soft menace is directed at me this time. I shrink in my seat.

We're going into a run-down suburb, Westdale or Ferndale or something, a place with a lot of little tiny box homes. It's a place I never go. We wind through the streets, deeper and deeper.

It's hard to even look at him. That means acknowledging what's happening to me. This is real. I may never make it out of this alive. That's what I think when I turn my head to the side, glance at him from beneath low lashes. Which makes his gray Henley and dark-wash jeans seem way too ordinary. If this were the day I was going to die, wouldn't he be wearing something more dramatic?

But that's just wishful thinking from my panicked mind. He can hurt me wearing anything. I'm so deep in danger it's hard to breathe.

He slows on a far block and turns. The van headlights hit overgrown weeds and the charred remains of a house. The place burned at one time, long ago.

He circles around and goes into the alley behind it. He shoves it into park and does something to the wires that make it shut off. He turns to me. "I'm gonna get out and deal with this guy. If you move out of this seat, I'll kill you. And if, by some miracle, you manage to get away, I'm going to kill everybody you called on this phone in the last month. Can you guess how? I'll give you a hint. A meat hook is involved."

I suck in a breath. He doesn't bother to wait for my answer. He gets out, yanks open the back door, and drags the man out—I can tell by the thuds. More punching sounds come from behind the van. The groans and garbled pleas sound worse and worse.

I huddle in my seat, listening to a man get beaten to death.

Bile rises up in my throat. I have only a few seconds to decide what to do—throw up in the van or throw up outside. He's told me not to leave. He's threatened my life, threatened to snap my neck. But I have an entire lifetime of my mother's voice in my head. I have sixteen years of decorum forcing me to fumble for the door handle and push my way out.

I make it two feet away before dropping to my hands and knees and throwing up in the weeds behind the place. For all I know, he'll kill me for this. For all I know, he'd have killed me for doing this in the van. He's insane.

There's not much that lands on the ground. A bottle of smartwater and some strawberries don't leave a lot to vomit, but my stomach still heaves again and again until I'm sore, until I'm choking on bile, wrung dry.

I sit back on my feet, wiping my face, panting, one

hand on the rough concrete, head down. The sounds back there have changed. There's this grunting and a grinding sound, then a crack. It makes me want to throw up all over again.

If he's going to kill me, I'd rather not see it coming. I guess I hope he does it fast. That's what they always say in movies.

I hear a thump in the back of the van and then the sound of the door shutting. Footsteps coming toward me.

I force my breathing to slow. He's behind me. I stay still.

"You've never seen shit like this, have you?" he asks, his voice almost conversational.

It makes me shiver, how he can sound so normal after killing a man.

My voice is low. "No."

"You've only seen—what? Parties? Fancy shit?"

There's judgment in his voice and something else. Curiosity? I can use that. I *have* to use that, because it's the only tool I have. I sit back on my knees, brushing my hands against each other to wipe off the gravel. My white and pink dress is stained with blood and dirt. My cell phone is in his pocket. If I want to survive this, I need to persuade him to let me go.

"Parties," I force myself to say in agreement. *Make him see you as a person.* "Tonight was my birthday party."

He doesn't say anything.

I look up at him. His face is cast in shadows by the moon. Demonic. Unforgiving. I wonder how I look to him, down on the ground in a dirty alley.

"Please just let me go back there," I whisper. "Nobody has to know."

He lowers to his haunches and brushes a strand of slick hair from my face. His thumb lingers on my cheek, brushing over my skin. "You're right," he says, voice musing. "No one saw me take you. No one even knew I was there. No one has to know."

"What does that mean?" I whisper.

He stands, sucking in a ragged breath. My heart pounds as his eyes move over me.

I've never felt so helpless, so alone. I'm a sacrifice, kneeling at the feet of a beautiful, brutal demon.

He tips his head at the van. "Get in."

Chapter Two

~Stone~

S HE SHOULD RUN, scream, get away from me, but she doesn't move. She's frozen, thinking I'll kill her, thinking she's seen too much. If it was just me, I might let her live, take my chances, but I have my guys to protect.

If I can't be sure of her, I should kill her. There's no choice. I can't endanger the rest of the crew. And I can't endanger the mission. I tell myself that it's her fault, that she shouldn't have barged into something that didn't concern her, but it doesn't work.

"You don't have to do this," she says.

So she knows.

The way she's kneeling there in front of me, trembling, I'll admit it gets me off a little. I like her this way, her pretty pale dress all smeared with dirt and blood.

That's me—dirt and blood.

"You can just leave me," she says, voice trembling.

I shake my head and say it again. "Get in." Because leaving her body in this place with that scumbag

Madsen's? Or at least, the largest portion of Madsen's body? It's not how she should be found. Definitely not how *he* deserves to be found—with someone like her.

Well, so am I—but I'm still alive. I'm taking her.

She doesn't move; she just whimpers a little. Her mouth isn't all that far from my cock, which is just a little bit dangerous because I'm already rock-hard off killing him.

She doesn't notice; she's looking up into my eyes, wanting to find some shred of humanity, something to give her hope, I guess. Like maybe I have a heart of gold or whatever other bullshit thing people like her think about people like me at times like this.

I hoist her up by the arm. She gasps as I pull her close. I like how it feels, so I yank her right up to my face, near enough so her breath is a tickle on my neck. I have her now, and it's a heady fucking feeling.

"Get the fuck in." I shove her toward the door, and she scrambles in. She sits herself down in the passenger seat in her party dress, but she can't quite bring herself to shut the door. Because it's a little like closing her own coffin lid.

People can sense that shit.

I go, thinking to close it for her, but then I pause because I like the way she looks, sitting there in her perfect dress with the perfect blood and grime, torn and tattered. I did that to her.

"Is he dead?"

"Take a wild guess."

She swallows. And then I do something that shocks even me—I grab the seatbelt and stretch it across her body and buckle her in. The seatbelt makes that loud *click* only seatbelts make. It feels good to belt her in. As though I'm protecting her with that belt but also keeping her in there, like she's mine.

She swallows visibly. "What do you want?"

I tuck another strand back behind her ear. She's warm and so damn soft. What I want is this exact moment in time, with her there and me here. "Doesn't matter what I want."

I say that a little bit for me. I don't want to kill her, but she's seen too much.

She stares at me with those brown eyes. Her hair is the color of tea. The tops of her tits are smooth like eggs. This girl herself is like an egg, I think. Perfect and unbroken.

I back away and shut the door. I get in my side and peel the fuck out of there, taking the main road south, toward the highway.

I can tell by her eyes, and by the quality of her silence, that she's plotting her escape. I flick the locks on the doors. Another satisfying sound.

She turns to me, stunned.

"Gotta love these service vans," I say, but my heart

isn't really into taunting her. I tell myself not to look at her anymore. It'll make it too hard to kill her.

I wasn't even that into killing Madsen, and he deserved to die for what he did ten times over. He's not only part of the group that stole our childhoods—he's also one of the guys who helped frame my brother Grayson for murdering a cop last month.

He's sitting in lockup. Awaiting trial.

If they'd set bail we would've paid it. Even a million bucks, we'd get it and pay it no problem, and then we'd hide Grayson where they'd never touch him. Guess our enemies were a little too smart to let that happen.

It's not too late, though. Our lawyer says we just need enough evidence for reasonable doubt to get him off.

Just.

Madsen knew he was dead either way, so he gave us nothing. But I won't quit digging. Grayson needs me. There are other guys out there to question. And if he ends up being convicted, we'll find a way to overturn it. Or maybe just break him out.

Whatever it takes.

Grayson isn't my blood brother—our bond runs deeper than that. He's a brother from the fiery hell that was our childhood. A kid I swore to protect.

So no, I didn't get a name, but Madsen had to die. Now he's dead. Madsen's death fulfills a promise I made to another brother of ours—Cruz.

Madsen put all of us through a lot of hell, but mostly he focused on Cruz back when they kept us all in that basement. And one night I looked Cruz right in the eye and I swore to him that I'd bring him Madsen's ring. The ring would mean that Madsen was dead, that he had paid for what he did to us.

It's important for guys like Cruz to see me keeping my promises. To see that they have a leader they can count on. And Cruz seeing that Madsen's really dead, that's important, too, because when a guy fucked you up that much, you can't just be told he's dead—it's not the same thing. You need evidence.

She's twisting the torn, bloody fabric of her dress—twisting and twisting. "I can give you money."

"I don't need your money," I say.

"There must be something."

"Nothing you can give me."

There's a silence. And then a whisper. "It's my birthday."

I make the mistake of looking over at her again. This pure, perfect girl dropped into the middle of my hell, trapped and strapped, under the total and utter control of a predator. Yeah, I know how it feels.

I force my eyes back onto the dark highway, lights blurring by. "So Madsen was some kind of friend of yours?"

"Who's Madsen?" she asks.

"The guy you tried to save."

Her pretty lips are a round *O*.

"He deserved to die," I say.

"I don't know him. I think I met him…he looks familiar…maybe a friend of my parents'…"

"He was at your fucking birthday party."

"Three hundred people were at my birthday party."

"What? You invite your parents and their friends to your party? I thought kids were supposed to rebel or something by your age."

I sense her staring at me now. "It's sweet sixteen. It's not really my party. It's…a social event. He probably works with my dad, or he's in the industry or the city."

"What the fuck," I say. "Maybe next time you should invite two friends and get drunk by the river or something instead of hanging out with a scumbag like that."

There's a silence. "Will there be one?"

"What?"

"Another time?" Her voice is quieter. "Another birthday?"

I don't want to think about birthdays. "We'll see," I say.

"What does that mean?"

"It means we'll see." What it means is that there's always a chance the van could get hit by lightning or a bus, and I die and she survives. It's a cheat of an answer, but I don't want her to fall apart before we get wherever we're going. I'm thinking about drowning her in Big Moosehorn River. It's a good way to go. Fast. Clean.

She lets out this ragged sigh.

Her dress looks like it's from another country, or maybe another time—I don't know shit about dresses. What I do know is that, from this angle, there's something dried on the mound of her tit—dried tears, I think. I imagine licking that little spot off.

I won't do it, of course. I'll kill her, but I won't break her like that. I look again. She seems pale, almost green. "You going to be sick again?"

She shakes her head.

"You sure?"

"Don't worry."

"Come on. You look a little…I don't know…"

"Well, you don't have to worry, because I've eaten exactly two strawberries. So it's not as if—" She waves her hand.

"What the fuck is that? Two strawberries?"

She shakes her head like it's too hard to explain to me.

"You need something to eat. That's your problem."

She gives me this incredulous look. "That's my problem? Really?"

"It sucks to be hungry. That's all I'm saying."

"It does," she says.

"You should eat."

"Got any fries?" And then she laughs. It's the way you laugh when things are fucked up beyond belief.

There's this buzzing in my head. I'm staring at her like an idiot because she's beautiful when she laughs. Her laugh, her smile, it all gets me by the throat. And the exit to Big Moosehorn River is up ahead, but I pass it by.

Her laughter turns into sniffles and sobs. She leans her head against the passenger-side window. Hopeless.

"We're gonna get you something to eat," I say. "There's a Burger Benny up at the next exit. Okay?"

"Okay," she whispers, trancelike.

I'll feed her before I kill her. It's the most messed-up thing I've done in a long time.

I shove a caterer's cap low over my head as I pull up behind the truck in the drive-through line. "I don't have to tell you to act right when we go through here, do I? Do I need to remind you how many people will die if you don't act right?"

She just watches me with this wounded, piercing look that's a little bit hot. Her light brown eyes shine with tears.

Doesn't matter how wide and brown her fucking eyes are, though. "Tell me you get it."

"I get it."

I stare at the lit-up menu. You'd think I've never ordered a fucking hamburger before. There was a time I hadn't. I didn't grow up with goddamn Happy Meals. The first time I experienced a drive-through, I was fifteen and fresh out of the basement after six years. Fresh from our violent escape.

I mostly remember the strangeness of it. How tinny and mechanical the voice on the other end of the machine sounded. Like a robot or something, rushing me to pick.

Back then I had this sense that I didn't even belong in the world, as if it had spun on without me and I didn't have a place. And that tinny voice, demanding my order, like a fist around my throat, the kind that leaves bruises the other boys pretend not to see.

"Burger combo," I say because the fist never really eased up. Because she should know how it feels, taking what you can get. That's all she's doing now—taking what she gets.

"Would you like a drink with that?" the voice asks.

I consider asking what she wants, but that feels too personal. What kind of soda does she drink? Or maybe she's too rich and fancy to drink soda.

"Two colas. Anything," I say into the speaker, and then I drive forward before I get the total.

"Don't I get to pick my last meal?" she asks, real quiet. She's looking straight ahead, her face in profile.

I study her nose and her chin, the slope of her neck. I suddenly want to know what she smells like up close. I want to press my face into the vulnerable skin of her neck and breathe deep.

My body gets hot just thinking about it, and I hate that. I hate that feeling that rushes through me, that thickness in my dick. I hate that she makes me feel this way.

There's a part of me that wants to tell her this isn't her last meal, but I won't do that. And anyway, she should find out what it's like to scarf down what's in front of you, knowing there might not be more. Knowing you might not be alive even if there is. I want her to understand where I'm coming from.

"You want to die hungry, die hungry," I say.

The window slides open, and some punk kid reads the total without even looking up. I dig the cash out of my wallet and hand it over.

It's when he's passing back the change that he sees her. His eyes fasten on her tits, pushed together by that fussy dress.

"Ketchup?" he asks, voice pitched high.

"Yeah," I growl because I don't like the way this horndog's looking at her. She's just a fucking kid. Why's he looking at her tits like that? And she's in the passenger seat of my van. Mine.

Mine. The word comes out of nowhere, but it's true.

She stays quiet, staring ahead. She might as well be a mannequin in a store window. All except for the tear tracks shining in the moonlight.

I grab the food and drinks when the punk hands them out, shove the stuff into her hands, and pull away. No one else gets to see her. It was stupid letting anyone see her, linking us together—a fucking witness. She knows I killed Madsen, and now that punk saw me with her, a daisy chain that leads to me in jail.

Even so, even knowing how dangerous she is, I'm mostly mad that another guy checked her out.

The van bounces on the speed bump, and she lets out a small sound of alarm, clutching the bag like it's a damn roller-coaster bar. And then we're on the freeway, heading back to the Big Moosehorn Park exit.

The ride smoothes out. "Open it," I tell her.

Paper crinkles as she unpacks the food and holds it out like I might take it from her. Her hand looks small, especially holding the big wrapped burger. And she's trembling.

Fuck. What am I doing with her? Why isn't she dead?

"Eat it," I tell her. I'm ruining her. That's what I'm doing with her.

Her life was charmed—a pretty little rich girl at her sweet-sixteen party. Then she got a glimpse of me. Now she's facing death or whatever the fuck I want to do to her. Which is a lot.

She's this pure thing in my control, and I'm bloody

and horny, and I want to devour her. I want to press my face to those pushed-up tits above the edge of that dress and fuck her hard and fast.

Skin smooth and pretty like an egg.

But here's the thing about an egg: when you break it, you get everything you want, but then it's not smooth or perfect anymore. It's just this dead thing.

This is something I know a fuck of a lot about, let's just say.

And yeah, you can put yourself back together, but you're never right afterward, not really. You're cracked and misshapen and definitely not smooth and nice like this girl.

There should be some smooth and nice things left in this world.

"I'm not—" Her voice cracks. "—hungry."

I know she's thinking about what I said, about her dying hungry. Maybe she'd rather go that way, all focused on it. People like to think they'd be prepared for death. They don't want to be caught off guard. Me, I've always been the opposite. There's no honor in death, no clean way to go. It's always messy. Always painful.

Catch me by fucking surprise. Fight me.

I think it at her, as if she can hear. As if she'll suddenly learn how to use my gun, to take it from me. But she can't. She's completely defenseless.

"Did I ask what you want to do?" I say, nice and soft.

"Open the wrapper and eat."

I only get to see the flash of her eyes, the light of anger, before she looks down. She puts the burger in her lap—I imagine it warming the tops of her thighs. She unfolds the paper slow—a small act of defiance.

It gets me hard, the way she's fighting with the only weapons she has. The way her small hands fold around the messy burger and pick it up.

The way her mouth opens wide.

CHAPTER THREE

~BROOKE~

THE BURGER TASTES amazing, juicy and salty on my tongue. God, how long has it been since I had a burger? It feels like forever, those two strawberries a distant dream.

I don't want him to see how good this is for me, how desperate I am. I want to swallow the entire burger, that's how much I want this. Except then he'd know. I can feel him watching me, weighing me. I can feel his gaze on my skin like a brand, hot and possessive.

We're going through woods now. Some kind of backwoods road.

I need to get away, form a plan, push back for once, but I don't know how. Do I try to fight him? Or do I somehow smash through my window? Dive out of a moving vehicle and run? In a full-length gown?

The headlights catch a wooden sign for a hiking area up ahead. The sign is cut ragged on the edges to look rustic. Disney rustic. We're in the state park, I realize. "I was here once," I say. "With my Girl Scout troop."

"Don't." His rumbly tone makes my chest tighten. Even his voice is overwhelming, taking over everything.

"Don't what?"

"Try to humanize yourself. It doesn't work on people like me."

I want to tell him I wasn't doing that—I wasn't doing anything at all, just saying a thing that came into my mind—but he probably won't believe me, and I don't want to get him angry. I've seen him angry. I mouth the word *okay* and take another bite, hating myself for wanting the burger more than anything else in that moment. *Gluttony*, my mom would call it.

Some of the juice drips down my chin. I wipe it quick, embarrassed. "Sorry," I mumble out of habit, feeling him watching.

I can't imagine how I must look in this torn dress, stuffing my face. I should have stood my ground about the burger. My mother would have refused, even if she were starving.

I take another big bite and close my eyes, enjoying the comfort and satisfaction of food entering my belly. A better person might not taste it. A better person might be focusing on her circumstances, but this burger is the best thing I've ever eaten. I take another bite. I chew, eyes closed. I swallow the goodness. I'm dissolving in rapture.

A rough sound comes from the driver side. I risk a look, steeling myself for the judgment in his eyes, the condemnation. I'm so used to this that it shouldn't hurt, but it always does.

His face is in the shadows—all I see is the unruly outline of his black hair. Suddenly the glow from the headlights reflects off his face. The breath goes out of me. It's not judgment I see. It's something else.

I look away quickly, feeling as if I saw something I should never have seen. Something new in his eyes. Hunger, raw and feral. My heart pounds the way it did back in that alley, when I was listening to the *thwaps*.

I reach into the bag and grab some fries, stuffing them into my mouth. I don't even care.

Something bad's going to happen, and nothing matters anymore…and the fries are warm and salty and delicious. I've been hungry forever. This is my last meal, the one he chose for me.

And it's perfect.

The dress cuts into my stomach, squeezing me. It's a vise grip, squeezing the life out of me, but I can't stop eating. There's not enough room in this dress for food or life, barely even room for breathing, but I don't care.

For a second, it's just me and this rich, greasy, forbidden meal and not him looking at me like that. I stuff more fries into my mouth, ravenous. Screw it—I'm eating all of them.

Tears in my eyes. I'm a mess. For once it doesn't matter.

I make a tray on my lap with the bag, and I squeeze ketchup all over the fries and eat them that way. The road gets really bumpy just around the time I finish my meal.

I force myself back to reality. Everything's dark around us, no lights at all except for our headlights. I see something glint up ahead, and I realize it's the river.

The road stops at the river. Whatever's going to happen, it'll happen now.

And that's when the buzzing in my head starts. This animal buzzing—maybe it's panic. I can't get a breath. He stops the van at the river's edge, and I'm gasping for breath.

He looks at me. "What's going on with you? What's wrong?" He sounds angry.

"I can't breathe," I gasp. "I can't get a breath. This dress. I shouldn't have…" I try to suck in air, but I can't. I press my hands to my belly. "No."

He's got this strange look on his face, like he's alarmed, like I'm a wild animal trapped in his car with him. Isn't that funny? Like I'm the animal. I would laugh if I could breathe.

"It's too tight…I shouldn't have…"

"Loosen it."

"I can't just…" I feel dizzy, crazy. Suddenly heavy hands are on my shoulders, turning me, pushing me to the door. His fingers are at my back. He's unzipping my dress. The sound echoes through the tiny space. "No," I beg. "Please don't."

"Shut up." He yanks the zipper all the way down to the base of my spine. I feel the cold on my skin, the release. The rush of air into my lungs.

I hold the front of the dress to me and turn, shrinking back, as far away as I can get from him in this tiny space. I stare at him, eyes wide, backed into the corner where the seat meets the door.

"Better?"

I just watch him. "Are you going to rip the rest of my clothes off now?"

He snorts. "Any dress that makes you choose between breathing and eating isn't worth wearing."

"I'd rather keep it on."

"Don't worry. I'm not going to rip it off you."

I keep it at my chest, heaving breaths. I don't believe him. I can't.

"I'm not going to rip it off you," he repeats. "Okay? That's not where this is going."

"Where is it going?"

He moves his hand to the armrest on his door. Everything slows. I jerk as a *pop* at my back tells me he just unlocked the doors. "Get out."

I watch him, afraid to move. What will he do to me outside?

"Do it. Get out. And don't even think about running. You won't like what happens. Do you understand what I'm saying?" He lowers his voice to a whisper. "You *really* won't like it."

With shaking hands, I open my door. He opens his, eyes on me. I start to climb out.

He's one step ahead of me, shutting his door, a devil in black.

The van's still running. He left it running. What does that mean? That he's going to kill me quick? That I'm not even worth turning the engine off for?

He's walking around the front, quick steps in the glare of the headlights. He freezes and turns my way, alarmed, as though he just realized something.

It's like a cord is connecting us—in that instant I know what he's thinking. I could slide over. I could take the van.

And I do.

I slam the door behind me and scramble to the driver's side to lock him out. I yank the front of my dress up as I settle into the driver's side. I'm shaking as I release the parking brake. I kick off my heels and fumble for the pedals.

I've taken driver's ed, but I don't have my license yet. Still, I know where stuff is. *Get it in reverse!* I tell myself. *Press the brake pedal. Find the shift thing and get it in reverse!*

He bangs on the window. I find the brake and grab

the shifter. Something grinds as I get it in reverse.

He's pounding on the window. No—punching it.

The van jerks to life, and I'm backing away. I'm going fast, driving crazy, but I'm doing it—backing the way we came. I see him illuminated in the headlights, running after me, powered by pure fury.

I can't let him catch me now. I won't like what happens—he promised as much.

I keep going backward. I can't see anything. I'm hitting and crunching things. He's catching up.

A loud *clunk*. My neck jerks as the van slams to a stop.

He's closing in. I shift into drive and move forward. He jumps to the side as I pass, but then he's back, driving his fist into the passenger-side window over and over. The glass breaks with a *crackling* sound.

I step on the gas, but he's got the door open. No!

He gets in, smashing over me like I'm not even there. He jams his foot over mine, onto the brake. He shifts it into park and gets out, yanking me right out with him by the arm.

"That wasn't smart at all."

I clutch my dress to my front as he shoves me forward.

I fall onto something hard—a downed tree, maybe. He's right there, picking me up.

I kick and struggle, but he just lifts me into the air,

squeezing me so tight against him that I can't do anything at all—one arm under my knees, holding my legs together, and one around my shoulders—and he's somehow got my arms pinned together.

"No," I beg.

"Shhh," he says.

"Help!" I yell. "Help!"

"Nobody'll hear you out here, little bird," he says, sounding almost sad. Not angry at all, like I expected. He killed the other guy out of anger, but me he's killing out of sadness. It pours out of him as he walks to the river, carrying me there. "That's what you're like, you know? A pretty little bird and you keep singing, thinking someone's going to understand. But all we hear is a song."

I hear the slosh of the water around his feet. He keeps going, eyes dark, fixed up above, like he's concentrating really, really hard on the moon.

"Please."

"Stop talking." Still he stares at the moon, wading into the river. He keeps walking, deeper and deeper. I gasp when the water hits my bare feet. He seems to clutch me a little tighter.

He's going to drown me.

I struggle with everything I have, but it's like fighting steel.

He doesn't react to the cold, rushing water at all, just

goes deeper and deeper. I feel its icy fingers climb my bare back where the zipper to my dress gapes open. I hold him tighter.

I get a new idea—I won't let him go. He can't drown me if I don't let go of him. But then I realize he probably can. He can do anything.

If he goes deep enough, he'll be able to breathe and I won't. I'll drown and die, clinging onto him.

And then I'll die and stop clinging to him. And he'll let me go.

No—he'll let my body go. I'll just be a body.

I kick and fight for all I'm worth, but he just clutches me harder. My pulse races. It's the weirdest thing, somebody killing you while they're holding you so tightly.

I try to remember the last time somebody held me so tightly, and I can't. Certainly not my parents. Things have been bad with them for a long time. Halfhearted hugs and air kisses. My friends would never hug me like this, with every muscle.

Just this guy. And he's murdering me.

So this is what you have to do to get a hug around here? I think wildly. *You have to die?*

My face is hot, and I realize I'm crying. I push my face to his shirt, which is still warm. A weird last consolation, like the food, clinging to my own killer.

He'll be watching the moon, still. He won't ever look

at me again. Nobody will ever see me alive ever again. They'll just see my body. The water is up to my waist and knees, up to his chest.

I imagine floating off, my dress billowing out around me, floating off. They'll find my body mostly naked. "Can I ask you one thing?" I say.

"No," he growls.

"Please?" I say. "Can you zip my dress back up?"

He stops walking. "What?" The water rushes around us, freezing.

"I don't want them to find me…"

He stands still for so long I think he doesn't understand. Or maybe he's not going to do it. Why would he? Then he turns and goes to the shallower water and sets me down. Water rushes around my ankles. He looks at me hard. "Hold up your hair."

I hold up my hair and turn around. He pulls my zipper up a tiny ways, or at least he tries. The zipper won't budge. He tugs at the dress, trying to get the two sides together, just like my mom did a world ago. But the sides won't come together, and the zipper keeps cutting into my back. He swears, and I hear a snap and see the flash of metal. I suck in a breath and pull away, but he has my dress, and he yanks me back. There's a rip and a snap again. And then the sound of a zipper going up.

He cut the dress. I imagine a tear down the back of it. But at least I won't be naked.

"Thank you," I sob.

He presses down the sides to get it looking more together, I suppose. "Fuck," he says. "*Fuck.*"

We stand like that for a few seconds that may as well be an eternity. I'm lost in the harsh sounds of our breaths. Isn't it strange how they mingle, even though he's working against me? Even though he's about to extinguish mine? All I can feel is the cold water at my legs and his hands hot on my hips.

The world goes upside down as he hauls me up over his shoulder.

And carries me out of the river.

He sets me down on the bank and stands over me, dripping wet, burning green eyes rimmed with thick black lashes. "You remember what I said about your phone? It's still in the front seat of the van."

I'm huddled at his feet. I don't know what he's saying.

"How I could kill all the people you called last? Remember?"

"Yeah," I say, shivering in the cold.

"But there's a chance I won't kill them. If I read in the news about a girl found in the woods. She witnessed a murder outside her party, but she didn't see the guy's face. She tried to call 911, but he came up behind her and he put a bag over her head—a pillowcase or something. He drove her here, and she got away. That's all she knows. She remembers nothing. She never saw this." He points to the white scar design on his arm. "She definitely doesn't do something stupid like tell the cops what really happened when they promise to keep it out of the paper. Because he finds out."

It dawns on me slowly. I don't know why I take so long to get it, except that I'm freezing from the river and in shock from the violence—and *full* for the first time in years.

He's going to let me go.

It doesn't feel real that he would take me captive. It feels even less real that he would let me go.

"I won't," I whisper. "I won't tell."

I don't know whether I'm telling the truth. I don't know what I'll say if my mom and dad are looking at me, if a police officer is asking me questions. It's a future that may never happen. It's more of a dream than even this.

He must see uncertainty in my eyes or hear it in my voice. He shoves large wet hands into my hair and pulls me up to face him. His grip brings tears to my eyes, but I don't whimper. I don't fight.

His mouth is close to mine. Almost like a kiss, that's how close.

Is this how you get your first kiss?

I can almost feel his lips, his breath tactile against mine. We're both breathing hard, both fighting. I know why I'm fighting—for my life, for tomorrow. For a

ANNIKA MARTIN & SKYE WARREN

future I can barely imagine. I don't know why he's fighting, why he could kill that old man but not me.

His voice is low, fierce. "I'll find them, but I won't kill them right away. I'll kill them slow and I'll make you watch."

The images flash through my mind, my mother on the ground, my father bleeding. My friend Chelsea crying, bewildered. *Thwap.*

And only then do I know for sure—I'll never let that happen.

I grip his arm. It's still wet from the river. My hand is wet too. We're slick together, but I hold on tight. This is important. I need him to understand how serious I am. I need him to see that I mean it. "I swear to you—" My voice is trembling but not with fear this time. With determination.

The intensity in his stare doesn't lessen one bit. He gives me a shake with my hair.

I know what he wants. "Your scars," I say on a gasp, because the pain in my scalp burns. "I'll never tell a single soul about your scars. I swear to you."

I don't bother swearing to God. I think a man like him doesn't have faith in anything.

He's studying my eyes, hands tightening around the back of my head. He's not sure. Second-guessing his decision. I can't let him do it—I can't.

I'm good in school, an A student. This is what we do

in school—we get told things and tell them back. I do it now, just for him.

"I was hiding, calling 911, and he came up behind me," I whisper. "He put something over my head and forced me into a vehicle. One of the vans, maybe. We drove around forever. I was so scared, I don't remember anything, or how much time passed. Nothing. He said if I took it off, he'd kill me."

He watches my eyes. "He stopped and got out once, but that's all you remember."

"He stopped and got out once," I repeat. "I don't know where we were. That thing was over my head."

"They can't make you tell something you don't remember," he says.

"Okay," I say.

"Did you hear any other sounds?" he asks.

This is a test, just like they have in school. I can do this. "That's all I remember." I let the hysteria I feel creep into my voice. "We just drove around and stopped once."

"He let you out here, and you whipped the sack off your head and ran."

"I whipped the sack off my head and ran."

"What direction?" he asks, fingertips digging into my skull, gemlike gaze fixed on my face.

"I don't remember," I say.

"Did he chase you?"

"I don't know. I ran."

He releases me. I stumble back, fall onto the mud.

He just watches me. "The people you love are counting on you to keep that up."

I swallow, afraid even to move. He has no reason to leave me alive, no reason to trust me. Even if he believes I mean what I'm saying, he can't be sure I'll keep my word. Leaving me alive is a risk. He's a stranger, he's an *animal,* but he's taking this risk to let me live.

Something drops by my hand onto the riverbed, a clatter of metal on plastic. I don't look down.

I'm afraid to know what he's left me.

"Find the nearest woman," he says gruffly. "Tell her what I told you."

He turns and walks away without a single backward glance. The van makes a turn as it pulls from its perch, headlights flashing onto me, lighting up my torn dress and blinding me all at once. For a second I think this might be it, that he's decided to run me over instead of drowning me. Then the van turns away. It jolts and bounces its way back onto the road. In a matter of seconds, the red taillights fade into nothing.

It's surreal, being out here alone. Like this really was a bad dream.

My ruined dress proves otherwise.

A laugh bursts out of me, hysteria and grief and leftover fear. I'm not safe yet. I still have to get out of here. I have to hope I don't run into some man who would take advantage of my state. *Find the nearest woman*, he told me. As if he was worried about my safety.

I look down at the small silver thing on the white river rocks. *A knife.* He left me something to protect myself with. As if somebody like me knows how to use a knife.

Chapter Four
~Stone~

I GLANCE AT my watch. *Dead.*

The water must have gotten inside. The hands are stuck at eleven and twelve. It's late, well past the time I should have checked back in with my guys. They'll be worried about me. They'll be pissed.

I don't mind pissing them off, but I don't like making them worry.

Any other time, I would have headed straight back to the hotel. Or at the very least, I would have found one of the few pay phones that are still around and called the secure number. Instead I'm sitting here, hidden by brush and a goddamn rock face, soaking wet, watching.

It didn't take her long to find someone. She'd only walked a few yards down the road before a car slowed down. I could see her dark nipples through the pale wet fabric of her dress. I tensed until an older woman got out. Not that I trust women, much. But I inherently distrust all men aside from my crew. I watched from my hiding spot while the girl gave her sob story, crying and pointing to the river.

It wasn't the stuff about Girl Scouts that got me, or the way she ate the fries, or the way she struggled to stay alive once she knew what I was doing. It was her desperation to be found with her clothes on. Fighting for that last bit of dignity, even when she was losing everything. That's what spoke to me.

You always hang on to what you can.

You never let them take everything. Some people don't get that. They think dead is dead, and it won't matter if you're dressed or not, if you kept your dignity at the end. When you've seen as much death as I have, you know it matters.

I keep to the shadows while the woman pulls a jacket from her back seat and presses it around her. And makes a call. An ambulance, maybe. I should already be gone from here. The girl will find her way back home. She'll be safe, most likely. But the world is a scary place. I know that more than most. What if she met someone worse than me? Someone who wouldn't feed her a burger and then let her go? And so I stay, watching, longer than I should.

I see Brooke talking, shaking her head. That's her name, according to her phone. Her password is one-two-one-two. She really needs a better one than that.

The woman is looking around. Sensing somebody watching, maybe.

I made a gamble, but I don't think it's a bad one. Brooke's a good girl, the kind who'll cut out little pieces of her own heart before hurting anybody else. She'll protect her people from me. She thinks I'm a monster, and she's right.

By the time the red and blue lights flash over the treetops, I should have been gone. I shouldn't be within a mile of cops if I can help it. It's not only about the danger to me, but about the fact that I could lead them to the rest of the crew.

Fuck.

It's because of the girl. Because of the strange feeling I get when I look at her, the tightness in my chest. Which proves I shouldn't be near her either.

I back away through the trees, making myself invisible.

It'll be a long time before they get organized enough for a search, and by then there won't be a trace of me. Except when I reach the end of the woods, where I left the van, something feels off. I move slower, silent and so damn careful. That's when I see it parked about half a mile back from the white van. A dark sedan. It's not a white cop car with reflective lights and bold lettering. No, I recognize the make and model. This is a detective's car. And there's only one detective who would be watching the radar close enough to suspect Brooke's call had to do with me.

Detective Rivera has been a thorn in my fucking side.

And now he might catch me. I'm alone out here. No backup.

There's the crack of a twig ten feet to my left. He's in the woods with me. For a second I'm worried—about the crew and what they'd do if I landed in jail. Who'd be there to watch over them?

This spurs me into action. I crash through the woods, heading west, where there's nothing but miles of trees. No use being quiet when he already knows I'm here.

Then there's a bark. Fuck. He brought search dogs?

I turn toward the darkest part of the forest and plunge inside.

CHAPTER FIVE

~STONE~

"**C**RUZ WON'T WANT that. I'm telling you," Knox growls as he signals and merges onto the highway. "You should have left it in the woods."

"The search dogs would have found it," I say, rubbing the place in my leg where one of them bit me. He took me down, and it was a close call. I had a knife, but I didn't want to hurt the beast. It wasn't his fault he's good at his damn job.

I got away. Barely.

Made it to the city where I could dial Knox for an extraction.

It was too bad I lost the caterer's van before I could torch it, but Knox's ride is a lot nicer; a vintage Porsche that's probably had blood in it a few times over the years. At least I had the ring in my pocket when I left the van behind.

"He wants it."

"He won't even look at it." Knox is wearing a crisp purple button-down and slacks, like he's going to some swanky hot spot for happy hour after work instead of picking up his boss from a manhunt.

"He'll look at it," I say. "You'll see."

Cruz needs somebody in this fucking life to come through for him. That's my job. With all my brothers. Make sure they get what they need. Sometimes that means vintage cars. Sometimes that means closure in the form of a bloodstained ring.

I pull it out and take another look. It's fat and gold with some emblem of a fancy university imprinted on it. This is the ring I promised to bring him as I held his shaking, sobbing body, and now he gets it. It took a good twelve years, but I would have searched for that fucker for another twelve if I had to. I mean to keep each and every promise I made back when we were kids, back when we were being made to do things with men that no kid should ever be made to do.

Our success in hunting those scumbags down is part of why they hit back, framing Grayson for that murder. It was a smart move; even I can admit that. It distracts us from hunting them down. And no jury will pass up the opportunity to slam a cop killer for life. Even if the supposed cop killer is innocent.

But it won't work.

Even if Grayson's convicted, we'll keep hunting them. We'll just have all the more reason to make them sorry.

"You're crazy if you think he's gonna want to see it. The same ring he saw all that time in the…" He trails off at the word *basement*. He doesn't like to say it, doesn't like to think about it. He prefers fast cars and oblivion. Every guy in the crew needs something different.

What do you *need?* a soft voice in my head asks. A voice that sounds a lot like Brooke. But I ignore that voice. I don't need anything.

"He gets the option," I growl. "That's the fucking point here. And someday we're gonna get to all of them. They all die. Begging on their knees. I don't care what it takes."

Knox glares into the distance. With his knowledge, he could easily have a job at some tech company. Something that has a fitness center and stock options. He would fit in there, but he prefers to run with the crew. Most of us do. There's too much outsiders don't know. Too much *we* don't know to ever really fit in out there.

Knox doesn't like that I dumped the body back where it all started. He thinks it's intense that I'm keeping the promises, but I don't give a fuck. Those promises are all that keep me going.

The guys need their leader to follow through, even Knox. Especially him. I'm the stability they never got. I'm their personal fucking angel of vengeance.

"You sure the kid didn't see anything?" he asks again. Maybe he smells the lie on me, I don't know. It's fucked up that I'm lying about this, but I have her handled. That's what's important. She's a good girl. She follows the rules. She'll do what it takes to protect the people she loves.

I guess that makes us alike in some perverse way.

"She won't be a problem," I say.

I feel Knox's eyes on me. "A pillowcase in a caterer's van?"

"Or maybe it was a potato sack. What the fuck do I know? She's got nothing to say, and that's all that matters." I was vague about it when he first picked me up, giving him the story Brooke and I created together— that's all she'll be able to tell the cops, I assured him. I said I dumped her in the park. At least that part is true.

What I don't tell him is how it felt to feed her. How hard it got me when I buckled her in. How it felt to hold her against me in that swirling water. How she asked me for that one small favor and my whole plan fell apart.

I think about what I promised her—that I'd kill the last people she called if she talks. And I think about how much it would hurt her if that happened. I'm not sure I would do it, which is fucked up. I'm all about keeping my promises. She's already changing me.

I think about her face as she ate, how hard it got me, watching her pleasure. It stirred something dark in me, something I'd rather forget.

We don't do connections with women—that's a pact

we all made early on. No girlfriends, no families, no children, no white picket fences. We're too far gone for that, too ruined, too twisted. We're brothers to the end—out for vengeance. Most of us guys, we hit the city streets when we need to get off. No girl ever comes back to the hotel—that's another rule.

Sex is purely physical. Nothing to get worked up about.

Until I watched Brooke biting into that fucking burger, watched how her sad eyes lit up.

She was just so hungry. Hungry for food. Hungry for affection. You never really think about how rich kids might be hungry, too. In their fancy houses and their fancy clothes.

She had been starving.

We're winding through the dark, littered streets of poverty-stricken North Franklin City. The part we're going toward, you can barely call it poverty-stricken— that would imply regular people actually live there, and regular people definitely don't live where we're going.

The part of Franklin City we live in is more like a post-apocalyptic war zone, all crumbling buildings and trashed streetlights.

We live in the Bradford Hotel, which looks like a boarded-up, bombed-out hull of an old-timey hotel. Unless you know what to look for—a tiny sliver of light seeping out from a gap in the metal covering on an upper window—one of us needs to get to that.

A break in the chain-link fence that surrounds it, just big enough for a car to nose through. Tracks in the rubble that surrounds the place, leading to an underground garage that used to be your basic hotel basement.

We don't live under the radar so much as off the radar completely.

We head down and park next to Cruz's Formula One turbo. One of the problems of illegally obtaining more money than you know what to do with while living entirely off the radar is that you can't drive around in the fan-fucking-tastic cars you get to buy. Too flashy, too obvious. But you can still collect them. Making up for the toys we never got as kids, I guess you could say.

We head up the stairs through the trashed, abandoned lobby. Knox kicks aside a rotting crate.

We left this part of the ruined hotel ruined for the benefit of curious bums and thrill seekers. To make everyone believe this is just an abandoned hotel instead of the headquarters of our operation. To make people think we're broke and not hoarding a few mil in a bunker underneath the building in addition to our offshore accounts.

We head through and on up into the place where we actually live. The only home our tribe has known since we broke out of that basement. I was fifteen, the oldest of them, when we killed them all and got away.

ANNIKA MARTIN & SKYE WARREN

We enter a huge, airy room full of couches and computers. Ryland is kicked back on the sofa in the corner with his phone, earphones in, playing at something. Calder—the saint, we call him—is in the corner, eyes closed. Not asleep—meditating. And I can tell you, he's not meditating for world peace or anything. He just sits there, cold as ice, blond hair falling around his shoulders. He'll stay that way until he's good and fucking ready to talk.

Even Nate is here, his dark brow furrowed, his brown eyes concerned. He always looks concerned, because he knows that what we do here is fucked up. Today is no exception.

There's a glass on the center table, full of water. Someone's drink.

I go over and drop the ring into the glass. It lands on the bottom with a soft *clink*. Blood spreads through the liquid in a slow crawl. A spider web of pain and vengeance.

Ryland yanks out his earbuds. "What the fuck?"

"It's pizza day," I say by way of explanation. Pizza day was a special day. A reward for good behavior. It made us sick to be rewarded for shit like that, but we couldn't help looking forward to it. That's what this is— a sick reward.

"Don't think I'll be drinking water anytime soon," Knox says mildly. He still doesn't approve. He's more into the tech side of things. No one's better than Knox. Even without the education we all missed, he's a genius.

"It's like a goddamn head on the mantel," I say. A trophy.

Ryland makes a face. "Is that…?"

He remembers the ring. Ry likes to stay on the fringes of the group, taking off for days or even weeks on his bike, but he remembers the fucking ring. We all do, but it's Cruz who saw it the most.

"Go get Cruz," I tell him, ignoring his weak stomach. It's okay. I have a strong enough stomach for all of us.

I hear footsteps, and I know Ryland is coming back with Cruz.

Cruz is a huge motherfucker, muscles like molten steel, black hair shaved close to his massive head. Our toughest fighter. Our smartest planner—he can look at a building and see exactly how to get in. Look at a group and know exactly how to take them down.

There are tats climbing up both his arms. Script that goes up around his neck. Any sane person would cross the street if they saw him coming, but I still see the kid from the basement.

That's who this gift is for.

His curious look means Ryland hasn't told him yet. That's good. I've got a flair for the dramatic sometimes. At least that's what Knox says, which is rich coming from him.

It's important, what happened down in that basement. If we tried to go about our lives, to pretend we're normal, it would be like it wasn't important.

Like what happened down there didn't matter.

"I made you a promise one night," I say. "A promise about Madsen. What I'd do to him. What you'd get to have. You remember?"

He turns his gaze down to the glass. Tendrils of blood reach up from the ring. "Fuck," he breathes. That's Cruz, always cool, always tough. Even in this moment of goddamn closure, he's the tough guy.

What happened down there matters.

Cruz steps closer to the table. A mix of emotions plays across his face—fascination and fear, hope and regret. "The ring. The fucking ring."

"It's so you know," I say softly. *So when you see him in your dreams, you can be sure it's a dream—because he's dead. He's gone from this world, in hell where he belongs.*

A choking sound comes from Cruz, the only sign of weakness I've ever heard from him since we grew up, since he got built. Since he put ink on his skin, a skeleton screaming in agony for every single man who ever touched him.

Knox goes to him, stands there next to him, a silent witness by his side. My throat is tight watching them. They're so different, the way they look, one of them all starched and sleek, the other one rough and wild, but they fit together. I'm glad they have each other, that Cruz has this moment and that Knox is there with him. "It's done," Knox says, soft, his voice unsteady. "He can't ever hurt anyone again."

But what he means is, *he can't ever hurt* you *again.*

Ryland comes up, too. He stands there with them, just off to the side. Always off to the side, that's what he is. But he's here, and that's what matters. Nate comes over, too.

Even Calder is watching, no longer meditating. No longer apart from us.

I'm the leader. I'm supposed to be detached. Supposed to be strong. It's an emotional scene, but I don't feel like crying—and that's a good thing. I tell myself that it's good, anyway.

Cruz turns to me, his eyes burning. "Stone."

There's something in my chest. It's not an emotion exactly. It's more like something hard and impenetrable and heavy. He doesn't look pleased.

Was Knox right? Maybe he would have preferred to forget. "If you don't want the ring, I'll throw it out the fucking window," I say.

"I like the ring. I just never thought—"

It takes a minute for his words to penetrate, for the intensity of his voice to pierce the haze of doubt. "You never thought what?"

"All those nights in the basement, you swore we'd get out. That we'd hunt the fuckers down. You told me you'd bring me his ring, and I never believed it." Cruz swallows hard. "I never let myself believe in it, even when we got out. It didn't seem real."

It feels like my body's running an electrical current, sharp and hot. "Believe it, brother."

We're out, and we've been out. We're not ever going back. Which is why the fact that Grayson might go to prison is such a blow. I've failed him, failed all of them in a way. But I'm going to fix it. And then I'll make sure no one ever fucking finds us again.

Cruz comes at me—I don't expect it, and because I'm not expecting the hug, it hurts. Cruz doesn't know his own strength sometimes. I don't flinch away. I clap him on the shoulder. "Fucking believe it."

"Thank you," he says after he pulls away, voice raw.

"Get the fuck out of here," I tell him.

He gives me a small smile before looking at the ring one more time. The whole room pauses, giving him a moment while he studies the trophy of the man who hurt him.

The man who regretted it at the end.

Cruz leaves. I let out a breath.

"Melt it down," I tell Knox.

"Fuck," he says, but he doesn't argue. He's the youngest now that Grayson's detained, so I make him do the shit work. He still makes a face while he picks up the glass and takes it out of the room.

"Good work," says a deep voice from the corner. *Calder.* The saint has decided to speak today. His bright blond hair is long and straight; he's dressed head-to-toe in black, kind of like a priest. If priests were fucking terrifying.

"Thanks."

"Messy," he adds. "Did anyone see?"

I bristle at the implication that I would be so sloppy, that I would let someone witness me doing that—even if it's more or less what happened.

And I hate that she saw me like that. Beating on him in the parking lot. She saw me feral and angry and broken.

"No one," I answer before leaving the room.

I want to be alone now, on the roof of the Bradford, looking out at the city, but Nate follows me.

Out of all the guys, he's the only one who lives a regular life. The only one with regular morals. He doesn't think killing is okay, even for someone as monstrous as Madsen.

Which makes it a surprise when he says, "You did a good thing."

I look sideways at him, at his hard profile set against a dying sun. He's wearing a worn work shirt and jeans. Work boots that are coated in mud. He spends his days healing sick animals in his vet practice outside the city. "That's something, coming from you."

"Cruz needed to see that ring. You could tell, looking at his expression. Even though he acts tough. I know how much it costs you, keeping those promises."

A bark of a laugh comes out of me. "Doesn't cost me a damn thing."

"No?" he asks, damnably soft. "You don't dream about the blood, then."

I growl because he's right. "Save the doctoring for the animals."

"You don't need my help. You don't need anything, right? I get it. Except the truth is, you're made of the same flesh and blood as all of us. You need help, too."

I wave my hand, dismissing his words. My bones turned to stone over a decade ago. My blood to dark sludge. I'm like the abandoned hotel we stand on top of. Some of the pieces are still here, but most of me is gone. I only have one purpose now, and that's making sure all the guys get their revenge.

"Who is going to fight for you?" Nate asks softly.

I don't turn around as he leaves me on the roof. Alone, the way I like it. The way I need it to be.

CHAPTER SIX

~BROOKE~

I'M CURLED UP on the living room couch. The blanket on my lap is cashmere, soft as a cloud, but I don't want it. I could push it off, but my mom would just tuck it around me again. I don't really have the heart to tell her I don't like it. Not when she's trying so hard to take care of me. Not when this is the only way she knows how.

"Are you thirsty?" she asks me for the fifth time this morning.

I'm not, but I give in and tell her, "A glass of water might help."

Nothing is going to help, but the way her eyes light up for half a second makes it worth the lie. I know she's doing the best she can for me. She's canceled her hair appointment, her bridge club, her charity meetings. I wonder what she's told them, but not enough to ask. I don't want to find out that I've suddenly come down with the flu.

I stare out the living room window, wishing I'd asked

for something that would take longer. A glass of orange juice, but freshly squeezed. I don't want a drink—I want space. That's strange considering I would have loved this kind of attention a day ago.

A lot has changed in a day.

She's on her way back with a glass of water when the doorbell chimes.

Worry flashes across her face, and then she changes direction and goes to the foyer. I listen, mostly disinterested, while she opens the door. I'm expecting some hushed whispers and a thinly veiled reference to the housekeeper having a day off. A few of her society friends have already dropped by, their concern masking blatant curiosity.

I went missing from my own sweet-sixteen party. It's gone from blood in the water to floating limbs.

Instead she's coming back in, and there's someone behind her. Two someones.

Men. Not friends. They look official.

My heart beats faster. Suddenly I'm desperate for that glass of water she's still holding. In fact I wish I'd taken one of the sleeping pills the hospital sent me home with, so I could avoid this altogether.

One of them nods in greeting, his dark eyes somber. The lines on his face tell me he's normally expressive, even though I can't read a thing in his expression now. "Ms. Carson. I'm Detective Emilio Rivera."

The other detective dips his head and introduces himself too.

"Hi," I mumble, not quite able to meet his eyes. I already talked to cops at the hospital. They were uniformed officers with uniform questions to match. Something about this man's presence tells me he won't be as easy to fool.

It's crazy, the guilt and fear I feel. Like I did something wrong when I was the one held at gunpoint. *He* did this to me, by making me keep quiet.

My mom sends me a worried smile. "Are you up for questions? They said it wouldn't take long."

"It's fine," I say because I'd rather get it over with.

She offers the detectives something to drink, which they refuse. Then she flashes us all a nervous smile and escapes from the room—taking the glass of water with her. I lick my lips.

Suddenly my mouth is completely dry.

The detectives sit down on the plush chairs across from me. The one named Emilio Rivera leans forward, clearly the man in charge. It's the way he holds himself, the way he speaks first. The way his eyes seem to take in every square inch of me, like I'm a puzzle he's going to solve. I barely even register the other man, because this one seems to take up all the oxygen.

"Ms. Carson, we're very sorry to hear about your ordeal," Detective Rivera says. "I know you must be tired, but we're in charge of the investigation. It's important that we speak with you."

Unease clenches inside me. "I already talked with cops. Told them what I remember."

His expression doesn't reveal much, but I get the sense that he's looking at me. Looking *into* me, like he knows I kept some stuff back. "It helps to hear things in your own words," he says. "And sometimes you can remember things later that were fuzzy at first."

"I don't," I say, too quickly.

His eyes narrow slightly. *Damn it.*

I'm messing this up because it feels wrong to lie to the cops. It feels wrong to lie to my parents. I've been raised with a lot of luxuries, especially before the construction business started to tank. But I was also raised pretty strict. Brought up to be obedient, to do and say the right thing.

Lying makes me feel like an accomplice to a crime. An accomplice to my own abduction—and to the murder of that man, Madsen. I don't even know the name of the man who took me, who carried me into the river, but I feel linked to him now. Partners in crime, almost. I hate it, but I can't tell on him.

I can't endanger the people I love.

"I just—" I twist my hands together, looking down at the plush throw over my legs. Even with my mom in the next room, I can't bring myself to move it. Even sweating, I leave it there. It covers me. I wish I could pull it over my head. "I was wondering about the man who got hurt."

Now those dark eyebrows rise. "We have an identification on the man who was murdered. His name was Gerald Madsen. He was a guest at the party. *Your* party."

I nod, my throat tight, because my mom already told me this. I don't remember him, which makes me feel horrible. Did he try the foie gras before he drew his last breath? He wasn't close to my dad, not close enough that I'd met him before, but he was still one of the guests.

Detective Rivera stares at me. Waits.

Worse, I can't help but feel guilty about the party Mom worked so hard for. All those nights in secret at the bakery, earning nine-fifty an hour so she could pay for caviar and champagne. So she could make the evening a success, but now it's not.

Because of him. My abductor. It's a failure, because of *him*.

Detective Rivera studies me. "Do you remember anything?" he finally asks. "Anything you might have heard? Anything either one of them said? Even if it seems insignificant."

I take hold of the blanket, running my thumbs over the smooth fabric. Mr. Madsen's face is etched into my mind. The way he looked tied up in the back of the van. "I heard the fight, I guess. I was hiding, trying to call

911, and the man who took me came up behind me. He put something over my head."

"You told the officers it was a bag."

"Soft. Like a pillowcase."

"Are you sure you didn't get a glimpse of your attacker's face?" Rivera's voice has dropped, becoming almost persuasive. That scares me the most, as if he already knows I did see his face and he's just trying to persuade me to tell.

But I believe that man when he says he would kill me for telling about him.

I believe he'd kill the people on my cell phone, including my parents. My friends. He'd make it hurt, the way he made that man hurt. Gerald Madsen. "The bag was over my face," I whisper. "And before, it was dark." I flash on the anger, the fury as he beat Gerald Madsen half to death.

"He made a stop before the river. Do you remember anything about it?"

I'm thinking about the drive-through.

Do they know about the drive-through?

I furrow my brow as if I'm trying to remember things to help him, but inside, my heart is banging out of my chest.

Detective Rivera sits there, watching my eyes. He doesn't smile, doesn't bother to put me at ease. He stares for what seems like an impolitely long time. I would never stare at somebody that long. Is this part of what detectives do? Try to make you feel like a bug under a microscope? Like they can see everything?

Of course it is.

I think about that kid at the drive-through, the way he leered at me. I thought my captor was going to reach up through the little window and drag him out and kill *him*, too. All for looking at me like that. It felt…strange. Like a twist of fear, but something else, too, deep in my chest.

Something wild and raw.

"Is something coming to you?" he asks. "We need you to tell us everything you remember, even if it seems insignificant or…" He glances toward the kitchen, where my mom is, and lowers his voice. "Or embarrassing."

I shake my head, thinking about the little house in a nowhere suburb. "I didn't know where we were."

"What about sounds? Could you hear anything?"

I close my eyes. It's a welcome break from his scrutiny. "It was quiet," I say. "I thought about running, but he said he would kill me if I got out or…" I gesture to my head, because supposedly I had a pillowcase on my head. "He said, 'You want to live, you do not move.'"

This, at least, is true.

"His voice," the other detective asks. "Young? Old?"

I shake my head, picturing the scar design on his forearm. Like crossed axes. I think about the question.

ANNIKA MARTIN & SKYE WARREN

Young. Old. He seemed both. I open my eyes. "I don't know."

"Did he have an accent?"

"No."

"Did he make any calls?"

"No."

"He said nothing else? In all the time he took to drive around…"

"He told the man—Mr. Madsen—to shut up a few times."

"Why? Was Madsen saying something?"

"No. More like groaning. In pain. Maybe scared. I don't know."

He keeps pushing. "What about at the end? At the river?"

I shudder, remembering the freezing water against my skin, how hard he held onto me as we went deeper. This is my chance. I could tell the full truth right now. Rivera already gave me an out by saying some people remember things later.

But I won't do that to the people I love.

"I kept my eyes closed. I thought he was going to—" My voice cracks, and a tear runs down my cheek. The emotion is real, but it's also convenient. I don't have to talk anymore. I can't.

"You closed your eyes so you couldn't see…" He crosses his arms and frowns like he's confused. "Except you had a pillowcase over your head," he points out, unmoved by my tears. "Or is that after it was off? That you closed your eyes? Because if you had the pillowcase over your head, it wouldn't matter if you'd closed your eyes."

"I don't know," I say, feeling the panic rise in my chest. "I don't remember."

"Did your abductor take the pillowcase off you at the end, or did you take it off?"

I don't know what to say. I didn't work that part out, and the detective knows I'm hiding something—I'm sure of it. Then I remember what *he* told me—*They can't make you tell something you don't remember.* "I don't remember," I say again. No explanations. He can argue anything I tell him, except for that.

"Were you out of the vehicle at that point?"

"I don't remember." I cling to it like a lifeline. *Don't remember, don't remember,* even as the crystal-clear vision of blood and violence and unexpected mercy plays in my mind.

"Do you know how you got out? Can you tell me that?"

Just then my mother appears. The glass of water is gone, and her expression hardens when she sees my face. "I'm sorry, detectives, but Brooke needs to rest. You'll have to come back another time."

Gratitude overwhelms me. She may have a problem

with my posture, but she loves me. She protects me in her own way. Even the lessons on manners and propriety are a form of protection for a girl in our set.

"Of course," Rivera says easily, standing, his demeanor full of respect and understanding. There's something in his eyes, though, that tells me he hasn't given up. A glint of suspicion that makes my stomach clench tight. "I'll come back another time."

Chapter Seven

~Brooke~

Seven months later

CHELSEA AND I step out of the hushed warmth of the Franklin City Natural History Museum into the cool April air. We've got tons of notes for our project, which involves making a model of a hunter-gatherer village out of putty and cardboard. Our village shows how people lived before they figured out they could grow crops and settle in one place. Our teacher said that anybody who added museum research would get extra credit, and Chelsea and I are all about the extra credit.

We head to the parking ramp across the street and take the stairwell up. "You need to tell your dad to get one of those 3-D printers," she says. "Can you imagine how amazing our village would be? If we could make tiny little tools like what was in there?"

"Yeah, I'll tell him. I'll get right on that," I joke. Sometimes I'm surprised that even Chelsea doesn't realize Dad's company is doing so poorly.

At least I'm doing better.

It's been seven months since my abduction. Seven months since my sixteenth birthday party.

Right after it happened, I thought I saw him around every corner. I don't think I see him around every corner anymore. I still see him beating that poor old guy to death when I close my eyes, though. I still remember the way he held me so tightly. Like we were both in danger of drowning in that river.

We get to the fifth level. She pulls out her keys, and I pull out mine. The lights flash on her white SUV, parked next to my red one.

"Tomorrow? Study hall?" she says. We both have first period free.

"I'm there," I say. "I promise I'll remember your blue sweater." I borrowed it, and I keep forgetting to bring it back.

She narrows her eyes, playful. She always acts like I'm trying to steal it.

"I swear! Unless I decide to wear it. I might wear it. Finders keepers," I tease.

She snorts and gets in and buckles up. I shut her door for her and thump on the side as she backs up and out, leaving me alone in the parking lot.

I walk around my car and click the fob. It unlocks with a soft *squeech*.

Just as I open the door, I see a dark form separating from a nearby pillar of concrete. A person, coming toward me, long strides eating up the ground between us.

Him.

I back up, going around my car, keeping it between us. I know not to get in. He'll shove a fist right through the window, because that's who he is. He stops at the driver's side. "You want me to drive? Is that it?"

My heart thumps in my chest. "What are you doing here?"

"Throw me the keys and get in."

"I didn't tell," I say, backing away from him and my car, too, praying for somebody to come. But there are barely any cars on this level. A red exit light in the far corner shines like a beacon in the gray cavern of the parking ramp.

"If you'd told, your people would be dead, wouldn't they?"

A cold finger trails slowly down my spine. "What do you want?"

"We're going for a little ride."

"I need to get home," I say, voice louder than it needs to be. Bravado. "I'll be late for dinner."

"They giving you something more to eat than strawberries these days?"

If that's some kind of sick joke, I'm not laughing. I'm backing up now, eyes on him.

He comes around the car and moves toward me, green eyes burning, dark hair curling at the ends. His jeans are faded, and his dark green shirt hangs open, revealing a black T-shirt underneath. There are specks of something light clinging to his shirtsleeves. His brown boots, too.

I think maybe it's flour, but a man like this doesn't bake things. It's too coarse for flour anyway.

It doesn't matter. Getting away, that's what matters.

I back into something hard—a concrete post. I move around it, trying to put as many solid things between him and me as possible.

He keeps coming.

My pulse whooshes in my ears. The distance between us shrinks. I spin around and run for the exit. "Help!" I yell as I burst through the door to the stairwell. "Help!"

If I can get down to the street, I'm free. There's life there. Cars, people.

I fly around the first landing and rush down the next set of stairs, footsteps loud behind me. I turn and descend the next flight, and then the next.

Suddenly a dark form hops over the rail.

Him.

He drops down in front of me, wrapping me in a bearhug and hauling me up, just like before, holding me tightly to his chest.

Except this time he has his hand over my mouth, sealing it. He doesn't like that I yelled. He seems stronger and huger than before. He's half a year older, so maybe he *is* stronger and huger. Maybe he spent the past months regretting that he let me go.

His fingers press into my flesh, holding me to the hard planes of his chest.

"I said we're going for a little ride," he growls. "What part of that didn't you understand?"

He carries me back up the steps. I wriggle fiercely. He just tightens his hold, bringing me back up to level five like I weigh nothing—a Neanderthal and his prize.

He carries me across the gloomy parking garage, back to my SUV where the door still stands open. He shoves me into the driver's side and pulls a gun from out of nowhere.

He has a gun.

"I'll use it if I have to. Now start 'er up."

I turn the car on. I'm trapped. *Again.* How did I end up back here?

The light from the interior of the vehicle illuminates his fierce features, all sharp angles that make me think of a diamond, strangely—how a diamond is formed under huge pressure, and it's beautiful but incredibly hard. It can cut almost anything because of the way it's made in nature. Stronger than steel.

He's a dark diamond. Green eyes bright and hard.

He bends over, nearing me. I suck in a breath and shrink away, thinking he's going to kiss me.

"Hey," he says, "you're okay." He pulls out my seatbelt and tucks it across me, buckling me in. And for a second, his diamond-hard face seems to soften. "Now I'm going to go around and get in, and we're going to drive out of here like a happy couple. Got it?"

I can't take my eyes off his gun.

"Stay buckled in like that and do what I say and I won't hurt you. Okay?"

I just stare at the gun, frozen. It's so huge and dark and so…there.

"Say okay," he says, his green gaze capturing mine.

"Okay."

He reaches up and touches my hair, just the end, twisting it a little, rubbing the strands between thick fingers. "Your hair is different."

The words tumble out before I can consider them. "I got blonde highlights."

"It looks nice." He shuts the door and comes around to the other side, gets in, and closes the door quietly. "Here's hoping your driving skills have improved since last time."

Despite my fear, indignation rises up in me. "What? I didn't even have my license yet! I was backing up through woods. Running for my life."

He shrugs.

I clench the wheel and pull out of the spot. I have no idea where we're going or why he came back. Part of me is terrified. I can't stop looking at that gun, even out of the corner of my eye.

Another part of me feels a sickening sense of familiarity.

When we hit the pay area, he points to the exact-change line. "I got this."

He hands me the money, and I throw it into the basket. The black-and-white striped arm rises. I look across at the woman in the credit-card payment booth, but she's talking to the driver in that car.

"Don't bother," he says. "People don't notice shit. They don't care."

Of course he'd say that. But he's wrong. "Some care."

"You go on and think so, then." His voice is unconcerned, easy. His whole body is easy, like we really are a couple on a drive. He tells me to turn left. He directs us toward the highway.

"Did you follow me here?"

"How do you know I don't just really love museums?" he says. "Maybe I'm a museum lover like you."

"I don't love museums," I whisper.

"Then what were you doing at one?"

"A school project. It's extra credit if you go to the museum."

"Aren't you a good little girl." He points, directing me to the highway on-ramp. "The hardworking ant."

I merge in. He said he wouldn't hurt me if I do what

he says. Still, I'm shaking a little. Shaking inside. It's fear. Mostly. I try for a joke. "Did you just call me an ant?"

"Haven't you ever heard of that fable? The ant works all summer, preparing stores of food for the coming winter, while the grasshopper lies around and sings and enjoys himself. Then the winter rolls in, and it's cold and harsh, like a fucking wasteland. And the grasshopper is shivering and starving, and he begs the ant for food and the ant says, 'You shouldn't have fucked around all summer.'"

"The ant doesn't give him food?"

"I don't know. That's where it ends. The grasshopper's sorry for being a fuckup, but it's too late."

I check his face to see whether he's joking. "Did you just make that up?"

"No. It's a fable. We read it in a musty old book somewhere."

"You and your parents read it?" I say. Though I can't imagine him with parents. Or with books.

He shrugs. "Just some old book in a box in a basement somewhere."

"I guess I *am* kind of the ant," I say. "Except I would share."

He grunts.

"Are you the grasshopper?" I ask. "The one who blows off all the work he's supposed to do? Just does whatever he wants?"

"Nah," he says. "I'm not the grasshopper."

"You're the ant? Preparing for the future?" I look over at him. I should probably be scared, but I'm actually curious. "Would you share?"

He looks out the window. "I'm not the ant or the grasshopper," he says.

"You can't be neither."

"I can."

"No, you can't. You either plan and think ahead, or you don't."

"Maybe I'm the winter, bringing all the hell," he says. "The winter nobody ever wants to see coming, but here I am."

With a little shiver, I put my eyes back on the road. "Do you really think that?" I ask softly. Because it would be horrible if somebody thought that about themselves.

"Drive," he barks.

"Where are we going?"

"Just drive."

We're heading north. With a sick feeling, I realize this is the highway we took last time we were together. The one that heads out toward Big Moosehorn Park. Why is he bringing me back there?

Oh God. Is he going to finish what he started?

Maybe he thought about it and realized he should have drowned me that night. My foot lets up on the gas pedal. I could be driving myself to my own funeral.

"I didn't tell," I whisper.

The car is slowing down. "I know you didn't."

"Then why…"

"Because. Because this is how things are going to happen. When I say jump, you jump. When I say drive, you motherfucking drive. That's how it is between us now."

"For how long?" I hate how small my voice sounds when it comes out. I hate how I always knew he'd come back, knew it wasn't over.

His gaze is dark with promise. He looks older than he did that night somehow. Less of a mystery, more of a promise. "Forever, Brooke. I let you live that night, and now you're in my debt. Understand? You're mine."

A chill comes over me, and at the same time, the heat of anger in my neck, my face. Not because of the threat of it, but because of the truth. He connected us that night in a dark, sick way.

He made me lie to everyone I love. Made me his.

Maybe it's the anger making me feel brave, I don't know, but I give him my worst *fuck you* look. The kind of look I reserve for when guys my age are being douchebags. The kind of look that puts people in their place. "I'll never be yours," I say.

It doesn't put him in his place.

He turns to me with full-on intensity. There's heat in his emerald eyes, but also a kind of wonder. And sadness, a little bit. I cringe as he reaches over and touches my hair again. "Too late," he says.

My pulse whooshes in my ears. "What are you going to do?"

The question feels alive in the air between us. Alive with speculation, as if I'd asked more questions. *Are you going to touch me? Kiss me?*

Are you going to kill me?

He's touching my hair. His hand brushes my shoulder, a ghost of a touch, but it feels electric, shivering over my body. Sweat trickles down my spine. My heart hammers in my chest like a wild thing under my stiff white school shirt.

He seems to be thinking about the question. Maybe he doesn't know. Maybe he doesn't want to know.

The Burger Benny sign looms up ahead, bright blue and yellow. Ever since that night, I get this weird mixture of feelings when I pass one of those signs, like when you remember a feeling from a dream and you don't know what it is. All you know is that it connects to some deep part of you.

I hate that we're connected like that.

He gestures with the gun at the exit for Burger Benny. "Get off there."

"I have to be home for dinner soon. They're expecting me. They'll be worried, and after last time, they won't wait and see. If I don't check in, they'll call the police."

"That's why you're going to call and make up an excuse why you're late."

"I can't just do that."

"Okay. Then call and tell the truth. You're driving your buddy around. The guy who killed Madsen."

My blood races. The more time I spend with him, the more trapped I feel. Telling them that would terrify them. And they wouldn't be able to help. No one can help.

"The guy you covered for," he continues. "That's who you're with. You know what accessory after the fact is? I'll give you a hint—it's not something you want on your pretty, perfect record."

He pulls his hand away from my hair and opens my bag.

"Hey!" I say.

He fishes out my phone and hands it to me. "Make the call, little bird. Make it good."

We're at a stop sign. I call the house number, getting voicemail, like I knew I would. I leave a message, saying that Chelsea and I are done with the museum but I'll be later than expected because she wants my opinion on a prom dress at Macy's.

I feel his eyes on me as he takes the phone from me. "Chelsea," he snorts. As if that's stupid or something. He opens the back of it and pulls out the battery.

"What are you doing?"

"Three guesses."

I focus on the road. "What do you want?"

"A burger. What are you going to have?"

He says it like we're a couple on a regular night, stepping out for a burger.

But we're not. I say nothing. He can pretend all he wants—I don't have to participate.

I catch sight of a cop car up ahead. My pulse speeds. I grip the steering wheel. We draw nearer to the cop. To the exit.

My abductor doesn't seem the least bit nervous. Casually, he reaches over and flips on the blinker, brushing my arm. A shiver goes through me.

His voice is casual. "Would suck to be pulled over riding with the guy you covered for, wouldn't it? After lying to your parents like that? Things would really look bad then."

When I glance over, he's smiling that beautiful, devilish smile I remember so well from the first night. I feel like a fish, and this guy, he drove a hook deep into my gut. And he can pull it whenever he wants.

It's about more than the fact that he forced me to lie.

It's about how tightly he held me in the river that night—every muscle wet and straining with the refusal to let go.

Nobody has ever expended that kind of intensity on

me. Perverse as it seems, it was something real after all the fakeness of the party. After the fakeness of my entire life.

The feeling of hating him and clinging on to him was like nothing I'd ever experienced. Like clinging to a leaky life raft even though it's going to drown you.

Clinging to your killer, that's a powerful and horrible kind of intimacy. I used to think of intimacy as chocolates and roses and sweet whispered words. But it can be blood and violence and darkness, too. That's something they don't teach you in school.

It drove a hook deep, deep into me.

The sensation of him has lived under my skin for the past seven months. The feeling of his fingers digging into my shivering flesh. The way his wet shirtsleeves clung to his bulging biceps. The hard intensity of his gaze, fixed firmly on the moon, like he couldn't bear looking down at me while he killed me. How severe and sure his grip became each time I struggled. The musical swash of the water against our bodies, a soundtrack to the most twisted dance ever.

And then he let me live, even when I could ID him so easily.

It felt like something beyond chocolates and roses and sweet whispered words. Something more genuine, somehow.

It's completely crazy—I know.

And I can never tell anybody, not even Chelsea. That's almost the worst part of it.

"My treat," he adds. Like this is a date.

I veer into the drive-through lane, heart thudding.

"Careful," he commands. "Prom's coming up. Saw the sign on the school. You going?"

"None of your business."

"I'll decide what's my business or not. You're mine, and that includes you answering every single question I ask—with the *truth*. You do everything I say and tell me what I want to know, and I won't hurt you, got it?"

You're mine. There's this tightness in my belly. It's not right. *I hate you I hate you I hate you*, I think at him, repeating it like that might make it true.

"Now, are you going to this prom shit or not?"

"Probably not."

"Why not?"

I look over at him, wondering how much he knows about prom. "I'm not old enough. It's for seniors. I can go if a senior asks me, but…"

"But what? No one asked you?"

He sounds a little indignant about that, and it makes me smile.

I think about Zach's fumbling kisses at the party last month. I'd liked him for so long, but his kisses had seemed as fake as my sweet-sixteen party. Kissing me like a prereq to some blow-off course he has to take. The way he touched me felt like the air-kiss version of touching. Like he wasn't really there.

Maybe I wasn't really there.

Zach asked me to go to prom with him and another couple, but I lied and said my parents thought sixteen was too young for prom, and that I'd promised to go to the movies with Chelsea. Then I'd asked Chelsea to go to the movies, just to make the lie true. Zach is the perfect boyfriend in every way, but everything with him feels empty.

Ever since the night of my sweet-sixteen party, nothing has felt real. Except the man in my passenger seat. He feels real.

"Let's get the usual," he says when we get up to the speaker thing. "Order two of the usual." He has the gun out of sight, but it's still there.

I glare at him. "We don't *have* a usual."

He lowers his voice. "Order. The. Usual."

Chapter Eight

~Stone~

Brooke orders two burger combos with Cokes. The burger combo—that's what I got her last time. I know better than to think it's a big deal that she remembered our usual.

I make her drive back to Big Moosehorn Park. I show her where to drive and the parking area I want us at.

We get out of her SUV. It's a nice enough set of wheels—a Lincoln Navigator. Red like cherries.

It's a warm night for April, but the ground is still cool and damp. I lead her to a grassy bluff a ways off the trail, near a few large trees. It overlooks the river where we were that night. No doubt she remembers that, too. "Here."

She looks confused.

"Wait," I say, laying out my leather jacket. "The ground is still a little wet."

"I'm not sitting on your jacket."

I give her a look. That's not how this goes. I know

she understands that, even if she fights me sometimes.

She sits.

I settle in beside her.

I eat my burger, but that's not what this is about. It's more about watching her eat. About doing the things from last time. Messed up, I know. I try not to think about it too hard.

It's been a fuck of a month. Grayson got convicted. They're moving him to a prison out of state—far away from us. They won't let him have visitors or even communicate with the outside world. I'd lay down my life to protect him, but now I can't even see him.

We're all going crazy. Sometimes I can barely sleep.

The worse things are, the more I think about that night with her last September.

To escape the worry and the rage, just for a moment. To lose myself in that good feeling I had with her.

I'd be lying if I said I didn't think about fucking her, too. I'd be lying if I didn't think about how it felt to hold her in the river that night. The way she trembled, this girl I had total control over. I could destroy her or save her. I could kill her or fuck her or do anything at all.

She didn't tell.

She kept our secret.

I was fairly sure she would. Still. It got me in a way that's hard to explain.

And I needed a hit of her again.

We questioned a guy at the old lumber mill in West Franklin today. He was a guy from the basement days. It was a miracle we tracked him down. We felt sure he knew who engineered the frame-up of Grayson, that he could give us something we could use.

The motherfucker wouldn't talk. I told him I'd run him through the wood chipper if he wouldn't give me something.

He didn't believe me, of course. Kept saying he didn't know who was behind it. So I made my guys hoist him up. I started feeding him in, hand first. He blurted out a few nicknames and then shut up. Done talking. I suppose he knew he was dead either way.

So I put him through.

They didn't want me to do it like that. Too messy. And with all the safety features wood chippers have these days, it's also a real pain in the ass compared to just shooting him in the head, but when I say something, I follow through. That's important to me.

Let them have the high ground. I can be the psycho they need me to be. I left them back at the Bradford to bitch about me. Too angry. Out of control. You have to let people bitch about you when you're the leader.

Doesn't matter.

They're safe. That's what matters.

Then I found myself driving to her. I told myself I'd just watch her from the car. She gets done with her last class at three fifteen on Wednesdays, and I thought I'd drive by her fancy girls' school.

They hang banners from the roof to show the world what the girls are up to, and this month the banners say *prom season*. Prom is a kind of dance, according to Wikipedia.

Then I followed her to the museum. I wanted to know what she was doing in there, and I thought to slip in, but I don't know how the fuck you blend in at a museum—you have to know something about a place to blend into it.

So I hung around in the garage until she got back. I told myself all I'd do was make sure she got out of there okay. Wouldn't want any predators to get at her.

Yeah. Too late for that now.

Even her hate feels good. *I'll never be yours.* I replay it in my head. That glare as she said it. Her fear, her hate, her friction. I shouldn't get off on it, I know. That's how twisted up I am.

"So did Detective Rivera follow up? Is he giving you any more trouble?"

Her eyes snap to mine. "How do you know about him?"

"I'm a bad guy. It's my job to know about the cops."

She fishes through her bag of fries, taking out a slim, crispy one. Maybe she likes crispy ones. "He didn't believe me."

"But he didn't go at you again?"

"No. My mom kind of ran him off."

"Your parents protecting you. That's good."

She nods, seeming sad.

"So they're leaving it?"

"Is that why you wanted to see me?" she asks. "To make sure you're home free?"

I can see the hope in her eyes. She wants that to be the reason I've grabbed her up and not something bad. She doesn't get it; everything with me is bad. "I'm asking the questions. Are they leaving it?"

"I have to go to a shrink. But she doesn't ask me about it directly."

"And you won't tell her."

"I said I wouldn't," she snaps. "I'm good for my word."

I nod. I like that. Keeping our word is something we have in common, but I don't say it.

"I never tell her anything."

"You should tell her how you feel, if you feel upset."

"Just leave it," she says, echoing me.

"What else? Everything back to normal otherwise?"

She drags another burnt french fry through the blob of ketchup she squeezed out into the side of her fries bag. If I'd known she likes them crispy, I would've ordered them like that and taken a look to make sure they did it right. "Pretty much. Except for self-defense classes."

"You're taking self-defense?"

She shrugs. "The shrink thinks it would be good."

"Is it?"

She eats the fry. "It's exercise, I guess."

"Show me. Can you hit? Did they teach you to hit?"

She pushes a fry into her mouth and looks at me suspiciously.

"I'll give you pointers," I add.

"No, thanks."

"It's not like you can hurt me."

"You want me to hit you? So you can give me pointers? Practice self-defense with the person who's the whole reason…" She doesn't have to finish the sentence.

"The whole reason you need to defend yourself? Who the fuck better to practice against, right?"

"I just want to go home."

"C'mon." I stand. "Give me your best move."

She just gazes up at me. The new highlights in her hair catch the setting sun, and there's a light dusting of freckles on her nose. She looks like an angel.

"Come on. Up." I want to see this. More than that, I want her to touch me. Doesn't matter whether that touch comes with pleasure. I'm more used to pain anyway.

"I can go home if I hit you? That's what you're saying?"

"If you knock me down."

I wait. I can tell she's considering it. She knows I mean what I say. She wipes her fingers on her napkin, tucks the napkin into the greasy bag, and stands, eyes wary. She's suspicious.

"Let's see whatcha got."

I'm expecting something half-assed, but she comes out with a big roundhouse. I slap it away.

"That's what they're teaching you? To try something like *that*?" I grin. "I don't know about these classes."

She looks wild and angry and kind of beautiful. "You think it's funny? Go to hell. You made me lie to everyone." She kicks me, hitting my knee.

"Ow," I say, laughing.

Suddenly she's like a little windmill, a flurry of hits and kicks. "I could barely sleep! And he knew!" Hit, kick, hit, kick. She's landing them. I'm laughing, surprised more than anything. "Everyone looks at me like I'm…" She hits again.

"Fuck!" I say, holding her off. "Okay!"

She doesn't stop. She's dead serious, going at me like a wild banshee. She actually connects a few times.

"Okay, okay." I grab her, get her under control. She's crying by the time I pin her to a tree. I have her arms trapped against her shoulders. She's breathing hard, frightened.

I dig in my fingers, just to let her know who's in charge. Having her under my control again, let's just say it's a good feeling.

Her breathing changes. Tears in her eyes. "They know I was lying."

"Okay," I say, "you're okay." I use my calming voice, a little trick I perfected down in that basement all those years, calming my guys down when things got rough, which was pretty much always. "It's okay."

"It's not okay." She kicks, and I move my leg to pin hers, getting real close to her. This level of control feels a little too good. A little dangerous. "I hate you."

"I know, little bird."

"They all know!"

"Did you tell them?"

"No! I said I didn't."

"Then they don't know," I say. "They have no idea. People are lost in their own miserable lives." I breathe her in. "Your self-defense classes, though. You don't try that shit on a person like me. Okay? What you were giving me out there, those weren't good moves. You can do better."

"And you know all about me," she bites out.

"Your best move with a guy like me? Get the fuck away. You had a chance to run back there, and you didn't take it. That would've been your best move." I press her harder, putting my whole body into it, and whisper into her ear. "All the hitting and kicking, it's just a lot of nothing to a guy like me. It's barely even trouble.

You get a chance to run, you take it."

I ease up a few inches and see the alarm in her eyes. It's good that she's scared. That's how it should be. I let off, and she moves away.

"Maybe I'll run now."

"Little late for that."

She pulls her keys from her pocket and backs away from me, back to her car. Her eyes widen as she realizes I'm not planning to move. She waves the little copper key like it's a knife. "You think I won't run you over? Ram right into you?"

Part of me wants her to do it. The same part of me that wants to crush any man who hurts her—even me. I like her strong and fighting. Powerful.

The more realistic part of me knows there's nothing a sixteen-year-old girl can do to a man like me. I'm too hard, too mean. She never stood a chance, not from the very first time I looked at her in that ridiculous party dress. I may never claim her, but she'll always be mine.

Her hands clench into fists. "What do you want from me?"

"That's a good question." A good question without a good answer. I can't seem to keep myself away from her. She's too good for me, too pure. *You made me lie to everyone.* I'm ruining her, and I have no plans to stop.

I take a step forward, and she's a smart girl. It's not hard to figure out what I might do to her.

"Wait," she says.

I don't wait. I step into her space, close enough to smell the strawberry scent of her shampoo, to feel her breath warm against my neck, to back her up to the cool metal side of the bright red vehicle. "You're so fucking pretty."

Her voice trembles. "Why do you say that like it's a bad thing?"

Because I can't stand her delicate eyelids and her bow-shaped mouth. She's so fragile, so breakable, and I'm a goddamn sledgehammer. "Don't move." I grasp her upper arm and hold her against the SUV, wanting her right there.

Her eyes are impossibly wide, staring up at me with fear. "I didn't tell," she whispers. "I wouldn't."

I know, and maybe that's what sealed her fate. Knowing that she lied for me, that she protected me. There aren't many people in the world who would do that. Only my guys. Nobody else. Even if she only did it to save her family, it's formed a bond between us.

Her hair shimmers with spun gold. I reach up to touch one of the bright parts. It runs through my hand like silk—no, something softer. Like liquid, a whisper of a touch against calloused fingertips.

She's shivering. *Terrified.* That should be enough reason for me to let her go. Only a monster would keep her pinned like this, captive so that he could feel her hair.

This isn't right, but all I can think is that she's listening to me. *Don't move,* I told her, and she's barely even blinking. It's like catching fucking sunlight in a jar. I don't want to let her go.

And you know all about me.

I know hardly anything about her—what does she taste like? What sounds can she make?

My pulse rages in my ears like a goddamn ocean. How messed up is that? I can kill a man and go out for a nice dinner right afterward, calm and serene, laughing with my guys over stupid shit. But pinning this fragile girl to the smooth side of her vehicle gets me churned up inside.

"Have you ever been kissed?" I whisper.

It feels like the time to whisper, everything intimate even when it smells like damp dirt. Or maybe because of it. We're getting primal here. This isn't a fancy party like she's used to. I'll never be that kind of man. This is who I am. Hard. Ruthless.

"I—I—" She stammers like she's trying to figure out the right thing to tell me.

"The truth," I say, laying steel under my voice. When I leave her again, all I'll have of her is knowledge. When I'm lying in my empty fucking bedroom at the Bradford, jacking off, all I'll have is this.

"Yes," she whispers. "At a party. He—"

I make a growling sound, and she stops.

I didn't mean to do that. It sprang from deep inside me, a raw part of me best left alone.

She digs into things I don't want dug into just by being who she is, just by looking at me with those big brown eyes.

Fuck.

My pulse rages.

"What did he do?" I make myself ask, voice mocking like I don't give a shit. "Did he touch your pretty tits? Did he come in your mouth?"

"What?" Her eyes widen, and that mouth—God, that mouth. Her lips part in shock. "No."

Isn't that what kids do these days? You read those articles about middle school kids getting pregnant. But what the fuck do I know about being a kid? Not a damn thing. I knew about touching and about cum. It's a kiss that would have shocked me.

A kiss. Lips on lips. Tongue against tongue. The mechanics sound simple, but the reality confounds me. I stare at the pink of her lips, the shape of them, wondering how they would feel against mine. Telling myself I have no right.

My hand slides through her hair and locks behind her neck, holding her in place. My other hand keeps her pinned against that vehicle.

Leave her the fuck alone.

I might have been able to walk away. That's what I

tell myself. Then her head tilts back, just the smallest degree, and her lips part.

And I'm lost. Everything inside me goes upside down. I bend my face to hers, a breath away.

And freeze.

Her breath heats my lips. The moment stretches out in rapid heartbeats. I stalked her, but she set the fucking trap.

And then I can't stop myself—I press my lips to hers. Lights explode behind my eyes.

God, she feels so soft—so soft, so good. I sink into the pleasure of her. She's warm, luxurious. She's all-consuming quicksand I never want to escape. Sweet and soft, like everything good.

I'm sinking into oblivion, and it's all I want.

I adjust my grip on the back of her neck, fisting her hair, my other hand gripping her shoulder. I love holding her like this.

Fuck, it's too much.

I pull back, blood racing. It's too much. It's not enough.

She stares at me with this stunned light in her eyes, arms dropping to her sides. Was she trying to push me away? If she was, I couldn't tell. What does she see on my face? Hunger? Surprise? Danger?

I fit our lips back together, higher and harder this time. Even better. No matter how our lips connect, it feels like magic.

I want a better taste, but using my tongue will change this. It will make it less pure, and her lips are fucking heaven.

A little voice says *why not*? I ruin everything I touch. Why not her? So I do it—I slip my tongue along her lower lip.

She gasps into my mouth.

I delve deeper. I take more.

I invade the fuck out of her, tasting her everywhere, exploring her mouth like it's the last thing I'll taste. I'm blown away by the sweetness of her, the surrender. I don't deserve it, but I take it.

I grip her harder, kiss her harder, lost. Only when the shadows crowd in from the corners of my mind do I realize I'm running out of breath. When I pull back, I'm panting hard. So is she.

I stare into her brown eyes, drowning in them.

She looks almost tender, but that can't be right. The kiss must have fucked me up.

The point of her tongue darts out to her lips, and I groan against the urge to kiss her again. I'm already rock-hard against her stomach, one second away from throwing her on the hood of the car and fucking her.

A small hand cups my cheek, warm and soft. Her eyes never leave mine. "You've never done that before, have you?"

Shock freezes me from the inside out.

I take a step back.

Her hand falls away.

How does she know? How does she fucking know? Nothing about me is finessed or gentle. When I fuck, it's hard and rough—and no one's ever questioned where I learned it, how I started.

Leave her the fuck alone, the voice whispers again. This time it isn't trying to protect her. It's trying to protect me. She sees too deep inside me. "You fucking serious?" I say.

She gazes, unblinking.

"You serious?" I go to her and grab her a little rough. I press her to the Navigator door, let her feel the ridge of my steely cock, let her feel how there's nothing nice about me. "You need to stop spinning fucked-up little schoolgirl fantasies about me."

She stiffens under me, no longer soft. She's scared.

"What the fuck good is it?" I demand. "What the fuck good is it to learn all that bullshit self-defense, or what I taught you about running from people who might really fuck with you, if you can't see what's in front of your face?"

Still she gazes up at me.

I jerk her a little, trying to shake the answer out of her.

"Okay," she breathes.

I stay on her, though. Funny how that works—here I am, back again, holding her close, enjoying her warmth and her softness once again.

Some string of logic twists around in my head, saying it would be good for her if I took her right now, right on the hood of her daddy's car, just to show her what the world is like so that she doesn't get the lesson from somebody else, somebody worse.

It's important to know what the world is like. She's in for a lot of hurt, this girl.

I close my eyes. This other part of me wants to protect her from that. Like maybe she never has to know what the world is.

I want that for her in a way I haven't wanted anything for a long time. I want her to not know how things are. To not know what darkness really is.

"Hey," she whispers.

I open my eyes. She's furrowing her pretty brows, drawing them together like dark, silky dashes. Dainty creases form at the inner edges. Her lips are pursed in a pout of concentration.

She removes my hands from her and brushes my sleeve. "Look at this. You have something all over your sleeve. Your sleeve is covered in…what is this?"

I pull my arm away, because I think it might be blood and I don't want her touching that scumbag's blood. But then I see it's not. "Oh. Just sawdust," I say.

"Were you making something? Doing woodworking?"

The hopeful look in her eyes kills me. That's what she thinks I do? Make nice furniture? All industrious and shit? Maybe sanding down my ventriloquist's dummy between shows at the children's hospital?

"We're out of here," I say.

Chapter Nine

~Brooke~

H E MAKES ME drop him on a gloomy corner in Franklin City. He melts into the shadows as soon as he's out of the car, like a shark disappearing into the murky depths of the ocean.

We only spent a couple of hours together, but it feels like I lived a lifetime in those hours.

I head toward the freeway that will take me back home, a deep suburb as far east as you can get from west.

I put my phone back together while I'm stopped at a light just before the freeway entrance.

The texts and voicemails flow in. Mom asking where I am. She hadn't gotten my voicemail. Then it's Mom saying I'm not at Chelsea's. Mom angry. Then Dad.

I quickly give them a call.

"Brooke!" Her voice is high, the way it gets when she's drinking or mad. I'm thinking she's a little of both. My throat clenches with worry—or maybe just grief. She's like this more and more.

"I just got your messages," I say. "I'm fine, I'm

okay."

"Where are you?"

"Just driving around," I say. That's what the man said to tell people. I wanted to drive around and think about my school project.

"You lied to us!"

"I knew you wouldn't understand, so I—"

"You lied! You frightened us out of our minds! Not to mention wasting the time of the police!"

A bolt of fear shoots through me. "I shouldn't talk while I drive," I say. "Everything's fine." I hang up, thankful for the excuse.

But everything isn't fine.

Detective Emilio Rivera is there when I arrive.

My pulse kicks into overdrive. He smiles at me in a kindly way, like an uncle.

My mother embraces me—partly for the benefit of Detective Rivera, I'm sure. I'll get the freeze or worse once he leaves.

Dad looks stern. "You gave us quite a scare, young lady."

I murmur something about not having ideas for my prehistoric village. "I thought I'd be home before you noticed." Part of me does feel guilty for all the fuss. I've been taught to be small and silent, to take up as little space as possible.

The other part of me is scared of what Detective

Rivera sees. His eyes are sharp despite the vague smile on his face. I have the impression of a mirror, one of those one-way things they put in interrogation rooms. He can see me, but I don't know what he's thinking.

"I'm sorry to waste your time," I tell him, heart beating too fast.

"It's no problem," he says smoothly. "I'd actually like to ask you a few questions."

"Questions?" My voice sounds as high and thin as my mother's.

"About the incident last fall. Your birthday." His tone is sympathetic, but I'm not fooled. He's observing me. Recording every detail in that whirring computer he's got inside his head. "We have some new leads that I need to follow up."

"This again?" Mother gives me a hard look, as if I asked for it to be brought up. "The incident is best forgotten, Brooke, you know that. You can't let it ruin your future. Or this family."

She leaves the room in a flurry of silk and Chanel No. 5. The guilt sits heavy in my gut, churning like rocks. Like boulders. I don't want to ruin this family. But how can I forget him? I can't.

You don't want to forget him, a voice inside my head whispers.

It's my darkest secret.

My father glances at his phone. "I've already missed

two meetings."

"I'm sorry," I say, because he pours everything into his work, and missed meetings can be disastrous.

He's already on the phone by the time he leaves the room.

I'm alone with Detective Rivera, which is both a relief and a source of fear. At least I don't need to put up an act for my parents' sake. On the other hand, Detective Rivera won't have to put up an act, either. Nothing about his outward appearance changes, but I feel the shift in the air, the hardening.

"Driving around?" he says, almost mild. "Where?"

"I don't remember."

"For two hours."

"I was focused on my school project." I remind him of the lie. "Lost in thought."

"Ah," he says with a patronizing agreement. "The prehistoric village. That's all right. I'm sure a car as new and nice as yours has a GPS system. We can pull up the logs, find out where you went. Maybe find some surveillance cameras along your route."

I hadn't thought about that. Worry mixes with something else—a sense of protectiveness. My eyes narrow. "Does it matter where I went? What does this have to do with the prior incident?"

"What indeed," he murmurs. "But yes, you're right. The prior incident. We got a hit on a partial fingerprint at a different crime scene. One that matches the one from your party."

My blood races. A different crime scene? A partial fingerprint? All I can picture is another white dress with pink flowers, another girl. Did he take her hostage, too? Did he make her drive him around? *Did he kiss her?* Of course those thoughts are crazy. He doesn't spend his days making lost little girls drive him around. And even if he did, I don't care.

I shouldn't care.

I twist my hands together, remembering how the man looked in the car. Dark and mysterious. Forbidding. "A different crime scene. That's scary," I manage to say. It's the right answer for someone like me. A victim.

It's also true. I'm scared of him, even though he excited me. Took me over. Reached inside to my pounding heart.

How much is it worth to feel alive? A little fear seems like a small price to pay.

Detective Rivera nods, studying me intently. "That's right. It is scary what he's capable of. And how they found the print—smeared in blood."

The words slither down my spine, cold and thick. "Blood?"

"There was quite a lot of it," he says conversationally. "That's the typical result when you run a human body through a wood chipper. It pulverizes everything, but it's messy. Don't know why they did it. It doesn't get rid of the DNA. We got enough tooth fragments and bone chips to test. Even fingernails." He's looking right at me, testing me.

My stomach turns over, vision darkening around the edges. The image is so gruesome it takes me a second to realize how callously the detective is talking about death. How pointedly. He's doing this on purpose.

"That's horrible," I say, heat pricking behind my eyes.

"Horrible," he agrees. "Have you been to a lumber-yard recently?"

No, but I can imagine what they look like. I can imagine the fine white specks of wood that gather against a blade, how the sawdust might hang in the air. How it might sprinkle over the green shirt or jeans of a man who visited. Could some sawdust have fallen off in my car? What if they test it?

I swallow hard against the dryness in my throat. "Never," I whisper.

Sawdust. I thought he might have a hobby. Building furniture in his garage or something. Like a regular man.

He isn't a regular man. He's a killer.

"These are dangerous people," Detective Rivera says. "The man who took you last fall—he's part of a very violent group. The accomplice of a convicted cop killer, Brooke. Not somebody you can trust—not ever.

Certainly not somebody you'd want to know."

"He put a bag over my head," I say, voice rising with panic, because we didn't think of a lie for me to tell this time around. A cop killer? Tears heat my eyes. "Why do you think I know him?"

He looks right at me. "I don't know. Do you? Know him?"

I feel my spine straighten. I know how he kills. I know how his lips feel when he kisses. I know how his green eyes can burn bright as cut emeralds, but then how they can turn soft and sweet when you least expect it. But I don't know his name. You don't really know somebody if you don't know their name, right? "Of course I don't know him."

Detective Rivera waits a long time. Does he want me to say more? Does he really not believe me? But he doesn't know for sure. He's not a mind reader. He can't make me tell anything. He can't make me say anything at all.

Suddenly Rivera stands, making every muscle in my body tense. "I think you know more than you're telling me, Miss Carson. And when it comes to Stone Keaton, that's a problem."

Stone Keaton. It takes me a moment to register that that's his name.

So I know his name now. The knowledge doesn't soothe me, not with the image of sawdust on his arms still fresh in my mind.

Stone Keaton.

"He's a suspect in multiple homicides," Rivera continues. "And I'll tell you, he's the kind of guy with nothing to lose. The kind of guy who'll do just about anything to avoid arrest. Including hurting people— friends, officers, family. Makes him very dangerous. Very dangerous to know."

"I understand," I say. Though part of me doesn't— not really. He could've killed me that night, but he let me go. *You're mine,* he said, like I'm something that belongs to him now. He's a dangerous killer, but I'm his. Maybe I should feel scared.

Or maybe he's the one who should feel scared. The police think he has nothing to lose, and that he'll never let himself be taken in. It seems like that's the kind of person they might shoot. Does Stone know? Probably. He knows all about the cops. He said so.

Rivera gets a call. He says he has to go. I ask him whether he wants to say goodbye to my parents, but he doesn't—he seems like he's in a hurry, so I show him to the door, smiling politely and saying goodbye as if he's a family friend who dropped by to borrow the boat hitch instead of a man who thinks I'm protecting a killer.

I shut the door after him and press my nose to the beveled glass window that's set into the massive mahogany door. I watch him head down the walk. He gets into his car and leaves, and all the while I'm turning his name over and over in my mind. Not Rivera's name, but Stone's. Stone Keaton.

Stone.

CHAPTER TEN

~STONE~

Five months later

EARLY SEPTEMBER IS hot as fuck, even in the Bradford Hotel. Which is saying a lot, because it's a brick-and-stone behemoth that usually stays cool. Of course we tapped into the grid when we first moved in, got AC blowing into the parts where we live—the deep interior parts we fixed up and tricked out, posh as a palace. Actually better than a palace, because there's nothing fussy—it's all nice rugs and good, sturdy, oversized furniture guys can lie around on, and of course the best gaming consoles and computing shit money can buy.

But whenever you go outside, it's a wall of heat. And we're out there a lot, chasing leads on the Grayson thing. Working overtime to hunt those assholes.

I think about Brooke all the while, thinking about that day at the park. Mostly I remember how perfect she felt in my hands, the way her belly felt when I pressed my rock-hard cock against her, pinning her like a butterfly against her cherry-red car door. It was fucking heaven—the kind of heaven I have no right to. Which is always the best kind.

Even the way she tasted was perfect—its own entire category of taste, not mint or berries or whatever bullshit, but pure, warm, soft, breathy Brooke.

She was stiff at first, like she was surprised, but then she softened. That's the thing that churns in my mind the most—churning like the angry fucking sea—that moment she went from stiff to soft. The moment her little body let me notch right into her.

She's fragile as a bird, but she let me hold her, like a sickening little token of trust. She doesn't know what she's getting into with me. She has no fucking idea.

Her skin is so soft. She's just so pure. It's fucked up how pure she is. It's fucked up how much she doesn't know and how untouched she is. Her skin is *literally* like silk. It makes me want to drive my fist into a brick wall over and over and over.

I churn on her silky, untouched skin while we lurk around in the heat, loitering in dark service alleys. I think about her while we linger outside expensive restaurants, in the shadows of the courthouse, cock hard, mind racing.

The whole train of thought is just dangerous, because when you're lurking around places and dealing with the kind of people we're dealing with, you can't be wanting to smash things or grabbing random guys and driving their faces onto a wall just because you're in a screwed-up place.

But I need to keep an eye on Brooke. Make sure she's not talking to the cops. The secrets we share are my private leash on her. I let her live, and now she's mine.

We follow different men around Franklin City. Sometimes we follow Governor Dorman himself. We didn't know his name back then, but we remember his face. Because trust me, young and drugged as we were, we remember the face of each and every one of the men and women who paid good money to perv out on us over the years.

I'd love nothing more than to show Dorman the end of my blade, and I'm sure we could get him alone without a lot of trouble, but we have to be smart. We have to think about freeing Grayson.

So we track guys. We've been hurting a lot of guys to get information. Like the one we ran through the wood chipper. The nicknames he gave us—Jimmy Brass, Johnson, Keeper—don't mean much. Yet.

Sometimes when I can't sleep, I head out into the streets in the middle of the night, driving around.

More often than not, I find myself in East Franklin City, outside her big brick mansion with the circular drive and rows of pine trees like soldiers guarding the estate. I look up at her dark window and imagine her sleeping peacefully. Dark lashes resting on her pretty cheekbones. Light brown hair with those angel-bright highlights splayed all messy on her pillow.

It's her birthday in a week, and this is stupid, but I'm making her a present. A carved hummingbird. I probably won't give it to her, but I started making it, and I knew it was for her, even though I didn't say it to anyone. I didn't even say it to myself at first. I just grabbed a blunt serrated knife and a block of wood and started carving.

I taught myself how to carve in the basement. We never got real knives, for obvious reasons, but a butter knife or two would make its way down there, and if you scrape the shit out of a piece of wood, you can make something. If you do it for hours and hours over many days and weeks, you can make something fucking amazing.

I work on it on stakeouts. I work on it sitting in gloomy alleys. I keep it wrapped in a cloth in my pocket, though its spindly legs are getting fragile enough that I should probably put the thing in a box.

It's on a Tuesday, the day before her birthday, that I get a break. One of the clubbing guys we pay for information tells me he heard from the grapevine about some rich guy who was asking around about a hitter who'd take a job to kill a cop last year. Said that the guy plays high-stakes poker in the back of a midtown bar on Tuesdays. Limo and everything.

I get the location and go by myself. Partly because Calder and the rest of the guys are out following up on some other lead. Mostly because something about it smells off, almost as if it's too easy. I decide just to have a look at who this is. If I decide he's somebody who needs to talk, or maybe somebody who needs to hurt, I can do the hurting, too.

It's almost better this way—I don't always like my guys seeing what I do. And the things I've been doing, let's just say they're not getting rosier.

Grayson's been inside a few months, and I'm feeling desperate. Whenever there's something gruesome to do, I make sure I'm the one to do it.

The way I figure, every time that it's me, it doesn't have to be one of them.

That's how I end up behind a sleazy midtown bar. There's a faded pub sign out front and piles of moldy crates in the back. It could be any old bar, any illegal poker game.

I watch a customer get out of a taxi, his movements cautious, his gaze wary as it darts around the street. He doesn't match the description I got. I'll kill a lot of guys if I have to—I need answers. If I don't get answers, I'm not sure that I can control myself. Maybe that's a sign that I should bring in the guys.

But I don't.

Better if only one person has to see. One person to

hurt people.

I raise my fist. The knock echoes through the alley.

A man opens the door. Greasy wife-beater. Big scowl. "The fuck you want?"

"The game. I want to play."

"You know the secret word?"

A secret word? Like this was some fucking exclusive nightclub. I resist the urge to pull out my Glock to prove a point. Instead I pull out my wallet and give him a glimpse of the thick wad of green inside. "Yeah, I know it."

He snorts. "Good enough. Game starts in two hours, strictly speaking."

"And less strictly?"

"High rollers don't show up until midnight."

That means I have some time to kill. I give the fucker at the door enough money to keep him silent, at least for tonight. He assumes I want to hustle at the game, take them unaware, and that's fine. No one needs to know my real purpose until it's too late for them to do anything.

There's a park down the block, the kind with statues and gardens. The statues are covered in graffiti from the neighborhood gangs. The gardens dried up a decade ago.

Now there's only a network of bums and drug dealers. They give me hard looks but don't come close. It isn't the fact that I'm carrying that keeps them away.

They can see that I'm like them. Made hard and merciless by years at the bottom of this city. Everyone here was made in a basement of their own.

I find an unoccupied bench with a plaque, unreadable from the rust. Someone once built this park with care. Someone loved it. I kick away a used needle with my boot before sitting down.

This spot gives me a good view of the side entrance, but I don't need it yet.

The men I'm interested in, the ones high enough to matter, they've got more money than God. I'm done dicking around with the grunt workers, the men desperate enough to take cash for dirty work.

I should wait in silence. Maybe light up. Play fucking Candy Crush on my phone. Anything but dial the number of a pretty little rich girl. I shouldn't even know her phone number, but my mind's like a fucking bulldog when it wants something. It knows the numbers forward and backward, as sharp and strong as her shining eyes or the freckles across her nose.

"Hello?" Her voice is clear and soft. Beautiful like her. She's a sparkling pond, and I'm black ink. The only thing I'm good for is ruining her.

I'm silent a long time. Long enough I expect her to hang up.

Then she says something that makes my heart stop. "Stone?"

How the fuck does she know it's me? It's been five months. And how does she know my name? "Have you been talking to the cops?"

"Detective Rivera was waiting for me when I got home. My parents had called him when—"

When we went on that little joyride last spring. A little kidnapping. "He told you about me?"

"Not much. Your name. And he asked me about…" Her breath shudders over the line. "He asked me about a lumberyard."

The fear in her voice burns me. She might as well be flame. "And you remembered the dust on my arms, didn't you?"

There's a rough sob. "Tell me you didn't do it."

"That would be a lie, princess. And I don't lie to you."

In the silence I can hear her breathing. I can hear her wondering. "I wish you would," she says finally. "I wish you'd lie."

I know what it's like to pretend. I'm done with that, though. "We don't have anything between us. Not promises or nice words. This is all we have. The naked truth."

The word *naked* hangs over the phone line, hard and weighty as a rock. I didn't mean for the words to be sexual, but as the seconds of silence tick by, they become that way. As if I expect things from her. More than a kiss or a touch. As if I'll make her fuck me.

"That makes it sound like I'll see you again," she says breathlessly.

Is she still afraid of me? She should be, after what Rivera told her.

"Probably. And I'll make you drive me around. I'll keep you until I'm done with you, but I won't make you fuck me, understand? That's a promise."

"He said you'd kill anyone to stay free. That you have nothing to lose."

"Yeah, that just goes to show he doesn't know shit about me."

"So that…wasn't you? At the lumberyard?"

I hate the hope in her voice. "I didn't say I wouldn't kill. I said I have something to lose."

"Oh."

I would kill for my guys, no question. To protect them. For revenge. Even as I think about it, the picture of her smile forms in my mind. They aren't the only people I'd kill to protect.

"I can't answer every question. I can't tell you every-thing." It would put her at risk as much as me. If Rivera thinks he can use her as leverage, he won't hesitate. "But I can promise not to lie."

There's silence, where I can hear her thinking.

I know whatever she says next will be her test of me. A test I'm suddenly desperate to pass. I've never gotten close to a girl. Never wanted to. Quick fucks when my body needed a warm, wet place. That all changed the night she witnessed me killing someone. The night I let her live.

There are a thousand incriminating questions she could ask me. A million sins I've committed, both things I did on purpose and things that were done to me before I even understood.

"Will you hurt me?" she finally asks. "If you see me again?"

And I breathe a silent sigh of relief, because this is one question I can answer. "Never," I tell her, my voice dropping with promise. "I'd cut off my hand first."

I may not know how to date a girl, how to make love to her, but I damn well know how to protect someone. I've been doing that since I was old enough to fight. It was only ever supposed to be for the boys in that basement with me, but somewhere along the way, she burrowed into my dark heart.

Was it when she stood up to me in her torn party dress?

Or when her brown eyes softened looking at me across the front seat of her car?

I've become obsessed with her. With the shape of her eyebrows. The feel of her skin. I'm stalking her in a way that would make her run straight to Detective Rivera for help if she knew about it.

There's this Instagram video where she's in a floppy hat and little orange shorts, blowing bubbles at her friend Chelsea. You can't see Chelsea—she's holding the phone, backing away, wanting to protect her phone from the bubbles. Brooke is happy, eyes shining, coming at her with bubbles, a brightly feathered bird captured midflight in all its glory. The clip's all jerky, and both of them are laughing and kind of screaming, but it's the good kind of screaming, not the bad kind.

I watch that fucking thing over and over. Forty-six seconds.

I don't have an Instagram or Facebook account or anything—none of us do. Because what the fuck do we want with that? But we use fake accounts for researching people and casing places. It's great for knowing where people are or when they're on vacation.

Or seeing what Brooke is doing.

It's a hot night, and I really want her to be in those shorts. I need to imagine her like that, breathless and laughing and so goddamn beautiful it makes my chest ache. "Where are you right now?"

"Why?" she asks, suddenly on guard—I can hear it in her voice.

I stare across the park at the moths swirling around a streetlight, around and around and around like idiots. "Because I want to know, that's why."

"In my bed," she says, hesitant. "Reading."

"What do you have on?"

A longer pause this time. "I don't know. Just a T-shirt."

"That's all?"

"Why are you asking?"

"Because you make me feel like there's something to fight for." The words come up out of some dark, twisted part of my soul. They feel both too raw and perfectly right.

There's a long pause. Then, "Panties," she whispers. "That's what else I'm wearing."

My cock is hard as steel, hearing her say the word *panties*. "What color?"

"Blue," she says, sounding breathless, her voice husky. I'm attuned to that kind of shit, with people's voices. While other kids were learning to ride bikes, we boys were listening for signs of heat-roughened voices in the adults around us.

Like fucking rabbits, alert to every threat in the jungle.

"They're both blue," she says. "It's a sleep set."

"A sleep set," I say, as if it makes perfect sense that you'd change into a special outfit for sleeping. I just pull off my shirt and leave on whatever jeans I wore that day. It means I'm ready to fight at any time of night.

I like that she has special sleep clothes. I like to think of her relaxed. Safe.

"What kind of blue? Light or dark?"

She makes a little humming sound. "I'd say…azure."

Azure? What does that even mean? I can't tell if she's fucking with me or being serious anymore—that's how far apart we are. "Is azure light or dark?"

"Oh. Medium, I guess." The words come out shyly. "The color of the sky when there aren't clouds."

I'm suddenly thinking about her silky skin. I'm thinking about me pressing her against that cherry-red car, my cock at her flat belly, her tight little ass cheeks squished against the warmth of that metal. Blue cotton straining and stretching. Azure.

"You know what I think, Brooke?"

"What?"

"I think there's a part of your panties that's dark blue."

"No, they're completely blue. I mean, medium blue," she says, her breathless voice betraying her. "With white lace."

"I happen to know for a fact that there's a part that's darker than the rest."

"I think I would know." I can hear the slight smile in her voice.

"You want me to prove it?"

Silence.

"Put your hand between your legs."

"Stone!" The way she gasps my name gets me even

harder.

"Do it."

"I don't…I can't…"

"Yes, you can. It's so easy. Just slip that pretty little hand—your fingernails are painted pink, aren't they? Slip them down over your panties. Touch yourself. See if you're wet."

"No," she says on a sigh, but I know I'm winning.

"Okay, okay. Look, how about something easy. You know that line of skin above the elastic band of your panties? Right below the hem of your top? You're going to trace that with your finger."

She says nothing. It's just soft breath. She's not doing it, but she will. I'll make her. It's wrong, what I'm doing, but I tell myself it's better she's doing it to herself than me doing it to her. Better her soft, silky fingers on her instead of my fingers, rough and brutal and scarred as the moon.

"I don't know if I want to do this," she says.

"You do want to do it. You know how I know?"

"No."

"Because I'm a bad guy, a criminal, and I can tell things other people can't. I can tell when somebody's heart is beating like crazy the way yours is right now. I know when they say they don't want to do things, but they secretly kind of want to."

There's a soft sound, like a whimper.

I push harder. "I live outside of the law. That is where I live, little bird, and that's where you went the first night with me. And you think I can't see you, but guess what? You're in my fucking living room, and it's my hand you're going to press between your legs because you belong to me."

She lets out a shaky breath.

"Are you scared?"

"I don't know," she says.

"I think you do know. Honesty works both ways. I won't lie to you, but this doesn't work if you lie to me. This all falls apart." It's a threat. A push. "And you don't want that, do you?"

"No."

I push aside the relief I feel that she wants this. That she's fucking glorious and sexy and desperate in it. A beautiful girl like her, turned on by fear. Like the fucking holy grail for a bastard like me. "So tell me. Are you scared?"

"Yes."

"That's good. But here's the thing—you don't ever have to worry about anything when you're mine. I've got you. You're safe, and you're going to touch yourself until you come."

Her breath catches.

"Did you ever make yourself come before?" I ask.

There's a silence. Then, "Yeah."

"Now you're gonna do it for me."

"But…what about you?"

I pause, considering the question. There's no way I'm touching myself in the middle of a seedy park. The question means more than that, at least to me. *What about you?* It means, *what do you want from me? What's the endgame here?*

Of course there's no future for me and a girl like her. No future for me at all. I'm going down in a hail of bullets. As long as I can free Grayson and take as many of the assholes who kept us in that basement with me, I'm content with that.

That means all we have is the here, the now. The imaginary touch of my hands on her pale skin.

"I'm there," I say, my voice hard. "I'm with you, my hand on your stomach, my fingers edging under the band of your panties. Do you feel me?"

There's a gentle rustle of fabric. A hitch of breath. "Yes."

In that one word, I see everything—her hand slipping into her panties, her wide eyes in the privacy of her bedroom. Her other hand clutching her phone like the dirty little secret that I am to her. It feels like victory, like I'm so fucking proud, so fucking pleased, that it doesn't even matter what happens tonight. Doesn't matter if I find the people we've been searching for forever. And that makes her dangerous.

"Now lower," I say. "I bet you have hair, don't you? Springy curls a little darker than the hair on your head."

Her whisper comes out in a rush. "Omigod."

"You're doing good," I say. "It probably feels a little coarse to you, but it would be a fucking cloud against my cock."

She makes a high-pitched noise. "You can't—"

"There's nothing I can't do to you, baby. That's what you need to learn. Your body belongs to me. Your mind belongs to me. Every part of you is mine for me to touch. Even that swollen pink slit. Slide your fingers down. See how wet you are."

A moan. "This is wrong."

"You love it. Imagine how shocked your mother would be. How angry your father would be. Every person in that fucking birthday party, smiling for you, looking down at you like you're some little kid. And meanwhile you're fucking yourself with your fingers, hungry and slick, desperate enough to come for a criminal."

Her breath comes faster. "I won't."

"Won't what?" She's already doing it.

"What you said. I won't come."

Despite the aching in my cock, I give a soft laugh. "*Come.* Is that the first time you've used the word like that? How about another word? Like climax. Orgasm. Do you want to orgasm, little bird?"

"No," she stutters, but it's a lie.

I could call her on it, demand honesty, make her admit how much she wants this, needs it. But there's something delicious about pushing her against her will. "Doesn't matter," I say. "Whether you want to come or not, you're going to. Those fingers are so wet, aren't they? Your body knows who it belongs to. Me, sweetheart. You're mine."

A black car pulls around the block, crossing right in front of me. Chrome gleams in the moonlight. All the hair on the back of my neck rises. My body is revved up by arousal and pure violent impulse.

Her soft moan is a balm to my cold anger, thawing me out enough to say, "Now find your clit. You know where that is, don't you? You play with yourself at night, finding all the places that feel good. It must be hard now. Hard and sensitive. Pinch it. Right now."

She makes a hoarse sound. "Stone. Not like this. You're not…with me."

Because I'm already standing from the park bench. I'm halfway across the weed-riddled sidewalk. How does she know that I'm withdrawing? How can she sense that I'm not there anymore?

I shove the questions aside, because they don't matter. She doesn't matter. Not really. A pretty face. Sweet brown eyes. A smoking-hot body. That's all she is to me. *That's all she can be.*

And I can push her away more effectively with words than with a gun.

I slip along the side of the building, using the shadows to disguise myself. If I really wanted to be stealthy, I'd hang up, but I need to finish this. For both our sakes.

"Oh yes, sweetheart. I'm there. I'm holding your hands down to your cunt, telling you to fuck yourself. Shoving my cock in your throat until you've got tears down your cheeks. Until you've got saliva running down your chin. You're crying, but you don't dare stop touching yourself."

Her cries grow louder as I speak, her breath faster.

"And it feels good because it's so wrong. You're coming on your hand, spilling that sweet juice all over your slippery fingers. Even while I'm taking away your air, making you choke."

She comes on the word *choke*, her body reacting on primal instinct, squeezing her throat until she breaks apart.

Like I've done a thousand times, I detach from the moment. I store her moans and cries in a secret place, balm for every dark thing I'll do in the future. By the time her body finishes spasming, her inner muscle clenching, her breathing exhaled in a low moan, she's already a memory to me.

"Very nice," I say, my voice clipped.

I stare down the alley where the black limo has

stopped in front of the private poker game. Early. This is a high roller, but he isn't coming after midnight. Because the guy at the door lied to me? Did the guy decide to have a few drinks before the game?

"Stone?" she asks, sounding lost.

Her voice seems small and distant over the phone line, like it's across an ocean instead of just the city. "Now you sleep in those wet panties, understand? Keep them on and pretend I came inside you, that I'm leaking out all night long."

Before she can respond, I click the end button on the phone.

The light in my phone goes out, leaving me in darkness. I erase the call history—nobody needs to know about Brooke except me—and I turn my attention to the back entrance of the pub.

The dark car is pulling away. It moves around to the edge of the park and pulls over. That'll be the driver, settling in to read or watch something on his phone or smoke or whatever, waiting for whoever it is to finish his game or his business inside. Is this the guy?

Is the game starting?

This is a fact-finding mission. If I don't recognize anyone, I'll just sit down and play. You get a really good sense of different guys off playing cards with them, especially if there's money involved. I take the safety off my piece. Nothing has to get bloody here. It's just me figuring out who might've hired the guy who framed Grayson.

Still, I like to be ready.

I'm back at that door. It's the same bouncer, and he gets a nice, crisp bill for letting me in. "Game's just starting to roll." He nods his head toward a staircase.

I don't like this. Something about this feels rushed. Not my presence here, but the dark car. The break in schedule. I just don't know what it is.

"They have their five yet?" That's how many they'll need to start, but it's not really why I'm asking.

He hesitates. He doesn't seem to like the question. "Yeah, but one of 'em'll play out."

I watch him an extra beat. Is he nervous? And upstairs. Not the best. Better than the basement, though. That's an old weakness, my reluctance to go below ground level. Not that I'd let it stop me.

I turn and head up. At the top, I knock on another door.

It opens, and right then I know it's wrong because the guy backs way away, but it's too late, because somebody rushes me from behind, pushing me in. *A setup.*

Four guys materialize on either side of the door, which gets slammed quick enough. Do they know who I am? Or is this about the game?

They have my arms before I can pull my piece out of

the back of my pants.

I go at them with my legs. I land a knee-cracking blow on the biggest guy, and get in a backward head butt on one of the guys holding me—his jaw, I think, from the way he cries out. If this goes bad, I'm extra fucked for that one, but that's what you do—when you fight, you fight.

Five against one. And they already have my arms. It'll definitely go bad.

I get in what blows I can before the beatdown. A fist in my face. Warmth explodes, followed by the taste of blood. Another fist drives into my gut, and another and another.

The biggest guy, a baldie with bushy blond eyebrows and a goatee and blood coming off the side of his lips, does the honors while the other two hold me.

"Fucking serious?" he says, smashing his fist into my mouth. The guy I got in the knee is down in the corner, back against the wall. He'll be trouble later.

I go into it, just go into the misery of it. That's what you do when there's no more fighting. You just want it over with, because you know the morning will come again. Or at least, you have to think that. I relax and take the pain. The broken ribs. The blood. There's no part of me that isn't battered, but they need me conscious. So eventually they stop. I let them push me into a chair.

The goatee guy puts his hands on either armrest and

gets into my face. One of his teeth is cracked. Did I do that? "You're gonna tell us what you know about Dorman, starting with thing one, and not ending 'til you're done." He gets closer. "And we know some of what you know, so there'll be no use leaving anything out."

Dorman, also known as Governor-elect Dorman, is the man who framed Grayson—or, at least, we only suspected it until now. But is he the one who directly ordered the hit of the cop and the frame-up?

I spit at the guy, but he's ready for it and backs up, then he advances and stomps my foot under the heel of his boot, and I just wish I would've hit him.

Chapter Eleven

~Brooke~

THERE ARE PLASTIC stars on my ceiling.

They've been there so long I almost don't see them. They glowed in the dark at the beginning, but that was a long time ago. I had a brief astronomy phase in middle school. A telescope is packed away in one of the closets, too expensive for someone who isn't serious.

I can still recognize a few constellations. I remember having my ruler out, determined to get the relative spacing right while the maid held the ladder steady. The little dipper. Gemini.

It feels like I've lived my entire life as a child, my protective bubble lined with plastic and glitter. And suddenly, with a single phone call, the bubble pops.

Imagine how shocked your mother would be.

Shocked, probably.

Disappointed, definitely. All her hard work to turn me into a society lady down the drain. The booster club would never let me in. It's a strange relief, even if they'll never know.

How angry your father would be.

He would be furious at all the money he poured into me, into my private school and my designer clothes. Like I'm an investment that will never pay out.

I never wanted to be a society lady. Never wanted to be an investment, but they don't ask what I want. Expectations. Requirements. A hundred different rules for me to follow, and I've complied with them all. They never realized that the pressure would build and build. That when I finally broke their rules, it would be by doing something as disastrous as this. As touching myself for a murderer.

Every person in that fucking birthday party, smiling for you, looking down at you like you're some little kid. And meanwhile you're fucking yourself with your fingers, hungry and slick, desperate enough to come for a criminal.

And I'd liked it. Loved it.

My body still hums from the orgasm, my muscles clenching even as the phone line went dead in my ear. How messed up is that? What's wrong with me that I get off with a guy like him?

I need to stop. I know that, but my stomach twists at the thought of never seeing him, never hearing his voice. It's a crush, like the one I had on Mr. Hernandez in the ninth grade. Silly and stupid, but the way my body felt when he spoke, I didn't feel silly. I felt alive.

The bedroom door swings open, no warning, my mother waltzing in like she owns the place—which she does. Even so, it's jarring, a shock. And my heart is still beating so fast and so hard, I can't believe she doesn't hear it.

"Where is that blue Armani?" she says, breezing into my closet. "We need to make sure it's ready for the party on Saturday."

Will she be able to tell? Can she smell it in the air? The faintest musk? A hint of sex? My body is completely under the covers, my right hand resting on my stomach. The phone slid down to my shoulder. I'm paralyzed. Afraid to move, like it will somehow reveal me.

Hangers clank. Fabric rustles. So much fabric. So many dresses. "Didn't you spill something last time? Was there a stain?"

Someone bumped me, sloshing apple juice onto me. Which is why wearing ten thousand dollars to an overcrowded hotel ballroom isn't the best idea.

Maybe it's because I'm afraid to move or maybe it's because I just came so hard I saw stars behind my eyelids, real sparks instead of plastic that doesn't glow, but I say, "Does it matter?"

All movement stops. My mother emerges from the closet, but instead of looking angry, she seems concerned. "Is this because of Detective Rivera?"

"What? No." Why is she bringing this up now? I don't want her asking me about him.

And I definitely don't want her calling him again.

"Are you sick?" she demands.

It makes my heart hurt that she would guess that. It's the only reason someone might not care what other people think.

"No, Mom. I'm fine," I say, looking away. My birthday is tomorrow, but that doesn't matter. It's all about the party on Saturday. I guess even my birthday can't behave properly. It needs to be fit into a more appropriate day.

"Well, what are you doing lying in bed? Help me find it."

I sit up, keeping my legs hidden under the covers, like I might have a scarlet *A* written across my thighs. There might actually be a small damp spot beneath me, which is really the same thing.

"Mom."

She spots a pile of clothes in the corner, eyes widening like she's struck gold. And for her, she has. It's not even fashion that makes her excited. It's status. "These should be hanging up. They'll wrinkle."

"And what if I show up with a wrinkle?" I ask wryly. "Or a stain?"

She gives me a side look. "Don't give me sass, young lady."

My brain is still blissed-out from the orgasm. From the rush of talking to him. That's the only explanation for my sudden rashness. "I'm being serious. What horrible thing would happen if my dress isn't perfect or my makeup? If I'm not a size two?"

Instead of snapping at me, she sits down beside the bed, her eyes soft. "Are you having your period? I know it can make you bloated. That tea…"

I cut her off with a groan. "I'm not having my period. I just don't understand why we do all this. Why we pretend so much. I don't even know how to be myself."

Her lips firm. "This *is* you. Brooke Carson. This is who you were born to be."

If I was born to be like this, why does it always feel like a struggle? Not only for me. For her. For Daddy. "I just don't want you to work so hard."

"It won't always be this way," she says firmly, standing up and returning to the closet. "Your father has a large development deal he's closing."

There's always some new deal on the horizon. Some new investment. Some new way to stall the debt collections. And we're always spending more so that no one realizes how close we are to ruin.

It's a miracle we've kept up appearances this long. A miracle that the glue on those plastic stars has held on all these years. Only a matter of time until they all fall down.

Chapter Twelve

~Stone~

I'M A BALL of hurt in a windowless closet. My hands and ankles are tied; even if they weren't, I'm a little too fucked up to move around just yet. But I didn't talk, and they don't know about the Bradford, which means my guys are safe. And they don't know about Brooke, either.

So everyone's safe.

Except me, of course.

And I feel more sure than ever that Dorman's our guy. The guy who framed Grayson, got him sent to prison. That's good and bad. Good because it's information. Bad because it might be hard to find the hitter and clear Grayson's name. Dorman's not just a guy; he's an organization. A machine.

Now I'm thinking about Plan B—breaking Grayson out of prison. It's not something I ever wanted to attempt. Breaking a guy out of prison is a bitch, but it might be easier than clearing his name at this point.

Considering what we're up against.

They relocated Grayson to a prison five states away and they don't let him have visitors or communicate with the outside world. Our lawyer got in once, but now he's barred, too.

Still, one time was enough for Grayson to pass along a message that he'd be looking for a *pet rat*—that's the term we use for somebody who can be turned, paid.

I don't know how Grayson's going to get a message out to us about this pet rat once he finds him, but Grayson's a resourceful motherfucker. Once he gets the message to us about the pet rat, we'll do what it takes to free him.

I calculate the time; I'm thinking it's around four in the morning.

Brooke will be sleeping with those little blue panties hugging her soft hips, still a little cool, still a little wet.

God.

I play the call back over in my mind for about the hundredth time—the way her voice sounded as she did everything I told her to, so sweetly, so beautifully. The outrush of breath when she got herself off.

The morning will come like it always does, but the connection I had with her for that moment feels like the only real light coming over that barren fucking horizon.

The little hummingbird I carved for her is still in my front shirt pocket, wrapped in a bandana. It's probably cracked. It fucks me up more than it should that the stupid thing is ruined. Clearly I have more pressing issues than a broken bird—men coming back to torture me, for one thing.

But I spent hours carving that little bird, and I really wanted her to have it.

I imagined leaving it somewhere wrapped up nice for her. It wouldn't have a tag on it, but she'd know it was from me. How many stalkers can one girl have? And she'd put it on her dresser in her bedroom. Maybe she would think it was nice.

I get a little sleep—not the easiest thing to do, bound like a side of beef, but when I wake up, my head is clearer. I find I can stand, move around. I get to work on figuring out the layout, the sight lines.

It's pitch-black, but that doesn't matter to me. I'm used to the dark. I function way better than most guys in the dark. My guys and I all do. Spend enough time in a dark basement and you come to know where bodies are just from the way the air feels on your skin. And hearing, too. You learn to tell exactly where people are from rustling, almost as if you can see them with your ears.

As soon as I manage to get my arms under my feet and to the front of me, I'm in business. I raise them up enough to find the light fixture and dismantle it, pulling out the bulb and smashing it. I use a shard of glass to cut my bindings.

And wait, assessing my injuries. Nothing major broken, but it hurts when I breathe. Cracked ribs. Worst of all is my foot, which is on fire. I'm thinking some bones in there got crushed.

The door rattles, bringing me to full alert. I crouch in a corner and hide as the door swings open. They try to turn on the light. Nothing.

One of them turns on his phone, and the other approaches, weapon drawn.

I grab his weapon arm and yank him all the way in, exactly what he's not expecting. I slam the door with my foot.

We're shrouded in darkness. And I'm a motherfucking ghost. He's lurching around like a fucking bull in a china shop.

He shoots, but I'm behind him. I grab his arm and ram my knee into his elbow, bending it the wrong way. In other words, breaking it. He cries out, because that's a motherfucker of an injury. His piece clatters to the floor. I grab his hair and ram that same knee up into his face, and he's over.

I grab his piece and go still.

A voice from outside the closet door. Just to the side. They're not so sure about coming in now. "Shane?"

I'm flat on the floor. I shoot the voice. There's a cry.

Shots come back, but they don't hear me like I hear them. I shoot. The other's on the move. I take one more shot.

A thump.

A cry. A groan. Silence.

I ease open the door. The two guys are done. I fish around in pockets for car keys. I need wheels for sure; the car I drove will have been towed by now. Maybe jacked.

I find the keys and get the fuck going, limping down the stairs.

The bar is quiet—not yet open. It's maybe ten in the morning. I go behind the counter and grab a bottle of scotch. I spot a black raincoat on a hook, and I take that, too, and head out the back door into the drizzly fall morning. The keys belong to a Jeep with little red dice hanging from the rearview.

I get in and pull onto the street, blending with the light traffic. People going to work. Meeting friends for lunch. Whatever the fuck regular people do instead of bleeding all over a stolen vehicle.

It takes two miles before I spot a pay phone. I pull into the gas station parking lot. Who uses pay phones anymore except for criminals? And cops can't tap them without a warrant. Kind of amazing they still keep them around, but it's useful today. They took my money and phone.

I use the change in the tray to put in a call to Calder. He's pissed I didn't check in, but I tell him I got a little fucked up, and that calms him down. I open the scotch and take a drink, let the warmth of it spread over the pain. Some old-fashioned anesthetic.

"We need Nate to come in?" he asks.

"Yeah," I say, my head swimming from pain and whiskey. More from pain, though. "Might need a Band-Aid. Maybe with little rainbows on them."

The last time I needed Nate was when I'd gotten shot, which is probably why Calder sounds worried. "Where are you? You need me to come get you?"

"I got wheels." I take another drink and look out at the midmorning traffic. Brooke will be heading to class, maybe with a latte in her hand. Or maybe something pink. A fancy drink that costs a stupid amount at the coffee shop. A pink mustache over her pretty lips.

Meanwhile I'm talking about getting looked at by a vet.

Nate runs a clinic outside of town. Looks at horses and shit. He tried to go straight after we got out. Tried to live a regular life. Even got his degree. Owns a business. Sometimes I feel bad dragging him back into this, but there's no one else I trust.

"How far out are you?" Calder asks.

"I don't know." I put the cap on the bottle and set it aside. Then I pull the little bundle from my pocket and unwrap it from the bandana.

I can tell right away that it's broken from the way it unwraps, its fragile little wing snapped, hanging on by a bit of wood fiber.

Fuck.

"You don't know where you are?"

"I know where I am," I say. It isn't really a lie. I'll figure out where I am, as soon as I figure out where I'm going. "I might make a stop before I head in."

"What kind of stop? You need to come in," Calder says. "Knox made bacon, dude. That thick-cut stuff. There's Texas toast. Not to mention the fact that you're fucked up enough to need Nate."

"Just a stop. And then I'm back." After I hang up, I get up close and personal with the rearview mirror.

There's a nasty bruise just starting to turn on my left cheekbone. My left eye is a little bit closed, and most of my bottom lip is fat. I lick my thumb and scrub the dried blood from the side of my mouth. It feels strange to give a shit, but I don't want Brooke to be scared.

I button up the raincoat over my bloody clothes.

I locate enough change in the change tray to grab a coffee and bagel at another drive-through place. The coffee doesn't do much for my pain, but Nate will give me something when I get back.

This feels more important.

More important than pain. More important than the guys.

Saint Mary's, the private school Brooke attends, is a three-story stone building right across from a huge East Franklin park—the nice kind with trees and benches and flowers and a duck pond.

The school is really old, with tall windows and grand steps that lead up to a fancy entrance under a curly stone-carved thing that says the school was founded in 1903.

Two purple banners hang down from the roof on either side of the entrance. Today's banners have pictures of hockey sticks. They tell the world that the girls who attend Saint Mary's won the state field hockey championship this year. I thought hockey was played on ice, but apparently rich girls play it in a field.

No boys attend Saint Mary's, so I guess Brooke's parents and I can agree on at least one thing.

I circle the tree-lined blocks near the school until I spot the cherry-red Lincoln Navigator parked on the street. Cherry red. Custom color. I grab an open space two behind, then settle down to wait. School's not out until three, but Brooke seems to have free periods in the middle of the day on Mondays, Wednesdays, and Fridays, and she sometimes leaves for lunch. If it's nice out, she grabs a snack at Panera and goes to study in the park, but it's windy and it looks like rain, so I'm thinking she'll go sit in the Panera. That girlfriend of hers sometimes goes with her, but not usually on Wednesdays.

It's her birthday, though, so all bets are off.

I swig the coffee and wait, trying to ignore the different areas of pain flaring in my body. My lip looks bigger and my bruises look darker every time I check them.

I wait. I'm starting to think I should trash this mission—the last thing Brooke needs on her birthday is me coming at her like a monster.

And then she appears, like a fucking dream, walking up the sidewalk in a plaid skirt and white shirt and jacket, glossy hair shimmering all around her shoulders. She fucking kills me.

Just walking, she kills me. I slip out of the vehicle just as she's getting into hers. I catch the door before she closes it.

She just gapes at me. Stunned. "Stone."

"Happy birthday, princess." I pull out the seatbelt and tuck it around her, brushing her hip with my hand as I click it into place. Her breath is a feather on my hair. I hit the Unlock All button on her door and then shut it.

I circle around to the passenger side, holding back a wince as I get in.

Her delicate brows are furrowed. "Are you okay?" she asks softly.

"I'm okay." And suddenly it feels true, as long as she looks at me with those pretty eyes. Brighter than the goddamn sky. They don't seem real. She isn't real.

Her gaze falls to my lip. "You're not. You're not okay."

"You should see the other guys," I joke.

She doesn't seem to think that's funny. I guess it's not, really. Considering.

"Let's go," I growl.

"I have to be back. They'll put out an alert on me. Maybe call Detective Rivera."

Fucking Detective Rivera. "Drive."

With shaky hands, she starts the thing up and pulls out.

I used to think heaven would be someplace alone, someplace secret. Where no one could touch me. Hurt me. Not that I would ever make it to heaven, but it was something to dream about.

But now heaven's the rumble of the highway, the faint scent of flowers.

"You need a hospital," she says, her voice low.

I sigh, strangely pleased by her concern. "What are they going to do that a vet can't do?"

She glances at me sideways. Then her gaze finds the bottle of whiskey in my pocket. "Have you been drinking?"

"Only a little."

"It's not even noon. And you shouldn't drink and drive."

"That's why you're driving," I tell her, even though that isn't why. It's because she always drives. I think guys are supposed to want to be in the driver's seat. They think that makes them in control, but they don't fucking know.

In the passenger seat, I can tell her to go anywhere in the world, and she'll take us there. The Grand Canyon or the Eiffel Tower. *Take us to the fucking moon.*

And all the while, I get to watch. Her delicate profile. Her slender hands on the wheel.

"Where am I going?" she asks, proving my point.

"Doesn't matter, sweetheart. It's what happens on the way that matters." I put my hand on her thigh, a subtle threat despite my injuries.

Tremors run through her body at my touch. Fear? Probably.

We both know I could overpower her, but I'm the only one who knows I wouldn't. Couldn't. I couldn't hurt her any more than I could hurt one of my crew. They're my family. And she's…something else.

Something new.

She navigates to the freeway.

"Left lane," I tell her, squeezing her thigh.

Her breath hitches, and she follows my order. "How did you know it was my birthday?"

"I know so much more than that. I know you're getting an A in chemistry. Good job, by the way. I know what type of shampoo you use. I know what book you're reading, the one on your ereader on your nightstand."

That's mostly thanks to Cruz's tech skills. It's crazy what you can find out from looking at someone's email.

Their Amazon order history. Her whole life is online.

She shivers beneath my touch. "That's scary."

"But I don't know the most important things. The things only in your head. Like what you think about school, what you dream about when you're alone."

Her lips press together like she's holding the information in by force. "You're not supposed to know those things about me. I'm your hostage."

"I don't have a gun to your head."

"You threatened my family."

I press my head back against the seat, closing my eyes. Part of me wants to tell her not to worry, that I won't hurt her, won't hurt her family. The other part of me needs her to fear me. It's the only barrier between us. The only thing keeping her safe.

She thinks it's scary being stalked by a man like me. What if I did more than that? What if I cared about her? Loved her? I'm not sure I'm capable of that, but I know it won't mean anything good.

"Take a left after the intersection." I shift, trying to find a way to sit that will make my ribs stop throbbing with that weird icy heat of intense pain. "What did they get you for your birthday? Your family?"

"The new iPhone."

"That's all? Daddy must be slipping."

She's quiet a moment. "A new dress. A necklace. And a spa day with three of my friends."

There's a tension in her voice that wasn't there before. In her body, too. I can feel it coursing, almost stronger than her fear. "You don't like them."

"The presents? No, I do. I mean, they're beautiful. Extravagant."

"And all for show." It's not hard to see what makes Mr. and Mrs. Carson tick. The huge parties and fancy clothes, all while they're drowning in debt.

She laughs without humor. "They picked who came with me for the spa day. All daughters of his work associates. I like those girls well enough, but it's not…"

"It's not about you," I finish for her. "And what would you want, if you could have anything?"

"Nothing that costs money, that's for sure."

"What, then?"

"Something small. Something meaningful," she says.

The broken bird seems to burn in my pocket.

"Something that shows that they see me," she adds.

I see you, I want to say, and then I feel like an asshole. Of course I see her. I'm fucking stalking her. Carjacking her.

I'm not the person she wants to see her.

She sighs. "I don't even know what it would be. What would I like? It feels like there isn't even a *me*, like Brooke Carson doesn't exist. I'm a prop as much as the dress and the necklace. A networking opportunity like the spa day."

"What about your friends?" I know she has plenty of them, far more than the ones her parents make her keep. They walk around the city in fuzzy boots and overlarge sunglasses, giggling like they don't have a care in the world.

"They'll probably get me something. We're planning to go out this weekend. Maybe they'll get me eyeshadow or a new clutch." She shakes her head. "Chelsea will find something fun, though. You probably think I'm ridiculous. Poor little rich girl, with all the expensive gifts."

Maybe I would have thought that, before I knew her. That first night, when all I had been able to see was a pretty dress and wide eyes. "Did you know that birds have different meanings?" I say.

She blinks. "What?"

"The cardinal, for example. It symbolizes truth and beauty. And the crane. It represents integrity. Honor."

"Which one would you be?" she asks, almost cautious.

"Me?" I consider a moment. "The eagle, maybe. Freedom. And pride."

"And a bald head?" she asks, a teasing lilt in that voice.

Her teasing note does something strange in my chest. I feel energized, suddenly. Too large for my body. *She trusts me enough to play.*

We're stopped at a light. I look over. "I'm not that old," I growl.

"Older than me."

That sobers me up quick. I'm older than her, both in years and in spirit. I lived an entire lifetime before I stepped foot outside that basement. "Older than you," I agree softly.

She gives me a curious look. "What bird would I be?"

I pull the broken bird from my pocket and hold it out. Her breath hitches. She takes it and runs her fingers over the wood.

"What is this?" she asks, holding the little thing in her palm.

"What does it look like?" I say, too harsh. "It's a hummingbird."

"You made it?"

I shrug, heart hammering inside my agonizingly painful rib cage. I spent the past twelve hours at the mercy of guys who wouldn't blink to see me dead, but somehow the stakes feel higher right now.

She looks into my eyes. "It's beautiful." She reaches over, touches my arm, sending ripples of warmth through me.

I shrug, like it's nothing, like her words and her gentle touch don't do things inside me. Like I'm not dying a little from it. I can force myself on her, the way I did through the phone, but it's another thing when she reaches for me. It's more raw somehow.

"What does it mean?" she asks softly.

"The hummingbird symbolizes movement. Change."

"Oh," she says, more a shape of her pretty lips than a sound. She takes her hand from my arm and touches the place where the end of the wing got bent. She tries to straighten it, but stops, seeing that will just break it more.

"In some Native American tribes, it means good luck if you see a hummingbird," I say.

Her eyes meet mine. "What if the hummingbird is injured?"

"Then you nurse it back to health," I say, my voice low. That isn't part of any bird symbolism that I know about, but it's the only answer I can give her. She's still looking at me, and I can't look away from her.

My lip throbs. My eye feels half-closed. No doubt I'm a sorry-ass sight, but you wouldn't know it from the way she looks at me.

The traffic around us starts to move. The light has changed.

"Am I broken?" she whispers.

I take the little thing from her and set it on the small ledge by the speedometer. "Drive," I tell her, not taking my eyes off her.

Her gaze returns to the road, her hands to the wheel.

She takes the left like I told her, heading for a long

stretch of road out of the city. There are tears in her eyes, but I ignore them. There's grief in her body, but I ignore that, too. Or maybe I'm not ignoring her. Maybe this is the only way I know how to make her feel better.

My hand returns to her thigh, pushing up her plaid skirt. Suddenly I'm touching skin. I thought she was wearing tights, but they're thin socks. They go way up her leg, until they stop. She's whisper-soft, like I'm in a dream.

"Oh God," she whispers.

It's as though she's whispering what I'm feeling. Because her skin is unbelievably smooth. Warm. I watch her face in profile, the rise and fall of her chest.

"Stone," she whispers.

"What? You want your leg back?"

"No," she says.

My pulse races. *No. She doesn't want her leg back.* I inch my hand farther up.

She turns to me. "Where are we going?"

"I don't know."

She stares at me a beat, wondering what kind of madman she's with, maybe. "You don't know?"

"Eyes on the road."

She turns to the road.

"I don't know a lot of things," I say. "Like whether you've fucked. Have you been fucked, sweetheart?"

The line of her throat moves as she swallows.

"Have you?"

"No," she says.

But she was kissed. She told me. It burns me up to think about other guys kissing her. Wanting her. Seeing her. I want to lock her up in a tower, like some kind of fairy-tale princess. I guess that makes me the dragon.

She turns back to the road. Says nothing. Drives.

"Have you been touched?" I move my hand higher. I feel her skin, alive with electricity under my rough calluses. "Like this? Anyone touch you like this?"

Her chest rises sharply. The air in the car seems to thicken. "Are you asking if I ever had a boyfriend?"

Right. Of course. I guess if you're a good girl like Brooke, it's your boyfriend or girlfriend who touches you. You don't have the touching without the relationship. "Just answer the question. Have you?"

Her words, when they come, are wild, breathy. "Not like this." She glances at me, and I feel her all through me just then. I feel her eyes burning into mine. "Not like *this*," she says again, emphasizing the word. As though this—what's happening with us right now—feels as amazing to her as it does to me.

I want to kiss her so bad it hurts. A physical ache in my chest worse than any broken bones inside there. I tighten my grip on her thigh. "Take the next left."

She flips on her blinker, takes the turn.

This next stretch is a straightaway south out of town. She takes a breath like she does when she's about to say something hard. I steel myself, sure she's going to ask for me to stop touching her. Or to go home.

She turns to me. "Do you ever think about just driving?"

"Driving where?"

"Nowhere. Get in a car and drive forever. Or at least, you know, until you're somewhere so far away that you're just new. A new person with a new life."

My gut twists a little, because that's something you say when you're unhappy. That's what you dream about when you want to escape. I know the feeling well. "Do you want that?"

"Sometimes," she says.

I think back to the basement. Us boys imagining all the things we'd do if we were free. Each of us with our own specific idea of how things would be. Knox imagined his own workshop full of robots and blinking lights and computers. Calder wanted to be on a mountaintop, seeing the sky all around. Nate wanted to be a doctor, a vet, and he would have his own farm, too. I didn't imagine things for myself, though. I just thought of my guys, safe. Free.

"What would the new life be like?" I ask her.

She says nothing for a long time. So long that I think she's not planning on answering my stupid question at all. Then, in a voice that sounds small and strained, she says, "I don't know."

CHAPTER THIRTEEN

~BROOKE~

I SHOULDN'T CRY in front of him. Nobody loves you when you cry, but I can't help it, because I don't know what the new life would be like. "I don't know," I say again, so pathetic.

"How would you want it to be?"

I shake my head. Stone is so free and wild, he can never understand. I get this intense rush of jealousy of him. It's crazy, because he's clearly in trouble. He's a criminal. He's beat up bad. But at least he knows what he wants. At least he's free.

"You can't just *not know.*"

"I can," I say in a small voice.

"You don't imagine it? Where you'd go? How it would be?" He sounds like he doesn't believe me. I don't know how to explain, and I *want* to explain. I want him to understand. I feel like he could. Crazy that, of all people, he could understand.

I decide to tell him the picture in my mind—it's all I have for him. The most honest I can be.

"There was this plant in my room. A vine type of plant," I say. "I was cleaning one day, and I put it in this box, and then I stuck something on top of the box and forgot about it. And then a while later, I found it again. It was mostly dead. It had grown all around, up and down the inside of the box, looking for light."

Stone doesn't interrupt me. He doesn't complain that I'm off the subject like Mom would, or even Chelsea. It makes me feel good. *He makes me feel good.*

I continue, "It was trapped, and all it could find was the sides of the box. It didn't know which way to grow. All it knew was the sides of the box."

My life is the box. My parents. School. The friends who are picked out for me. I can't imagine what I want outside of the box, can't even imagine a garden.

He's looking at me so strangely. "What happened?"

I put it in the sun, but it was too late. What leaves there were turned brown and then shriveled. "It died."

He says nothing, but I feel turmoil in the air of the car.

"Maybe it's stupid, but sometimes I feel like that plant," I say. "I'm growing inside this box, growing in this completely wrong shape plants aren't supposed to be in, because I can't see the sun. It's like I don't know anything of what I want. I think I would know what I wanted if I was out of the box."

"Because you feel trapped."

"Yes," I say, blood racing. "And sometimes I think, just drive. No more appearances to keep up. No more pressure. No more Detective Rivera asking questions."

He squeezes my thigh, sending waves of feeling all through me. His fingers are so near the spot between my legs, it makes it feel hot, like I want him to touch me there. "Brooke."

"What?" I turn to him.

His green eyes are soft and beautiful, even in that dark, scowling, beat-up face. And I get the sense that this is something important, something private he's sharing. "You can't do that," he says. "You can't drive away. You need to finish high school. Trust me—you want to be like a normal kid. You really, really do."

"I kind of can't believe you're telling me that." He's a criminal. He doesn't follow the rules. I can't imagine him worrying about what some piece of paper, some diploma says. "You, of all people. I mean…"

"What?" he says roughly. "The outlaw with the busted lip?"

"You have a lot more than a busted lip, Stone." I grin, but he doesn't crack a smile. My amusement fades. "Did you not finish high school? Is that why you're saying that? Do you regret it?"

He doesn't want to answer. I can tell—I don't know how. It's as though I feel him, feel the current coming off him. Negative to my positive, repelling me.

"My box didn't include high school," he says. "Let's put it like that."

"You dropped out?"

He shifts his fingers, making me throb between my thighs. "I never went."

I blink, almost distracted from the ache in my body. "How can you not go? There are laws about that."

"Do I look like laws apply to me?" he growls, shifting his fingers again, sliding up his hand.

The car is going the speed limit, but my heart is racing a zillion miles an hour. I'm watching the road, but all my attention is on his hand. My breath feels ragged. I really want to push myself into his hand, but it doesn't seem polite.

Classes start back up in less than an hour, but I feel like I've entered a different time zone where classes don't matter. When I'm with Stone, I'm out of that box. I'm driving to nowhere and everywhere.

With Stone, I really am free.

I look down at his hand, swallow past the dryness in my mouth.

"You don't want me to touch you?" he asks, low. There's a challenge in his voice, as if he's daring me to make him stop. And somehow I know he would stop, if I wanted that.

"No!" I say. "I mean, I do."

"But not right there?"

"I don't know," I say, face flushed.

"Yeah, you do. I think you know."

I look helplessly over at him.

"Say it, birthday girl," he says. "Where do you want me to touch you?"

I swallow. "You can move your hand up."

He lifts his hand off my thigh.

"That's not what I meant!" I look over, and he's giving me this half-smile that's devilish and sexy, a man instead of all the boys I know, a five-o'clock shadow instead of pimples.

"No?" he asks, almost a drawl. "You said up. Isn't that up?"

"Stop teasing. You know what I mean." I take a deep breath because he's going to make me spell it out. He's going to keep pushing me and pushing me. "You can touch me."

He puts his hand back where it was.

"Between the legs," I whisper.

He inches his hand closer. Not at all close enough. "Like that?"

"You're evil."

"I am," he says, kind of seriously. It makes me shudder—a good shudder.

"More." I swallow, force myself to say it. "Touch my clit. Do what I did to myself on the phone."

"Yeah?" He presses his fingers to the outside of my

panties, and I let out a shallow breath.

"More," I plead.

He curls his hand around me, grasping me between the legs. It's a starburst of feeling. "Oh my God. Stone," I gust out.

"You're so wet, little bird. So wet." He slides closer, whispering in my ear. "And you know how much I love hearing you say my name?" He begins to massage slightly.

I move with his magic hand. "How much?"

"A fuck of a lot." He grabs the wheel with his other hand. "A whole fuck of a lot."

"That's a lot," I breathe, made dumb by his touch.

His whisper in my ear is velvet. "You have no idea." He pushes his fingers under my panties now, under that panel. I suck in air as he touches my clit. "I'm your fingers right here," he says, sliding two fingers in small circles.

"Stone…" I say. "I'm trying to drive…"

"I'm your eyes on the road." He reaches across me and puts the car on cruise control. "Remember what I said? I got you." He pushes his fingers into me. "You ever have a cock in here?"

I squirm in the seat, shocked by the strange sensation of having him there. "No."

"What about a toy?"

A squeak escapes me. Visions of Barbies and Tonka

trunks flash through my mind. That's not the kind of toy he means. "No!"

"Not even a vegetable?" he asks, his voice low with a casual curiosity. "Maybe a nice, thick zucchini. You could have put it back in the fridge before anyone noticed, no one knowing what you'd done with it."

"I've never," I say, breathless with my denial.

"You must have fucked yourself. Put one finger inside. Two. Three. How many can you fit?"

"No, I—" Embarrassment turns my cheeks hot.

"You just touch your clit?"

God, how can he just say those words? None of the boys I've known talked like that to me. All the boys I've ever talked to go to Saint Matthew's, the boys' school we have dances and events with. Those boys ask to kiss me. They lean in from three feet away for a peck on the lips. They probably blush as much as I do during health class.

"Do you?" he asks again.

"Only that one time." On the phone with him.

"Then what?" he demands softly.

"The pillow," I choke out.

His fingers still, and he makes a sound, almost a groan. I'm starting to realize I can affect him as much as he's affecting me. When he speaks, his voice has gone pure gravel. "That's what you do, sweetheart? You put a pillow between your legs?"

I swear my face is going up in flames. It's a good

thing we're on cruise control, because my legs are useless. My entire body is focused on what's happening where his hand touches me. "And I just move my hips. Press my legs together."

"Yeah," he breathes. "Rub yourself until you come."

My hips are already moving, like I'm in bed under the covers. Like it's dark in my bedroom, the entire house asleep. Like I'm not in broad daylight behind the wheel of a moving vehicle with a man's hand between my legs. "I can't. Not here. Not like this."

"Yes, here. Exactly like this." His thumb brushes the sensitive place on me, as if to prove his point. And I can't deny what's happening. I'm sparking on the inside, light turned into sensation, the rest of my life a dark sky as the backdrop for this moment.

"Wait," I say, almost afraid of what will happen next.

Afraid of what's outside the box.

"No waiting," he growls. "Look at the sign. Exit four twenty. You have one mile to come. By the time we reach four twenty-one, you're going to be spilling your cum all over my fingers."

I shiver at his words, making a soft sound of surrender. The cruise control is set to sixty. My brain moves sluggishly, all the blood rushing elsewhere. One minute to come. One minute. Sixty seconds. "It's too soon."

"How long have you thought about me?" he murmurs, pressing his fingers deeper, rubbing his thumb faster. "How long have you been afraid of me, dreamed of me? Imagined me coming to you like this?"

"Forever," I say, almost a sob.

"That's right. You've been waiting for this. Now I'm here. I'm in charge. I have you."

My body moves on its own, pulled along by his knowing touch, his dark words. The scent of sex in the air.

The highway is mostly empty. Reflective stripes on the pavement flash by like blinking lights. From far away I can see the big green sign overhead proclaiming the next exit. *Almost there.*

"And I've been waiting," he murmurs. "Waiting to feel how soft you are, how wet. How much you want me. Do you know how incredible your cunt feels? Like fucking heaven. Like nothing that came before matters. Like I've never seen hell."

Before I can even process that, my climax rushes over me like an eclipse. It's an explosion of pleasure, blinding and yet dark. It blocks out everything but the sensation of his fingers on my clit. It's as if I can feel every ridge on his finger pad, as if I'm attuned to him in some permanent, inexorable way.

He rubs me softer and softer, pushing the climax on longer than anything I've ever felt. Every muscle in my body feels wrung out. I hear a whimpering sound and realize it's me. I'm collapsed on the seat, the insides of my thighs damp from my orgasm, his touch soothing now.

"There you are," he says with one last whisper of his fingers through my slit. "You're beautiful, sweetheart. You're perfect like this."

Something nags the back of my mind, something important he said to me in the final moments, but I can barely think. I can barely hold my head up as we speed along. His hand is still on the wheel, cruise control still keeping us steady. Even so it's a miracle we haven't crashed.

Slowly my hands fall onto the steering wheel. I turn on the blinker for the exit. Tap the brake to disconnect cruise control. I don't feel completely steady, but it's safer this way. I should be the one driving. "That was dangerous," I say, my voice shaky.

Stone leans back in his seat, his expression suddenly tense and brooding. "Yeah. It was."

And I know he doesn't mean the fact that we were driving.

I don't really mean that either.

He's dangerous to me because he opens the lid of the box, because he lets me see what's outside. He's the sun, a burning ball so bright it can blind me, and I don't even care. I want more. I'll do anything to feel more, even if it means I burn.

I take the exit and stop at the top of the ramp. From

up here on the overpass, you can see the highway stretching out into the distance, going for miles. I grip the wheel hard, reeling still—from the climax, from the freedom, from Stone's wild beauty. I always thought of the world as a kind of lush garden I was being kept secluded from, but it's more like a jungle—dangerous, wild, and fiercely beautiful.

He makes me feel wild, like I could go anywhere. I turn to him, pulse racing. "Where should we go now?"

He regards me strangely. He doesn't seem happy. Doesn't he see that I would go anywhere with him? That I'd give him anything?

"Left," he says.

I flip on the blinker. "What's left?"

He's silent.

I take the turn. "Now what?"

"Left again. Back on the highway."

"What? You want to go back?"

"Of course I want to go back. And so do you."

He's wrong. For one magical moment back there, I wanted to never go back. It felt good to imagine it. Good the way Stone feels good. I stop the car, right on the overpass, and turn on the blinker, but I keep my foot on the brake. "Us," I say.

"What?" he says. "Go on. Turn."

"Us. Far away from here," I say. "In a cabin in the middle of nowhere. And there are pretty things strung on the walls. Colorful rocks that we find in a river. And we eat the fish we catch. And we lie under the stars at night on this giant rock that's cool underneath us."

"What are you talking about?"

I swallow. "It's what I imagine. It's how it could be. The other life."

He's silent a moment. "Did you just come up with that?"

Does he like it? Butterflies flutter inside my belly, trapped and frantic. I need him to like it. To not say it's silly. Childish. Idiotic. Selfish.

He reaches out and touches my hair, slides a strand between calloused fingers—the same two fingers that were touching me in my most private part just a few minutes ago. But his eyes look sad.

Please don't say it's silly, I beg him in my head. I've never needed anything more. A car stops behind us and honks, but I don't care. I'm gasping for air, for light, holding on by a fragile thread.

He watches me wordlessly, soft green eyes rimmed with the sooty lashes. He repeats the motion, running that strand of hair through his fingers once again. "And your hair would turn light from the sun. It would turn the pale yellow of the moon. And you would be even more beautiful."

Tears crowd my eyes, thick and bittersweet.

"And we would take walks," he says. "We would

collect wood to make a fire with every night. Sit outside and watch the sparks rise into the sky."

"Yes," I whisper.

"It's beautiful," he says.

I watch him, suspended in midair.

He nods his head at the highway. The road back home. "Come on. Your class starts soon."

"You said it was beautiful."

"It is, but we can't do it. We can't just drive south. That's not how it works."

"How, then?" I'm suddenly angry. Angry that he went along with me even in daydreams. "How does it work?"

"Right now, it works with you getting back on that highway."

I wait, trembling, my heart beating a rapid pulse against my ribs.

"Come on, Brooke."

I take my foot off the brake and turn. I head back, merging, putting on the speed.

"You know that's how it works," he says. "I shouldn't've—"

"You shouldn't've what? Given me ideas? A taste of something I can never have?" I grip the wheel so tightly, I think it might break. It's not like me, talking back like this.

He says nothing.

"Is that what you mean?" I ask, all twisted up in my chest, because I'll never have that life. He might have it, with some woman from his life. A beautiful streetwise woman to sit with him next to a fire in the forest.

"Come on, Brooke."

I shake my head because I know the answer. He thinks he shouldn't have done any of it. The certainty is a cold feeling in my chest. "Because I have to finish high school and be this person I'm supposed to be."

"You have to finish high school, that's for sure."

I stiffen my spine. "You give me things just to take them away. You're toying with me."

"I'm protecting you."

"I think I've been protected enough, thank you very much. My mother. My father. Even Detective Rivera. I've been protected practically to death." So much that I'm suffocating, like the plant in the box.

"Look at me," he says.

I shake my head.

He lowers his voice. "Look at me. Take a good fucking look. You think this would be a pretty look on you?"

Because I have to obey him, I look—hard. But I'm looking past the bruise on his cheekbone, past his fat lip and his puffy eye, nearly swollen shut now. I look past the carved lines of his face, the way he's made from rocks barely smoothed. Rough, unforgiving rocks in the shape of a human, more object than person.

I see his green eyes, soft and beautiful. I still feel his warm touch on my skin.

He frowns as if he senses my small disobedience. "The people I'm dealing with," he growls, "this isn't what they'd do to you. Or at least, not *all* they'd do. Do I want to protect you? Fuck yeah. Was it fucked up that I came to you? Seriously fucked up."

"No, it's not."

He makes a rough sound, as though it's impossible to quantify how fucked up it is that he came to me. Like even numbers can't express it. Not even formulas from Sister Aggie's third-hour trig class. "I shouldn't've."

"Then why did you?"

He glares over at me, and my heart does a flip-flop. He knew he shouldn't come to me, and he did anyway. Because he couldn't stay away.

He couldn't stay away.

"Doesn't matter," he says. "I shouldn't've. I have things to do, and they can't involve you."

"What things?"

"Things."

Doesn't he see how free he is? "You don't have to do anything."

"You're wrong there, little bird. There are things that need to be done that only I can do. I have people counting on me, same as you."

The Franklin City exits loom ahead. "Maybe I can

help you."

"Yeah? You know how to kill the monsters that come after your friends in their nightmares? Do you know how to glue somebody's world together when it was shattered into a thousand pieces?"

I grip the steering wheel more tightly, wishing I did, wishing I could help him.

"You know how to break a guy out of prison? When you can't even communicate with him?"

I look at him wide-eyed.

"Oh, don't worry, he's not actually guilty. He was framed—very expertly framed for a crime he didn't commit. That's the power of our enemies."

"Why are you fighting them?"

He shifts in his seat and rests his head against the headrest. It comes to me that he's tired and probably in a lot of pain. "Something that happened…you don't want to know."

"Yes, I do." I frown. "I'm not a child."

He looks at me a long time. Says nothing.

Hopelessness washes through me. I thought we had a connection that rose above age and every other difference between us. Does he see me as nothing but a schoolgirl after all?

I could drive for miles with a gun to my head, with his hand between my legs. But I can't keep driving with this awful hopelessness. A sign for a rest stop appears ahead, and I take the exit with a sudden pull of the wheel.

"What are you doing?" he asks, his voice harsh.

"I'm stopping at this rest stop."

He glowers. "Get back on the freeway."

His voice is gravelly with threat, but I know he won't hurt me. I pull into one of the empty parking spaces and turn the key.

There's no one around. A couple of half-empty vending machines stand next to the doorway to the restroom area. A few broken picnic tables off to the side, scrubby weeds all around. A line of 18-wheelers are parked along the far end of the lot, but I don't see any drivers.

The car quiets, making expectation loud between us. I get out.

Stone gets out his side, glaring at me over the hood of the vehicle. "What the fuck are you doing?" He slams the door.

"You can trust me. I won't tell Detective Rivera."

"Fuck Detective Rivera," he says with a hard glint. It feels like a threat.

"Why won't you tell me?" I ask softly. "Maybe I can help. You won't know unless you try."

He snorts.

"Why is that so ludicrous? Because I'm too young? Not strong enough? Because you're wrong." I circle the hood, strangely exhilarated. "I think you want to tell me.

I think you could use an ally. Somebody you can talk to. Somebody who cares."

A scoff. "And you're that person?"

I feel like my breathing is larger than my body. He has a hundred pounds of pure muscle on me, but I have this wild idea that I could fight him, and I could win. "Yeah, I'm that person. Tell me I'm wrong. Tie up my hands and shove me in the trunk. Do everything awful."

His eyes flash. "Don't tempt me, sweetheart."

My heart swells wide and bright like I'm the sun, too. That's how I feel right now. Not a plant that can live or die by someone else's whim. I'm burning all on my own. There's a way in which I feel Stone brings out the best in me. I want to do that for him—more than anything I've ever wanted. "I'm tempting you, Stone. I'm in your face right now, challenging you to let me in."

He wants me to be afraid of him. It would be so simple. A slap in the face. A twist of my wrist. He could hurt me so easily, but he won't. He'll stand there, looking fierce and unholy in the bright midday sun, completely at my mercy.

That's when I realize that he's the plant. The one denied light too long.

He's the one dying.

"Get in the car," he says. He makes his voice hard, but I hear need. Desperation. "Now," he growls loudly. His words seem to echo back from the brick structure and the 18-wheelers and the line of trees far away. They bounce around us, fierce and pained.

I put my hand on his arm, feeling the tremors in him. "Tell me what happened," I whisper. "You said you take care of your guys, but who takes care of you? I think you want to tell me."

Something shifts in him. I have the sense of gears in his head turning, a decision being made. His voice, when it comes, is pure threat. "You think you know what I want?"

Instinct sends me back a step. Another. I wasn't afraid of him in the car, despite his threats. Wasn't afraid when I challenged him in a deserted parking lot. When he was made of marble, I was safe.

Not anymore.

He's all man, flesh and blood, fury and heartbreak. "I—I—" I stammer.

"News flash—you don't." He takes a step toward me, fire in his eyes. "Now you know what's going to happen here? We're going to get back in that car, and you're going to go back to your school uniforms and your ridiculous little-girl dreams. This was a mistake, and this—" He points from him to me to him to me. "*This* is not happening again. Not ever."

I ball my fists so tightly my fingernails dig into my palms. My fists are the only part of me not trembling.

"Get. In." He points at my car.

The world seems to tilt. I shake my head—that's as much as I can talk right now. I could drive while I was orgasming, dangerous as it was, but now? I'm turned inside out by the ferocity of his words, the cruelty of his regard. I barely know which way is up.

I straighten my spine, compose myself. If there's one thing I've learned how to do over the years, it's appear perfectly polished when I'm crumbling inside. "Fine," I say. "After a stop in the ladies' room. If that's okay with you."

"Sure. You go ahead. You go on to the *ladies' room*." He says it with disdain, like he really hates me. Maybe he does. He doesn't want to see me ever again.

I turn and head across the walkway toward the shabby rest building, black patent leather shoes smashing over the clumps of ugly weeds that strain up through the cracks in the cement.

What was I thinking? Trying to connect with someone like Stone. He's so much older than me, and worlds different. How could I presume to be able to understand him or help him, much less have him want me in any real way? To imagine I'm anything more than a distraction. Insubstantial. One of the hors d'oeuvres passed around at my parents' parties. Instantly forgotten.

My eyes are bleary with tears when I finally step behind the cinder-block wall that marks the entrance to the ladies' room. Half the lights are smashed out, making the row of metal restroom doors look ominous, some shrouded in near darkness. There's one window high up, the screen clogged with leaves and dead bugs, probably.

My imagination conjures pictures of tired mothers with hyper daughters. Do they mind how run-down the place is? Or does it seem like part of the road-trip experience? My mother would lose her mind before ever stepping one foot inside. The only family vacations we had were to five-star resorts. First-class seats and private suites. More about proving a point than enjoying each other's company.

Water drips from the ceiling to a gray puddle on the floor. I step around it and go to the sink, run the water and splash some on my face. I don't actually have to pee; I just need to pull my head together. Will I be late to class? I don't know. I can't even think about it.

I grab a towel from the crooked dispenser, telling myself it's better this way. Better than sparkling bathrooms with luxury seating and perfect tile, potted palms thriving under skylights. More real.

There's a creak from the direction of the door.

I ignore it. I know it's not Stone. Coming after me to apologize or whatever is the last thing he'd do. And I'm hardly in the mood to fake-smile at another traveler.

Probably just a female driver from one of those trucks outside. I splash more water onto my face and gaze up into the mirror.

And freeze.

There's a huge man looming behind me, whiskery cheeks and a grizzly brown beard under a seed cap. His jeans jacket is cut off at the sleeves to reveal a torn T-shirt over massive tattooed arms. "Fifty bucks," he says. "For five minutes of those pretty lips." He's on me in a flash, hands on my hips.

I jerk away from his grip, moving sideways. "No, I'm not…"

He thinks I'm a prostitute.

"Didn't anyone tell you that little whores can't be choosers?" He grabs my hair and pulls me back and shoves me down in front of him. My knees smash into the cold hard floor. I try to scream for Stone, but the man is squeezing my cheeks with his fingers so hard that I feel every ridge of my teeth, cutting into the sides of my mouth, and all I can do is grunt and cry.

Wet seeps into the thin fabric covering my knees. I try to scream, try to push him away.

"Fifty bucks. That's some six hundred bucks an hour. More than a little bitch like you deserves."

He has his zipper down. The musky, moldy smell is suffocating. I push against his tree-trunk-like legs as he fumbles with himself.

"Don't like the looks of me? I'll teach you not to like the looks of me. I'll stuff your little lips so full my cock'll be coming out your ass—"

That's the last word he gets out before he's jerked backward. The motion is hard. Furious.

Stone. He crashes the man headfirst into the hard cinder-block wall. There's a yell. A crack.

I fall to my hands and knees, panting, reeling from what almost happened. From what *did* happen. A stranger had his hands on me. The dark, shadowy vision of him looms in my mind.

"You okay, baby?" Stone's touching my hair, touching my face—gently, as if I'm made of spun glass. Light as his touches are, I can feel him trembling. "Tell me you're okay," he gusts frantically. "Say you're okay."

"I'm okay." I don't know whether that's true or not. Am I okay? All I know is that Stone looks sick with worry, and I don't want him to worry. He shouldn't ever have to be afraid.

The trucker is up, though. And coming for Stone.

Before I can even utter a warning, Stone is whirling on him. The trucker is bigger than Stone by far, but Stone goes at him with explosive fury like I've never seen. He drives the trucker back into the wall. The trucker's body jolts from the impact. But he recovers fast enough to slam a fist into Stone's jaw.

I back up, looking around for a weapon, some way to help Stone, because the trucker is so huge and scary, and he's hitting Stone again and again, but Stone slips the next hit and drives his knuckles into the man's jaw, and then he punches hard, right into the man's neck.

The man starts coughing and staggering, holding his neck.

"You think you can touch her like that? Her?" Stone's voice sounds funny. Like a demon got into him. "Make her cry?"

Stone is merciless now, hitting and punching.

No longer bothering even to protect himself, the trucker falls to his knees, clutching at his neck. I know with a weird certainty that something inside that man is broken, and I mean, *really* broken. He might die. One hand flies up in surrender.

Stone kicks him in the face. The man's head hits the floor.

"Stone!" I scream.

Stone is on his knees, wild, raining down hits on the guy. He sees nothing. Hears nothing. "You would hurt her?" *Craaack.* "Hurt her?" *Craaack.* "Make her cry?" *Craaack. Craaack.*

The puddles on the floor are turning pink.

I scream because I think the man might be dead.

"Stone! Stop!" I grab him by the shirt. "Please! Don't kill him."

"He deserves it," he growls, pulling his arm back for another blow. I latch onto his arms from behind, holding him with all the strength in me.

My toes brush the ground as he lifts me. That's how

intensely he's fighting right now—he can turn, and my whole body lifts. I'm riding him instead of pulling him away.

It must register, though, because he twists to look at me. His brows are low, eyes glowing with fury. He looks like a demon, something that rises from hell to drag men down.

"Please," I say softly.

For a long moment we remain frozen, and I think I'm going to watch this man die. Then Stone's fist unclenches. He releases the man, who falls in an unmoving heap onto the floor.

Stone straightens, but I stay with him. I won't let go.

"He deserves it," Stone says again, quieter this time.

"I know, but *you* don't deserve to do it."

He looks bemused. "It doesn't hurt me."

It does hurt him, but I don't only mean physically. I press my hand to his chest, feel the ragged rise and fall. I wish I could calm him, soothe him. "It hurts you here."

"Ah, sweetheart." He covers my small, pale hand with his big rough one, knuckles dark with blood. "There's nothing in there. Nothing at all."

I won't believe it. I rise up on tiptoes, reaching for him. I'm not tall enough, not strong enough, but he meets me halfway, his lips impossibly soft in contrast to the hardness of his body. Our kiss isn't one that moves, not with lips or tongue, only a press of mouths—

something moves inside me instead. I know he feels it too, in that heart he claims not to have.

It's dirty and dangerous that we're kissing in this dark rest-stop bathroom, a man's blood drawing a pink trail toward the drain in the floor. This is the life Stone has led, and I can't flinch away from it any more than I can turn away from him.

When I pull away, his eyes search mine. "Did he touch you?"

My shoulders still ache from his harsh touch, the skin on my face crawls from when he pried my mouth open. I want to tell him no, to lie to him, but a shudder works its way through me, revealing the truth.

Chapter Fourteen

~Stone~

RAGE SHAKES ME from deep inside as I watch the fear flash through Brooke's pretty eyes. All I want to do is crack every bone in this man's body. I want to run him over with his fucking 18-wheeler, forward and back, again and again until he's paid the price.

Something deeper than vengeance keeps me steady.

I know too well the kind of pain, the *shame* that can follow an experience like this. And I'm more concerned with making sure Brooke is okay than with beating this man even more.

The realization takes me by surprise—her well-being is more important than the darkness inside me.

"We're leaving," I tell her. "I'll take you back to school."

She lets me lead her out of that dirty bathroom, a place she never should have been. Even the air here doesn't have the right to touch her.

I'm trying not to limp, not to show her how messed up I am. Nate would have a fit if he knew I went out beating on a guy in this condition. Kind of a shock the man didn't rearrange my face. Well, he would've had to do more to get through me to Brooke.

Sunlight beams onto the sidewalk, almost blinding, unaware of what tragedies unfolded only a few yards away. This is where we stood when I told Brooke I'd never see her again, when I mocked her school uniform and little-girl problems.

Guilt is acid in my veins. If I hadn't said that, she wouldn't have felt the need to get away from me. She would have stayed near me.

I guide her to the passenger door and open it. Is this what it feels like to be a gentleman? To take care of a young lady, to have her look at me with trust shining in her eyes.

"I'm not driving?" she asks, her voice small.

She's not in any shape to drive. And somehow I feel compelled to take care of her. Not to order her around, to tell her where to go, but to kill for her. Except a bloody body is the opposite of what she needs…much as I'd like to end that guy in there. "Get in."

"Are you okay? Did he hurt you?" she asks.

She's worried about me? "I was hurt already. Now get *in*."

Her eyes turn shiny. Is she going to cry? She should. She's been abducted by me, multiple times. Attacked by that fucker in the bathroom. This girl who deserves only silk and lace. It's a miracle she's lasted this long by my side. I never should have gone near her.

She surprises me by straightening her spine. Not a single tear escapes down her cheeks. "Is this the last time I see you?"

I wouldn't have thought less of her if she'd cried. My brothers in the basement cried when they were little. It's how humans cope with horrible things, which is how I know I don't have a heart. I've never shed a tear. I don't think I would know how. My body isn't built that way.

"I told you this would be the last time." The words rip out of me. It's not what I want. It's what she needs.

She turns, eyes huge. Wary.

Christ, this girl. I want to rip her to pieces so she can't look at me, so fucking innocent and brave. "I'm not angry at you. I'm angry at the world. You haven't figured that out yet?"

"Then why is this the last time?"

There's a shadow on her cheek. That fucker touched her. It's going to be a bruise. "Because all I do is hurt you."

"You don't hurt me."

"Have you forgotten what just happened in that bathroom? I'm not good for you."

"You protected me."

"I *brought* you here. I made you come here."

"I wanted to come."

"I don't have anything you want, little bird. You need to get that. There's no taking me to the movies. You can't bring me around to your prep-school friends or put my picture in a locket. And you sure as hell can't bring me home to Mom and Dad."

She touches my arm. "This is what I want."

I have to laugh, because women have wanted to use me for my dick before. I can rough them up a little in bed and walk away before morning comes, a dark little memory for them to use with their vibrators when their husbands can't get them off.

But this girl isn't using me for my dick. She doesn't want to fuck me—or more to the point, I can't let myself fuck her, even though there's nothing I want more.

She wants me for my company, and that feels strange. Satisfying. Sickening.

I pull away.

"Fine." She spins on her heel and gets into the car. "Take me back to school."

I love the imperious way she says that. Like I'm a fucking chauffeur. That's more like it.

In a matter of minutes, we're back on the highway, cruising toward town. Except I'm not planning on taking her back to school, not at first. Because I know what she's thinking—that we've still got something going on. That all she has to do is wait and I'll show up again.

I almost never see her with guys her own age. It's

always made me happy. The idea of her being with a ham-handed high school boy who can't appreciate her, some kid looking to get his rocks off, it fills me with fucking rage.

But what does it mean for *her* that I never see her with a boy alone? What if she's *waiting* for me? Comparing boys her age to me? Am I making a mess of her life without even being around? The thought horrifies the fuck out of me.

You don't hurt me. You protected me. I wanted to come.

She doesn't get it. She thinks I can give her something I can't. She needs to understand.

I'm heading *there*, of course. Without really even thinking about it.

She begged me to let her in. *Careful what you wish for,* I think.

Most of the guys have never been back there. A few try not to think about it. It's possible Nate goes entire days without letting his mind sink into the pain and hell and twisted-up feelings of that place. Working on his animals. I've seen him work all night to repair a broken wing on a fucking crow. And Knox, losing himself in all his tech. But I never turn away. Not ever.

We head southeast. To Ferndale, the scrubby little suburb with boxlike homes fronted by grass gone to seed. And near the very end of an especially decrepit block, the burnt remains of the house, jutting up from the ground like charred teeth on a long-buried demon.

She was a witness to me killing Madsen. Hell, she had a front-row seat to me almost killing her, for fuck's sake, but she still has things twisted around in her mind—I'm getting that now. Her and her campfire fantasy.

You don't hurt me. You protected me. I wanted to come.

She's looking at me like I'm a fixer-upper that maybe needs some sanding to smooth the rough edges. Maybe a bright coat of paint. She doesn't get that I'm wrong from the inside out.

"This place," she says. "Have we been here before?"

I pull around the corner, park along the side. No sense in having her car connected with this place. She doesn't want to get out. I go around and open her door for her, but she just stares up.

"Out."

She doesn't move. She senses something's wrong. She has no fucking idea how wrong. "Isn't this what you wanted? Me opening the car door for you? Me taking you home to where I grew up? A visit to the folks?"

"That night you killed that guy. We came here."

"Come on, little bird." I pull her out. Not rough. She comes. She just doesn't want to.

"This is where you grew up?"

"Grew up might be a nice way of putting it." I help her over the wrecked part of the fence, which is posted with no-trespassing signs, and lead her to the edge of the place. To the spot where you can see beyond the charred remnants of walls and into the basement.

It's just a deep, dark pit with a few cinder-block partitions here and there. There are dried leaves and garbage in the corners. Some scrub brush looming up toward the sky. "Come on."

I jump onto what's left of the steps, surprised when she willingly follows. I lead her all the way down and help her as we near the bottom.

She's too pretty, too pure to be down in this open pit grave where the best parts of us died. What the fuck am I doing?

Teaching her a lesson about me, I remind myself. Showing her what's in me. She won't wait for me once she sees this. Won't get in a car if I'm inside.

I flick on my iPhone light, play it over the dank walls, weathered and cracked. "You have your whole life ahead of you, but this is where mine started and ended."

She says nothing. I can't look at her. Already the place is closing around me.

I walk around the familiar corners, so different but so much the same.

I kick a rusted paint can aside and kneel by the metal carcass of the hot-air furnace, a rusted box just a bit smaller than a coffin, once painted blue, but now it's mostly gray from years of dirt and weather. I crouch there, remembering how it would heat up like a motherfucker in the winter.

I touch a rivet on the side. Cool. Dirty. "We'd be down here twenty-four seven. Well, more like twenty-three seven. They'd keep us down here except when they needed us. You know, when a guy like Madsen would show up. Sometimes women, but mostly men. They'd make us go upstairs. Clean us and dress us like little whores. Me and my brothers. And they *were* my brothers. Never mind that I'd never seen them before. That we came from different mothers, from different cities. We were a fucked-up family."

"Stone." Her voice is shaky. She's finally getting a clear picture of me.

"It's cool. While you were getting aspirin and Band-Aids for your skinned knees, we were getting the good stuff. I don't know what it was they gave us, but it made it like you weren't there. Sometimes we'd even get off with the customers. The line between feeling good and bad was pretty thin in this place."

I hear the soft intake of breath. This is hurting her, but it's better that I tell her what I am all at once. She needs to take on a little damage, or she'll keep holding out hope.

"This rivet would get really hot in the winter. I'd make the boys touch their finger to it. Like when they came down from up there in a bad way. Or like if they wouldn't stop crying. I'd tell them that if they touched this really hot rivet, it would take whatever happened up there and suck it out their fingertip and burn it inside the firebox. I convinced them that if they touched their finger to it long enough, it would make it like it didn't happen."

There's a sob from behind me, but I don't stop.

"It actually worked. Got a lot of burnt fingers, but I made them believe it." I scrub away the area around the rivet, revealing blue metal. "Took us six years to get out of here. We fought our way out. We were getting fucked before we knew what it meant, but when we killed, we knew what we were doing. Fucking bloodbath like you've never seen."

Still I'm not looking at her. I keep my attention fixed on the dirty furnace box. I listen to the hum of traffic. A distant train blows its horn, long and low. She's probably wanting to get the hell away from me right about now. Probably going to throw up just looking at me.

"We set this fire. We burned this place. Three men toasted to a nice crisp, but I can pretty much guarantee you, they were dead beforehand." I sniff. "Whatdya know, folks? Turns out that when a boy touches his finger to a bolt on a furnace, it doesn't actually suck out all the murderous fucking darkness."

I'm breathing hard.

I meant to use the story as a club to beat her off,

bring her down here to make it all more awful. Instead she's diluting the darkness of it somehow.

She's making the memories almost bearable.

I rub the dirt off the rivet. "Sometimes I would touch my finger there when my brothers weren't looking. I knew it was bullshit. I mean, hello, I made it up myself, right? But it worked with them, and sometimes, when I was feeling like shit, I wanted it to work with me, too— to suck out the bad and burn it away. I wanted to believe my own stupid lie." I lower my voice to a whisper. "I really wanted to. I almost sometimes could."

I don't know why I'm telling her. I'm supposed to be making myself scary, not pathetic. I turn, finally, because I have to.

Because she's the one bright thing in my life, even if she's not really in my life.

She's there, straight and tall, brown eyes shining, but not with tears. She's looking at me with admiration. "That's the bravest thing I ever heard."

I give her a cockeyed look. Like she made a joke. "You caught the bullshit about the rivet, right?"

"That's my favorite part. You helped them when they needed it most. When you needed help as much as any of them, but you were the leader, weren't you? You made it better for them."

My heart thunders. I absorbed all the darkness. She's not supposed to be making it into a good thing.

"How old were you when they…trapped you?"

I shrug. "Nine or ten. Most were younger. Grayson—the one in prison—he was like five."

She sucks in a breath and comes to me, throws her arms around me, as if to shield me from the world. She puts her face to my shirt.

This is wrong. I should shake her off, get her out of here.

I don't.

I rest a tentative hand on her back. "Shit, sweetheart," I say softly. "I'm ruining you."

"I'm sorry," she says, a broken litany. "I'm sorry, I'm sorry."

"For what?" My voice sounds remote to my ears. "A lot of bad shit happened in that basement. Which part are you sorry for?"

I feel her flinch. I unwrap her arms from me and step back. "You don't even know."

"Don't," she says.

"Are you sorry we missed out on hopscotch and multiplication tables or the class where they teach you to write in that curly way? Or that we got our souls ripped out our assholes? You really should try to be specific."

"I'm sorry for all of it," she says softly. "Mostly that part of you is still here."

My heart thunders. I see what she's doing. Trying to absorb the darkness. "We're outta here."

"You were brave. You saved those boys."

I push her toward the steps, help her up. "You only say that because you haven't *met* those boys."

"You still know them? That's cool that you stay in touch."

Stay in touch.

"What do you think, like we send each other birthday cards or something? We're fucking criminals. We're like a pack of wolves roaming the goddamn city. We're not even official people."

"What about your parents? Didn't you try to find them once you were out?"

"You don't get it. They changed us into monsters down there." I kick a rusted hinge with part of a shattered door still clinging to it. "None of our folks much wanted us before we went down there. You think they wanted us after? A few of my guys found that out the hard way. It can only be us guys. We're each other's family now."

"You don't imagine a future? Something you want to be?"

"We want to be the ones who slaughter the people who did this."

She sucks in a breath. "That man you killed. The first night. Madsen."

I hadn't expected her to connect it so quickly. Hadn't expected to hear absolution in her voice. "Don't get the wrong idea, little bird. I'm not some kind of vigilante. This isn't about justice. This is revenge, pure and simple."

Her pretty brows lower. "What's the difference?"

"The difference is, I don't care if they swear never to hurt another boy. And hell, you want to know the truth? I don't even care whether they knew what was happening. If they were involved, if they looked the other way, if they even did business with the assholes who ran this place, they're going to die."

A sad light in her eyes takes my breath away. "This is all you do? Track down the people connected with this and kill them?"

"What else should I do? Take up knitting? This is the only reason I made it out of the basement alive. The knowledge that I would make them suffer. There's nothing else. There can't be anything else. No distractions."

She regards me solemnly, like she's a hundred years old, ancient with patience and understanding, but so damn young it makes me want to punch the wall. Because she's living proof that I let distractions interfere with my mission. Well, only one distraction. Her. Driving her around as if I'm the one taking her hostage, but really it's the other way around. She's the one who keeps me coming back, even knowing I shouldn't.

We had to fight our way out of this basement, killing

and yelling and half sure we'd end up in a shallow grave before breathing in free air. Yet it somehow feels harder to turn my back on her. To ascend the ruined stairs, get back into daylight.

All the times I came here, it was to remember. Now I have to leave to do the same thing.

She doesn't follow right away, and I don't rush her. Let her look her fill. Let her remember how cold it is, the stench of metal and stale sweat that never quite dissipates. It's not like there's any other way out of there.

This is the first time I ever noticed the fireflies in the yard. Were they always here, mindless witnesses to men coming and going? Were they here the night we escaped?

The stairs creak with her ascent, shaky even under her slight weight.

"I want to help."

Her words hit me harder than a physical blow. There are a hundred things I might have expected to hear from her. Disgust or anger. Disappointment. "Why?"

"Because what you're doing is important. It matters. Like you said, I got a Band-Aid when I fell down. A sweet-sixteen party. But you were suffering."

I'm already shaking my head. "I don't need your fucking pity."

"I'm not offering you any. I'm offering to help."

"Help? You going to help us feed a few guys through the ol' wood chipper?"

She flinches but persists. "If that was all you needed to do, you'd be done, wouldn't you?"

I shouldn't find her persistence so fucking hot, but I do. "We need to find them," I admit. "The boys and where they're being held. And the men who are running this shit."

"I can help."

God, I shouldn't even be talking about this with her. "All the deals are done with a wink and a dirty fucking handshake. There's no paper trail. No records. Except…"

She puts a hand on my shoulder. My muscles flex beneath her touch, my body glad for her even while my mind tells me to shake her off. "Tell me."

"You know how they say follow the money? This is like that, except with land. There are a bunch of different owners of these houses. A network organized in secret by whoever is in charge of this operation. Buildings that are abandoned, where no one will ask questions. An endless supply of them."

"So it's someone who owns a lot of real estate."

"Not just one man. Five. Ten. Twenty? I don't fucking know. If we can find one of them, though, if we can get him to talk, that would be the key we need."

"Okay," she says, her voice matter-of-fact. "What do you know so far?"

What do I know so far—like this is a school project

she's going to help me with. "It's someone with connections in the city. The kind of person who can get permits rubber-stamped and cops to not drive down a certain street. This is way too dangerous for you to be a part of."

"I'm already a part of this. I stood in that basement. I touched that rivet."

She touched the rivet? Fuck. There's a strange sense of comfort I get from that, despite how fucked up it is. That she's one of us now, even though I know it isn't true. "We don't actually know that much. He's a goddamn ghost."

"Let me help."

I need to get her off this track, so I do the one thing that should work: insult her. "You're a high school kid, little bird. Unless you know someone named Jimmy Brass or Johnson or Keeper, you can't help."

A pause. "Keeper?"

"They have nicknames they use underground. That's part of what helps them hide. No one knows his real identity, so even when we question them, when we torture them, that's all they can tell us."

She's quiet behind me, and I turn to see her looking in the direction of the fireflies. She isn't seeing them, her eyes distant. What's she thinking about?

When she turns to me, her expression is guarded.

There's a strange sense of loss inside me.

But this is what I wanted, isn't it? For her to pull

away from me. This is why I brought her here. Now that it's happening, my chest feels like it's being crushed in a vise.

"I'm ready to go home," she says softly.

I pretend like it doesn't hurt. "You drive."

It will be the last drive we take together.

She stops at the driver's-side door before we get in. "Stone."

"Yeah, little bird?"

"Thank you for taking me here. Thank you for...trusting me."

It's only then that I realize how much I do trust her. The world is full of liars and cheats. Full of monsters with pretty fucking smiles. I'd never have taken anyone else here, even to push them away.

She's more than a distraction to me. She's a knife wound. A gunshot. A burn across every inch of my skin, making me weak.

How can I talk about revenge when she's stepping into the car, turning the key in the ignition, straightening the rearview mirror?

She's the rivet, taking away the darkness.

But without the darkness, there's nothing left inside me. I'm hollow.

CHAPTER FIFTEEN

~BROOKE~

MY PARENTS RENT a party room at the Highline Country Club for my birthday dinner the Saturday after my actual birthday. Seventeen years old. It seems like a lifetime since my sweet-sixteen party, even though it's been just a year. Luckily, nobody's paying much attention to me. Nobody notices my fake smiles, or how much concealer went into covering the bruise on my cheek from when the trucker attacked me. Everybody believed my lie about losing track of time and missing class.

Is he dead? Somebody would've found him by now. Or maybe he dragged himself back to his truck. It feels weird to hope that he's dead.

Most of all, nobody notices how I can't quite look my father in the eye.

You're a high school kid. Unless you know someone named Jimmy Brass or Johnson or Keeper, you can't help. His words stay with me even when I'm smiling and answering questions about how it feels to be seventeen.

ANNIKA MARTIN & SKYE WARREN

It feels like I've aged a hundred years, but that has nothing to do with three hundred sixty-five days passing. It has everything to do with what Stone told me.

My family doesn't have much money. We've been holding things together for a long time, sewing in the bottoms of designer bags to hold them together, paying for lavish parties like this while we live on plain chicken and rice. Which means we're trading on something else—our name. Our connections. It's almost a kind of lore, the stories about my father.

There was one story about him, my mother tells it every Christmas, about how a pregnant woman had come to his motel on a dark night. How the front desk had turned her away because they were full, but my father saw her. He gave her a room in the employee section, because it was too rainy to go anywhere else. She gave birth that night.

"The Innkeeper," my mother says, fond and definitely proud. "Except unlike the one in the story, this one has a heart."

My father grimaces and shakes his head. I thought it was because he was embarrassed that she brags about him. But what if it's because he's trying to hide the name? The Innkeeper is a distinctive name. How many guys would have nicknames like that? And would people call him Keeper for short?

It was a whole thing at our Christmas parties, Mom

telling the story. Dad as the innkeeper. And Uncle Bill as a shepherd; our family a whole Nativity set.

That kind of detail, it makes it hard to forget.

Hard to pretend I don't know.

Maybe it's a coincidence.

I toy with my steak, but it tastes like sawdust.

Our ride was three days ago, but after what Stone told me, I've barely slept. When I close my eyes, I'm awash with images of defenseless boys, trapped in the dark. Of Stone as a kid, with that same thick black hair, those same piercing green eyes, making them believe in fairy tales about rivets.

I dream about Stone beating that trucker who dared to touch me. Or Madsen, that guy he killed the night we met, bloody and half alive in the back of the van.

Except now it's my father. My father's groans. My father's garbled pleas for mercy.

The Innkeeper. Keeper.

God, I want those names to be a coincidence.

Except it's not just my mom. Everyone knows the story about my dad. It's something they call him when they're drunk on eggnog and brandy. *Pour me another one, Innkeeper.* Do they ever shorten that to Keeper?

My father fits the other parts of the story, too—Stone's looking for somebody who owns a lot of real estate. My father doesn't own a lot, but as a developer, he certainly has access to a lot of real estate, someone who knows which places are abandoned. Someone with connections in both law enforcement and city hall.

Not just one man. Five. Ten. Twenty? Stone had said. Is it so far-fetched that my father could be one of them?

Mom gazes at me from across the table. She sits up a little straighter, which tells me she wants me to fix my posture. There are probably a hundred things about me she wants to fix.

I sit up nice and straight and glance at Chelsea. She gives me a sympathetic smile. She knows the drill of these birthday parties. She pulls out her phone and texts me. I sneak my phone under the table. A flower and a smiley.

I return her sweet smile. I text back a heart.

❖   ❖   ❖

IN THE DAYS and weeks that follow my birthday ride, I replay everything Stone said about Keeper. Somebody who'd found the abandoned houses. Somebody looking the other way.

...the only reason I made it out of the basement alive was the knowledge that I would make them suffer.

My dad would never knowingly let young boys be hurt the way Stone was hurt. But would he look the other way?

Stone got those boys out of the basement when he was fifteen, he said. He's around ten years older than me, so I would've been about five. And Madsen, one of the men who preyed on those trapped boys, was at my sweet-sixteen party. Which means my parents knew him. Granted, there were hundreds of people there, but still.

If somebody had gone to my father when he was first starting out and asked to rent a place off the books, no questions asked, would he have agreed?

Sometimes I think maybe yes. But I know in my heart he would never have said yes if he knew children were being hurt. I know that for sure.

But what if he'd thought it was for something less awful? Maybe illegal card games, a mistress, sports betting, things like that. Dad loves to bet on college football with his buddies.

What if he didn't know?

That wouldn't matter to Stone, though. Why should it? Children are hurt every day by people looking the other way. People not noticing, not caring. When you're a boy in a basement, looking away is its own kind of crime. He made it clear that he wants them all to pay.

I can never let Stone find out.

Not that I'll ever see him again. There was something final about that trip to the basement. He wanted to ward me off. Like the Mr. Yuck sticker on the bottles and jugs of detergents under the sink. A sign that I should probably listen to.

Poison. Stay away.

The worst part of it is that, after he told me about Keeper, he could tell something was wrong. He could tell I pulled away, and I know what he thought. That I'd decided he was too damaged after all.

Too much a monster.

I hate that he'd think that. But what can I do? Explain to him that it was really a suspicion that he's talking about my father? Tell him how the shock of it nearly made me throw up?

"Tell me about the Innkeeper," I finally blurt out to my mother.

She pauses with her teacup in midair, her other hand holding her phone where she scrolls through the newspaper's society page website. "What?"

"For Christmas. The story you tell every Christmas."

She looks at me oddly, a little worried. That worry has been there ever since the last time Stone took me, like one of these days I'll finally splinter into a million pieces. Sometimes it feels like that would be a relief.

"Oh, that." She gives me a small smile. "You've heard it enough times to tell it yourself. That's always been your father. A good man. Good to the bone."

Hope rises inside me, because a good man couldn't do what Stone said. He couldn't be involved in any of that. "But how did you know? When you met him, how did you know?"

"I didn't, really. I mostly liked the way he looked.

The way he smiled at me. The knowing part only came later. He rode a motorcycle; did you know that?"

That startles me out of my worry, because I have never heard Mom talk like this. "Really?"

"He was dashing." She laughs. "And sexy."

I wrinkle my nose. "Eww."

"Well, your grandfather was furious. He thought your daddy wasn't good enough. He didn't have much money. Neither did we, but we had our name and standing."

"I didn't know that."

"The heart loves who it loves, and my heart loved your daddy. But he worked so hard. Impossibly hard." There's a small line between her eyes; she puts cream on it every night because she thinks it makes her look old. It deepens now, and she doesn't seem old, only troubled. "Maybe too hard. He wanted me to have everything he thought I should have."

"And Grandpa came around?"

She shakes her head, but it's more like agreement. "He didn't have a choice. The old factory would have gone under if your father hadn't bailed him out."

I gasp, knowing how proud my grandfather is. We aren't close, but I see him once a year. He's a stern man. Cold but loving, somehow. "He did that?"

"Most men would have lorded it over him, the way my father had been so rude to him and then was brought low. But not your father. He is always kind, even when he doesn't have to be."

The doubt feels lighter now, like it's floating away. It can't be my daddy who's connected to crime and pain. There's a whole city out there. It must be someone else.

Anyway, Stone said *Keeper*, not *Innkeeper*. Those are two completely different words. It's a coincidence—it has to be.

I got worked up over nothing. Mom's always saying I do that. "I'm glad you told me."

"You probably know that the charities and foundations I'm on...some of them do good work, but most of them are just for show. Opportunities for society women to get together. Your daddy doesn't mind me doing them, but he donates as much as he can to charity. And unlike the story I tell at Christmas, no one knows about that."

Chapter Sixteen

~Brooke~

Weeks pass. Then months.

I don't know how I make it through the holidays, but I do.

I throw myself back into school once January hits. It's my junior year, and I need to keep up my grade-point average if I'm going to land any kind of scholarship to the local university.

Most of my friends will attend Ivy League schools, but no way can we swing it. Mom is already talking about how I don't want to go out of state for college, how I can't bear to be apart from my family. Making it sound like they'd send me to Harvard or Princeton if only I desired it.

I fixed the hummingbird Stone carved for me.

You can see where I glued its little wing, but I don't care. It's beautiful to me. I keep it on my bedside table next to a tiny replica of the Eiffel Tower I got the first time we visited Paris and a turtle made of sapphire, my birthstone, and some coins from trips we took. Stone's bird is my favorite of all my treasures.

I dream about the way he touched me on the ride we took. His hand between my legs. His other on the steering wheel. How free I felt for once. Flying.

Sometimes I think I see him out of the corner of my eye.

There's one snowy Saturday in March when I'm shopping at the mall with Chelsea, and I'm sure I see the flash of his face on the level above—dark hair, green eyes blazing down at me.

I dropped my bags right there, told her to wait, and bounded up the escalator, practically knocking people over.

When I got up there, he was gone.

And what would I have done if I'd caught him, anyway? How could I face him, knowing my own father had a hand in what happened to him? Well, I don't know for sure. I hope not.

I tell myself it's for the best that we stay apart. I think he and I both know it. Stone and I don't have to talk or be in the same room or even the same world to know people like us can't be together.

But if I could say one thing to him, it would be to tell him he's not a monster. I would tell him he's beautiful. And the bravest person I ever met.

Chapter Seventeen
~Stone~

Almost two years later

I'M SITTING ON the hood of my car at the entrance to the Sugarbeet Hills Campground, just another camper in the shade of the tall oaks, sneaking away to do phone shit.

But really waiting for Grayson.

Nervous.

Two years he was inside. I still can't believe it worked. All those months of planning, all that money paid to Grayson's rat. The whole prison breakout. And the way he got word to us through that ridiculous prison stories journal? Brilliant.

We fucking pulled it off. Knock me over with a feather.

But I won't rest until I see him with my own eyes. And he could have a tail, so I'm armed to the teeth. Things got messy. He had to take a hostage.

I pull the ball cap low over my head and keep my focus on my phone, but my awareness is everywhere.

Soon enough, I catch sight of the blue Honda rambling up the shady gravel road. My heart is smashing near out of my chest. Wait and be sure. Don't blow it now.

First thing I notice: it's two people. Grayson's still got that hostage with him. What the fuck? But my anger about the hostage disappears when he jumps out of the car, comes at me for a bear hug.

"Grayson. Fuck." I pull him to me, hold him a long time. It's not my style, but it's Grayson, and there are no words for how incredible it feels to see him. I pull back and clap his shoulder. "Motherfucker, looking good."

Actually, he looks older, harder.

That's partly on me. I should've seen it coming, him getting framed like he did.

I tell him about being pulled over on the way here. Ten hours I drove from Franklin City. But I had a fake ID. They let me go.

"The guys cannot wait to see you. Two words: party central. Whatever you want." I glance toward the girl in the car, sitting like a petrified deer, eyes staring ahead. Why does he still have her? He needs to get rid of her. "When are you going to do it?"

He shrugs. Mumbles. Grayson's always had a soft heart, though he wouldn't like me to know it. Not one for violence.

"I'll do it," I say. "Let me do this for you."

"I got it," he says.

I narrow my eyes, not liking this.

"She can still be useful," he adds.

Useful. Such bullshit. He never could lie to me. I shake my head. Getting attached to some hostage is the last thing he needs to do. Every minute he keeps her doubles the danger—to all of us, now that she's seen us together. "Grayson," I warn.

"Fuck you," he says. "It's not like that. I got this."

"Shoot her in the woods out there. No one'll find her."

He gives me a hard look. Yeah, it's a harsh thing to say. Extreme.

It's just that we don't do captives, and we definitely don't do relationships. We made that pact a long time ago. No women except to fuck. Allegiance to each other and nobody else. *One blade to protect my brothers, one blade for vengeance.*

I made myself stop seeing Brooke, and it feels like having my leg sawed off not to see her, touch her. Which just proves the point. That kind of connection? It's a weakness.

"It's under control," he growls. "And then we'll pick up where we left off. At the Bradford."

"You're not bringing her to the Bradford," I warn. "I'll tell you that right now."

He holds up his hands like that's the last thing he'd

do.

"She's a hostage," I remind him. "She served her purpose. You keep her, and it endangers you and your brothers." I give him a look. "Keeping her, it makes you like *them*." *Them* meaning the ones who took us. Are my words penetrating? I can't tell.

I grab the clothes I brought for him. His favorite old boots.

I watch the girl while he changes. She's pale, brown hair in a messy bun. Delicate features. Pretty.

Maybe he can't do it. Or maybe he's waiting for a better spot. I'm not going to fight him on this. Unless he tries to keep her. Then I'll deal with her myself—for his own good and hers.

I tell him we have leads on the governor. How we're going to make him pay. How awesome it'll be. He seems distracted by the girl. "You're okay?" I ask.

"Why wouldn't I be?" He gives me his classic grin.

We discuss logistics.

Ten minutes later, I watch him drive off with a bad feeling in my gut, like everything's about to change. Maybe it's a little hypocritical of me to warn him away from this girl when I've been taking Brooke hostage like it's a goddamn hobby.

But like I said, I stopped. More than a year and a half since I've touched her.

Every so often I let myself follow her around for a

couple hours. It's past the point where I can pretend it's about keeping her quiet. This is about needing to be close to her, even if it's twenty yards away. I look at her and remind myself of what I can't have.

It's what Grayson can't have either. He's my brother, but he has to live by these rules. This is how I keep all of us focused. This is how I keep us alive.

And it's working. Case in point: we're closing in on the players.

Jimmy Brass turned out to be a retired cop who did all kinds of work for them. Signed off on patrols that never happened. Made evidence disappear the one time there was a bust.

He never touched one of us, that I know of, but that doesn't matter. He's plant food now. Fertilizer. Six feet under. He put his dumb kid through college with money we earned with our bodies. He deserved what I did to him.

Now we're closing in on Keeper. There's an old paper trail someone forgot to cover up. A shell company that bought and sold a house—not *the* house, but the one next door. How's that for twisted? Can't have the neighbors complaining about kids screaming in pain.

Keeper bought that house and kept it empty on purpose. They hide behind nicknames because they're cowards, but I'm going to find him. I'm going to break him.

It's times like this that I really miss Brooke, when I'm tense, when I'm getting close to a kill. She has a way of making these things bearable.

CHAPTER EIGHTEEN

~STONE~

THERE'S A PLACE at the top of the Bradford where a greenhouse used to be. I never saw this place in its heyday, but I imagine it produced thick red roses to put on crisp white linens. Now it's my lookout.

I have a room in the hotel, like the other guys. Bare walls and a clean mattress. More than I could have hoped for when I was a kid, but the ruined greenhouse is where I spend most of my time. From here I can see all four corners of the Bradford. I can see the cross streets and the buildings beyond—abandoned, mostly, which is what makes this place perfect. Over the ridge of brick and metal, the city spreads out in front of us, bustling with headlights, with sound. The world spinning on without any idea that we're here.

That's the point, of course. If the cops knew about this place, they'd be on our asses. Some of our business interests are legal. Some of them aren't.

And Grayson, well, he's a fugitive since his prison break.

The Bradford is more than a place to sleep, more than our operational headquarters. It's a safe haven. And it's my job to keep it that way. That means keeping my finger on the pulse of the streets. I have a network of informants throughout Franklin City. A few cops on my payroll. There are a hundred ways I make sure this place stays secret, but I like to watch for myself. Sometimes it's the only way I can take a deep breath—with my gaze on the empty streets around us, making sure the crew is safe.

Something is off today.

I lift my face to the breeze, clench my hand around the rusted wrought-iron banister. What the hell is it? I'm about to go downstairs, to make Knox run his scans or whatever the fuck he does on the computer to find a problem I can fucking solve, when I see it—a streak of red.

For half a second, there's relief. Part of me always knows when one of the crew is away from the Bradford. I can feel it as surely as if I were a farmer sensing a goddamn storm rolling in. The red streak? That's Knox. The cherry-striped Shelby is his favorite car, which is saying something. He has twenty in his personal inventory alone, not to mention the garage he keeps for the rest of us.

His favorite, which is why I know he'd never grind the gears so loud I can hear the crunching echo off the brick walls a block away. Tires bounce onto the broken curb. The bottom of the car scrapes concrete with an ear-splitting screech.

I have my cell phone out, a calm sense of purpose washing over me. This is what the crew needs me for. For times like this, when I can be cold as ice.

The Shelby cuts the corner too close, sending mortar and brick flying into the street.

"Get Nate here," I say, knowing Cruz will be on the other end of the line, pinging the only brother who doesn't live at the Bradford on our secure line. "Nine-one-one," I say as the car comes to a haphazard halt in front of the hotel, where the old valet station would have been.

Fuck. I'm flying down the stairs, still talking.

"And find out what's happening on the police scanners. Some shit went down, and I need to know what they know."

I make a quick stop to grab Grayson.

"It's Knox."

Grayson doesn't argue, but I feel his tension as he follows me down the steps. "On a Tuesday?"

Every single one of us has our demons. Whether it's sex or blood or drugs. There's something we use to numb the pain. Or, worse, something we use to relive it. What happened back then fucked us up so we're not really human anymore. We're animals with damn-near unlimited funds and access to the world's worst vices.

Knox's demon is alcohol. At least it was until I sat him in a fucking room for a month, while he swore at me and called me every name in the book, and dried him out. He hasn't touched a drop since.

"No," I say on a growl, but the truth is, I don't know.

I don't know until I reach the car, its engine still running, and yank open the door.

The smell of rum doesn't greet me. No, it's metallic. It's blood. Knox is bleeding from a hole in his chest, slumped against the black leather, eyes glazed with pain and delirium.

"Fuck," Grayson mutters, and I hear the panic in his voice.

I hear the panic, but I don't feel it. Because this is who I am. Cold. Hard. Steady as a rock. "I'll pull him out. You grab his right side. We'll take him upstairs and stabilize him."

When you say words like that, that's what makes them true. The fact that I could say it so strong and clear, that's what Grayson needs to pull himself together. Maybe it's what Knox needs to hear deep in his shock-numbed mind.

We're in the main living room twenty minutes later, keeping the wound stanched, when Nate shows up, looking winded and pissed.

"If this is another one of your pranks—"

"It's Knox," I say flatly.

"Still? He needs an AA meeting, not a doctor."

"It's a gunshot," I snap. "You got anything in your bag of tricks for that?"

That spurs him into action. Nate gets off on healing people, though they don't let you near human bodies when you're not actually a person on any government records. But vet schools, we faked enough documentation to get him through admissions. He earned his diploma, and that's all he's needed to practice ever since. It's good, though. The animals. The farm. The fucking wholesomeness of it.

It's another hour before Nate's removed the bullet and sutured the wound.

Another two hours before Knox wakes up from the anesthetic. Those horse drugs don't fuck around. Which means I've been in the dark about what actually happened for way too long. Cruz has checked around enough to know there aren't any reports about someone matching Knox's description or even gunfire on this side of town. There's no disturbances on the perimeter. It seems like we're safe, but I need to know for sure.

Knox blinks up at me, still groggy. "Stone?"

"Yeah," I say, my voice hard. Like I don't care that he just went through hell.

"It was the…" He pauses through a labored breath, pain bright on his features. "The detective."

"Detective Rivera?" There's a sharp sting of disappointment. I would never admit this to the crew, but I thought that guy was clean. I don't usually trust cops, don't usually trust *anyone*, but I at least thought he was clean.

"Yeah, but not...he must have been following me. When I tried to make the deal, he was there. They thought it was a setup. Shot...me. Rivera tried to pin us down. Barely got out."

Jesus. Rivera may not have pulled the trigger, but he's going to get us killed pulling a stunt like that. The men we do business with, they aren't about cocktails and handshakes. More like guns and bloodshed.

They don't care about those boys in a basement somewhere. All they care about is cold hard cash, which is what we were going to exchange for information.

"Did you get it?" I ask, my voice tight.

A different kind of pain flashes over Knox's face. "I'm sorry."

Fuck. We need that information. Those guys won't come near us again after this.

We can't protect ourselves long term without information about what happened to us. About who framed Grayson. Forces more powerful than us need us quiet. Dead, preferably.

I want to swear and kick something. Instead I force down my feelings. Force myself to look at the bandage stained red. At the sheen of sweat on my brother's face. He's hurting. If I were still in that basement, I would have told him to touch the hot rivet, to let the pain out that way, because I was dumb and desperate.

Now I nod to Nate from across the sofa, and he injects something into the bag. Morphine, probably. It will take a few minutes to kick in. I grasp Knox's hand so he doesn't feel alone between now and then. "You ever seen a Shelby Cobra with an automatic?"

He lets out a strangled sound. "Blasphemy."

This is what we talked about that month I kept him locked up. Felt bad about it, like it was some grown-up version of the basement, but I didn't have any other choice. Couldn't let him drink his life away. Or endanger the rest of the crew. This was our grown-up rivet, talking about cars. I read all these books on pointless car facts just so I could keep him interested.

"There were only twenty ever made. Three-speed."

"You're shitting me."

I shrug. "Probably easier to drive when you get shot."

His laugh turns into a groan, and I keep up the steady stream of useless car talk for fifteen minutes. By then his muscles have turned soft, his lids lowered. His hand is burning hot in mine, but he doesn't let go. "You gonna stay?" he whispers.

He must know he's going under. He'll be asleep; what does he care if I'm here? But I can't tell him no.

"I'm not going anywhere," I say, thinking that maybe I'm the rivet now. Taking all the hurt inside myself. Maybe I always was.

CHAPTER NINETEEN

~BROOKE~

"**H**ERE."

I stare at the small foil packet in between the eyeliner and lipstick. Even though I've never seen one in person, I know what it is. A condom. It says *For Her Comfort* on the label, which is almost sweet of my mother. Except that she's not giving me a choice.

"I don't need that," I say, knowing that's the wrong answer.

She doesn't look surprised by my refusal. She doesn't look accepting, either. "It's normal to be nervous about this. That's why I want you to be prepared."

"Mom, I barely know Liam. And I don't want to have sex with him."

Disapproval flashes across her face, which is so like mine. The Botox has kept the wrinkles away. "He's spending a lot of money on tonight. The limo, the dinner at Bel Canto."

"So what? Does that mean he's paying me for sex?"

She looks horrified. And angry. "Of course not. This

is a completely normal thing that happens on prom night. There are girls who would love to go out with Liam McConnell."

The words slip out before I can stop them. "Because his family's rich?"

My bedroom turns ten degrees colder, and I shiver in my pale pink slip. My dress hangs on the back of the door, the perfect combination of sophisticated and sexy. I might even like it if I had chosen it myself. Instead it was planned for me, like everything else in my life. This is the first time Mom's let me wear black.

When she speaks, her voice is unexpectedly soft. "I'm not saying you have to do it, Brooke. Only that you should be open to the possibility."

I force a smile. "I understand."

"And if you have any questions about what to expect…"

God, she makes it sound like I'm getting married. It's prom night, and I feel like I'm being sold to the highest bidder. Liam isn't a bad guy. A little cocky, but what heir to a shipping fortune wouldn't be? We aren't close, though.

Honestly I was surprised when he asked me to prom, but it seemed like a good idea. Now that the little silver packet stares up at me, I'm rethinking that decision.

"I do have one question."

She doesn't quite manage to hide her wince. This

conversation is as uncomfortable for her as it is for me. "Of course."

"That story about Dad? The one you tell at Christmas, about him being like the Innkeeper from the Bible. Did that happen before or after you were married?"

She blinks, looking surprised by the question. "We were engaged at the time. That was when he only had a couple of motels to his name."

It's my mother's family that had money. My father had pure ambition and hard work. The business thrived until just a few years ago. I know that Liam might be the answer to turning things around. Such a mercenary way to look at my prom night.

The foil crinkles, and I realize I'm holding it in my fist.

My mother's blue eyes are pleading with me. "Brooke, I never would have suggested this if I hadn't met Liam myself. If I didn't know he comes from a good family."

"What if I don't want him?"

"You wanted him enough to say yes," she reminds me gently. "If you decide you don't want to do anything with him, then don't. This isn't a requirement. But if you're on the fence, remember all the things I've done for this family. That your father has done. We both make sacrifices."

Sacrifices. She could be talking about Daddy's long

hours at work. But what if he's sacrificed more than that? What if he's sacrificed his morals as well? What if he sacrificed defenseless children?

But he's my father. I won't give him up to Stone.

Which is why it's a good thing I haven't seen Stone again. Over and over I tell myself that.

My mother scowls at my feet, clad in black heels. "Is that a scuff?" She mumbles something about her kit and sweeps out of the room with an air of annoyance, as if I've been careless already.

I flop back on the bed.

It's been a year and a half since my seventeenth birthday. A year and a half since that last ride. A year and a half since he made me feel free, hurtling down the highway in the sunshine.

When I turned eighteen, I half expected him to show up, the way he did on my sixteenth and seventeenth birthdays. In truth, I more than expected to see him. I *wanted* to see him. I yearned to hear him call me little bird in that way of his, gravelly and surly, yet so strangely full of tenderness. I would've given up every brightly wrapped birthday gift to feel his hand on my thigh just once, a little bit too heavy, too possessive.

Stone was the only birthday present I wanted and the only one I should have never wanted.

I told myself it didn't matter what I did—Stone would either show up, or he wouldn't. That's his way.

Still, I parked in a shady spot near a shadowed door-way. After school I actually sat there, alone in the driver's seat, for fifteen minutes, checking Instagram.

I wasn't looking at the scroll of smiling faces and meals and blue-water beaches—not really. With every fiber of my being, I was waiting for him, trembling for him, butterflies in my belly, thighs smashed tight together, thinking of him.

An ache between my legs.

I felt sheepish about that when I realized it. What if he touched me there? What if he knew? But Stone wouldn't joke about something like that, and he would never say I was a slut.

He would like it, because my desire for him is some-thing real and true. Stone likes real and true things about me. He's the only one who wants to know my dreams. He's the only one who doesn't want me in my mask.

In the end, it didn't matter how long I sat in the car. My birthday came and went.

Stone never showed up.

It's for the best—I know that. Even as he could touch between my legs and feel the wetness there, I knew he could gaze into my eyes and sense my secret worries about my father.

Could I lie to him? I don't know. I wouldn't want to try.

Three hours and a hundred photos later, I'm riding

in the back of a huge limo next to Liam, across from Randall Wainwright and Kitty, one of the gorgeous Shaffer twins. They're nice enough, but kind of drunk, and Kitty managed to make me feel terrible about my dress by not saying a word.

Randall cranks *Lil Peep*.

Liam slings an arm around me and hands over a polished silver flask.

"No, thanks," I say. "I haven't eaten."

"But look, it says *drink me*," he protests.

I smile. "Where does it say that?"

He grins and changes his voice, like the flask is talking, blond hair flopping over his forehead. "Drink me, Brooke!"

I roll my eyes. Liam can be seriously silly sometimes, though I don't really know him that well. Liam and Randall go to the boys' school down the block from our girls' school, but in the upper grades, we share activities like band and theater and choir, and we do all our dances together.

"Drink me, drink me!" he repeats. Randall and Kitty are laughing.

I snort and take the flask. "I think you're the Mad Hatter, that's what I think." I take a fake sip.

"Oh, come on," Liam says.

I take a good swig this time. The liquid burns my throat.

Liam takes the flask back and drinks. Randall cranks the tunes.

Kitty shows me her nails, with tiny loops on the ends of them. "Amazing," I say.

We get a booth at Bel Canto. Liam and Randall have fake IDs. They order two whiskey sours each and then give them to us when the waiter leaves.

We get puffed pastry appetizers, and Randall is laughing about band kids. It's a five-course meal, the kind you order as a set. It's delicious and probably worth an entire car payment for most folks.

I have just that one drink—I don't like to drink the way some kids do.

Liam is actually really nice. He likes me, and he's always trying to make me laugh. He gives me the cherry out of every drink he orders, and he smiles at me when he puts his hand on my thigh under the table, watching my face for any sign of not wanting it there.

I smile back at him, signaling that it's okay. I try to imagine it feeling alive and exciting, like when Stone first touched me there, but really, Liam's hand just feels…wooden, in a weird way. Like there's no life in his touch. Flat.

But I let him leave it there, because he's taking me out to this nice dinner, and maybe he'll grow on me. I remind myself I didn't like hanging around with Stone at first, and he grew on me, right?

Understatement of the year. Stone is all I can think about.

But Stone can't be my boyfriend.

If anything, I should hate Stone for how he blazed into my life with all his heat and fury and passion. I should hate Stone for his intense gaze, and the way his eyes burn into my soul, and the way he kisses me—like he'll die if he doesn't.

Liam kisses me after dinner. More tongue, less passion.

It's not fair to compare them. Of course Liam would have less experience. I have less experience, too. It's actually kind of sweet. We can experience this together.

The prom is held at the elite boys' school down the block from our girls' academy. The theme is fairy garden, and kids from both schools have been collaborating on the decorations, though everyone knows it's just an excuse to meet each other.

And as the night goes on, Liam's kisses get more sloppy. During a slow dance it seems like he's making out with my cheek. "Got a hot tub room at Solange," he slurs.

I smile and nod.

Solange (you never call it the Solange) is where the after-party is; Solange is a boutique hotel on River Road Drive, just down from the Ivy Club, which is the exclusive private men's club that my father belongs to.

If the schools Liam and I attend cater to the most elite families in all of Franklin City, the Solange penthouse after-party is where the heirs of the most elite of the elite families will go.

I'm hoping Liam passes out before we get there. Even though he was nice to me, I don't want to have sex with him. The condom feels hot in my little black and gold clutch.

He grabs my hand and pulls me out of the ballroom, mumbling something about fresh air.

I'm wondering whether he's feeling sick. Some small part of me hopes he is.

I imagine myself playing Florence Nightingale, making the limo driver bring us to the 7-Eleven, where I'd buy him crackers and soda. He'd apologize, and I'd be so nice about it. And then he'd drop me off, and my mother would have no excuse to be angry—how could I go to Solange when my date was deathly ill?

"You okay?" I ask.

"Gotta get air," he murmurs, arm slung around my shoulders.

The limos are arrayed up and down the block. "Which one is ours?" I ask.

"Who cares?" he says, and his voice is lower than usual.

It sends a shiver down my spine, not completely unpleasant. It reminds me of Stone, that voice. Enough that I turn my face away and pretend he's with me.

So we keep walking. Suddenly, he's leading me into a darkened walkway between buildings, ivy-covered brick on one side, a chain-link fence on the other, a dim glint in the dark.

"What are you doing?"

"A little party of our own."

I slow down, tugging toward the street, the light. I'm not sure that I want to go back. Not sure that I want to go forward. "We're missing the dance," I say, stalling for time.

He pulls me deeper in, then pushes me against the bricks in the dark and makes out with my face—that's how it feels, like I'm a face to make out with while he paws my breasts.

My mother's words ring in my ears. *Be nice. Try. We all make sacrifices.*

"Somebody might come." But that's not what I'm worried about. No one will find us out here. And even if they did, they wouldn't care. Everyone in there will end up naked in a hotel room.

"Let them come," he says, running his hand over my dress, pulling it up, feeling my bare thigh above the stockings, reaching higher.

"Wait," I say, but what I really want to say is, *you're not Stone.*

The realization turns my insides cold. No matter

how long it's been since Stone left, even after I knew he wouldn't come back, I've been waiting for him. Ignoring all the prep-school boys for him. Keeping myself a virgin for him. How messed up is that?

In the end it's not my mother's words that move me.

It's the knowledge that I want Stone that makes me decide to have sex with Liam. I think if I let Liam inside my body, if I lose myself in this moment, I can finally forget.

I resign myself to this. I'm going to have sex with my prom date, like a hundred other girls tonight. I'm going to be completely ordinary, completely normal, completely unlike the girl who dreams about the man who took her hostage.

Except that Liam isn't kissing me anymore.

He's pulled back, looking at me, concern replacing some of the lust in his eyes.

Because I told him to wait, I realize. He's respecting my body, respecting *me*, and that's another thing that makes this so different. Stone never had sex with me, but I like to think that if he decided to, he wouldn't stop. Not even if I asked him to.

That's the way I fantasize about him, being hard and demanding.

"You want to go inside?" Liam says, his voice a little hoarse.

It would hurt him to go back inside, be a strain on

his body, but he'd do it if I asked him to. The knowledge sends a tendril of tenderness through me. "No. I want this."

To prove the point, I reach back up for him, curling my hands into the lapels of his tux and pulling him down to me. His lips meet mine again, and I can almost, *almost* be in this moment with him. I'm a few seconds away from letting go of those car rides. A single breath away from forgetting.

Suddenly he's off me.

There's a flash of hands and black leather. The shattering smash of a body against steel links. A delayed grunt of surprise. Protest. Pain. Liam leaning against the fence, a stunned expression on his face.

A hulking shadow stands in the alley between us.

"What the hell?" Liam says, pushing away from the fence.

"Walk away." Stone. He came for me. He watched me. And he's standing between Liam and me. I can hardly process this. It's like seeing a wild animal in the middle of a shopping mall. He doesn't belong here, but I'm so angry. Angry that he messed up the one thing that might help me get over him. Relieved, too.

"Who the fuck are you?" Liam demands.

Stone takes a step toward him, and in a matter of seconds, I'm flashed back to my sixteenth birthday party. To seeing Stone for the first time. To blood and death.

"Wait," I say, breathless with panic. "Don't kill him."

He turns to look at me, his face in shadows. Even in the dark, I can see his expression. Terrifying. And a little incredulous. "You think I'll kill him."

His voice is flat, and I realize I've managed to insult him.

The truth is, I don't know what he's going to do. He beat that man in the truck stop bathroom, but that was entirely different from this. I didn't want that man. And, for my own reasons, I wanted this boy.

"Please," I say, soft. It's only meant for Stone, that one word. Not for Liam, who's cursing and threatening to call the police.

Stone takes a step toward me, and I'm too glad to be scared of him. Maybe I should be worried that he'll hurt me, but he's protected me too much.

"I should leave you with him," he says, his voice still strangely flat. "So he can paw at you. Put his filthy hands on your body. That's what you want?"

I have the sense of being at the top of a mountain, that whichever way I lean now will determine where I roll, one word to decide my whole future. Stone will leave me here. That much is clear in my voice. If I tell him that I want to stay, that I want to lose my virginity to Liam, he'll let me.

"No," I breathe out, before I've even thought

through the ramifications.

Liam chooses that moment to wave the phone at us, the screen overbright in the dark alley. "The police are on their way, asshole. You have no idea who you're messing with."

My blood runs cold. The police. They won't take kindly to a grown man crashing a rich-kid prom night. "You have to go," I whisper.

"Come with me," he says, and it's the first time he's ever asked me that.

He's taken me hostage three times now. Sat in the passenger seat and told me to drive. But he's never asked me to come with him. The question sits between us, as precious as crystal, fragile as dew.

"Stone," I say, and it's impossible to mistake the longing in my voice.

I'm standing here in a dress my mother picked out, with the boy she wants me to lose my virginity to. With that foil packet in my clutch, a symbol of everything I'm worth to them. The dutiful daughter to make a sacrifice. What about what I want?

What about what I need?

Light bounces off the bricks, flashlights on cell phones. Then Randall appears at the entrance to the alley, his arm slung around Kitty, who's carrying a bottle of wine.

"We've been looking for you," he says, his voice

almost a shout. "It's time for Solange, baby!"

It's Kitty who realizes something is wrong. "Oh my God," she says.

Randall sobers up real quick. "You can take what you want. I have money in my wallet. I'll give it to you."

He thinks we're being mugged. And in the middle of this mess of teenage hormones and drunkenness, Stone stands like he's actually made of marble. Still. Cold. Unfeeling.

With a terrible shudder I realize he never had this. Prom night. Tux rentals. A limo.

He stands there looking so alone.

I take his hand in mine. He squeezes so hard I gasp, and I realize I was wrong. He's not unfeeling. Not cold. He burns hot with fury, with regret. "Let's go," I tell him softly.

"Come quietly and your pretty boy doesn't get hurt."

Stone's words ring loud through the alley, bouncing off brick, and I realize he wants it to seem like he's taking me hostage. Even though I already asked to come. I don't know why he wants it like this. Maybe this is the only way he can take me.

"No," I say, a little hesitant at first. "Don't."

"I won't let you touch her," Liam says, but he doesn't sound sure. And he doesn't place himself between us the way that Stone did. Doesn't defend with his body.

"What are you going to do about it?" Stone says, soft with menace. "Are you going to fight me? Going to throw a punch at me? Does it seem like you'd walk away from that?"

As threats go, it's effective. A visible shudder grabs Liam.

Stone grabs my wrist, his grip firm but not bruising. "He understands, princess. You don't fight me. Got it? That's the way you keep your friends nice and safe."

He drags me down the alley toward the street.

"I'm sorry," I tell Liam, hoping he'll understand. It sounds like I'm sorry that he was threatened, like I'm terrified and mindless. In truth I'm just sorry he didn't get the sex he deserves.

Stone pulls me down the street, with Liam shouting about the police, with Randall staring after us. Kitty whispers to me as I pass by, asking where I met him. She thinks he's some kind of bad man, the kind who would snatch a young woman off the street. She doesn't know he's so much better than that. And so much worse than that. Because he's done this before.

A white truck waits at the corner, a sharp contrast to the long line of black limos in the parking lot. I'm supposed to be in one of those limos, getting felt up, getting drunk. I'm supposed to be a regular eighteen-year-old girl, but instead I'm holding hands with a murderer.

My high heel twists in a sewer grate, and I yelp as I start to fall.

Stone catches me, pulling me into his arms before I can land on the street. One shoe stays stuck in the grate. The other flies off and lands on the pavement. I'm barefoot, and my feet don't hurt for the first time all night. It's enough to make me laugh. I must look like a maniac, wearing a ten-thousand-dollar gown while he has on a leather jacket with a T-shirt and jeans. Happiness courses through me, the certainty that I'm doing something right, even as I make the biggest mistake of my life.

Sirens sound in the distance. Liam hadn't been bluffing about the cops, but then that doesn't surprise me. But they got here fast.

"Sirens," I whisper. Meaning, *we have to hurry.*

The tender look he gives me melts something deep inside my belly. He opens the door and carefully sets me in the truck. It's not a limo, but it might as well be. It's better than that. He buckles me in, heads around to his side, and we pull out.

We're halfway down the block when I see the flash of lights bouncing off the buildings to the right of us. They won't catch us. Affection fills me as I look at Stone's hard profile. They won't catch *him.*

"You came for me," I say, still stupidly excited about that.

He grunts, turning onto the freeway and merging with the other cars and trucks.

I run my bare feet along the rough carpet at the foot of his truck. There aren't any old wrappers tossed into the bottom, but it's not exactly clean either. There are too many rips and burns in the fabric for that. "Where are we going?"

"Somewhere quiet. We need to talk."

It's ridiculous, but my mind goes to the silver foil in my clutch. I have a condom. Protection. This was the night when I would lose my virginity, and now I'm with a man who can take it.

"Talk about what?" I ask in a voice I hope is seductive.

He gives me a sideways look, dark and severe. "Your father."

My mouth goes dry. I look down, twisting the soft part of my clutch. I'm not good at hiding my emotions. And right now they're lit up like a neon sign, flashing *guilty guilty guilty.* "My father?" I say as lightly as I can. "Why would you want to talk about my father?"

"It's serious, what I have to tell you, little bird."

The sirens get louder. Closer. I give him a frantic look. He glances in the rearview, once, then again. His voice calm and steady as he says, "We're okay."

"You sure?"

There's a grim look on his face. What does he know

about my father? Does he know he's the Innkeeper? Keeper? Is he going to hurt my father? I've gone from joy to dread in the space of a heartbeat.

He's pulling off the highway. It's the Big Moosehorn Park exit. But instead of heading down to the river, we go the other way, up a road that turns into dirt and rough gravel. It's a bumpy ride up here, jolting me out of my panic.

"Where are we going?" My voice comes out small.

"A place I like to sit to think."

Ten minutes through the woods, twisting and turning through it all, and he's pulling over in front of a tiny cottage. Ten minutes of wondering what Stone could possibly want to say to me except the worst thing in the world. Ten minutes of wondering how I can plead for my father's life.

He looks over at me. "You can't tell anyone this is here."

"How would I even find it again?" Except I remember the path by heart.

He leads me around to the back, to a door with the hinge broken off. "This used to be a ranger station before they built the nice one down by the road. I fixed it up two summers ago."

It's old but clean. He lights a gas lamp, and then another. "Remember my friend Grayson, who was framed for murder?"

"Yeah," I say. "Your friend in jail."

The place glows, tiny and cozy. A red plaid blanket is thrown over a small couch. There are books and papers around.

"Well, he's out now."

I turn to him, forgetting my nervousness. "They let him go? That's great, Stone! You were so worried about him. He was like a little brother to you."

He tosses me a bottle of water. "Let him go…that's not exactly how I'd put it, little bird."

"Oh my God." If they didn't let him go, that means he left on his own. A prison escape? Stone's expression is unrepentant, which means he probably helped.

"It's all good." He grabs what looks like a giant sketch pad from the table and settles down on the old couch, sinking into the cushions. It looks like the most comfortable place in the world.

I sit next to him. It feels strangely natural, like I've been here forever.

He sets the pad on his lap but doesn't open it. He just slides his hand over it. Thinking. There's something different about him, but I don't know what.

"It's amazing to have Grayson back," he says finally. "I didn't let on to my guys how worried I was about him. Things are…different with Grayson. Not really in a bad way. I think he grew up a little. Calling his own shots in some ways…"

He looks over at me, pinning me with that intense gaze, eyes deep pools of green that seem to go on forever. It comes to me that what he said about Grayson calling his own shots is significant in a way I don't understand. Like maybe it changed something for Stone, too.

Or maybe for us. Because something is definitely different. It's been a year and a half since I saw him last, but it's not just that. He doesn't look different, but he feels different. Stronger and more solid. More purposeful.

The air seems to heat and thicken between us.

"But he's back," I supply. "I'm glad. However he got out, I'm glad, Stone." I find that I mean that.

"Me, too," he says. My breath stutters as he reaches up and slides a strand of hair from my face, grazing the side of my forehead with his knuckle. The small touch burns, sends waves of heat through me. "You look beautiful tonight," he says. "So goddamn beautiful, it kills me."

"You look beautiful, too."

He narrows his eyes, as though I said something silly. He tugs at the frayed collar of the soft-looking green T-shirt under his leather jacket. "Good, because this is my best T-shirt. Special occasions only."

He's being sarcastic, but the T-shirt goes with his eyes, and it looks soft, and the collar is perfectly worn below his thickly muscled neck. His pulse thrums beneath his jaw line, and for a moment, I imagine pressing my lips to it. Would his skin feel warm? "I mean it, Stone."

He keeps his gaze on me for a long time, and I'm acutely aware of us alone, here in this simple, masculine space that feels so much like him.

He seems to remember himself. "There are things I need to tell you, Brooke."

I nod, tense again.

"We…had a talk with the man who helped to frame Grayson," he says.

A sense of something darker—something unsaid—arrows through me. *Had a talk.* They'd do more than talk with the man who helped to send Grayson to prison.

Is the man still alive?

"We got some new info. It's bad." He pauses, runs his hands over the pad. "There are other boys out there—right now. Being held, just like we were."

My stomach turns over. "Where? Right now? Can you get them out?"

"We don't know where they are. *Yet*," he growls.

There are kids being held in a basement like the one I saw. Touching a burning hot rivet as their only sign of hope. I can imagine the heat against my finger. "Did you tell the police?"

He looks at me like I said something outrageous. Like I asked whether he told the Martian delegation or something. "This city, you have no idea, do you? The police have been the best protection these guys could ever have."

"Oh."

"It's up to us," he says. "They're out there, being kept in a hole like we were, nobody giving a fuck. Or at least, that's what they're thinking. But they have us. They don't know it, but they do."

He's silent for a bit, staring down at that pad.

They have you, I think. And it makes them amazingly lucky. I don't know where the thought comes from, but I'm thinking it with all my heart.

"We're going to find them," he continues, "and we're going to make everybody who put them down there sorry they were ever born."

I nod, swallow past the dryness in my throat. I can't believe my father would knowingly be involved in the horror of boys being imprisoned like that. But what do I say if he asks me point-blank about Keeper? I can't let him hurt my dad.

There's no way my dad is a part of this. Even if he let someone rent a property way back when, there's no way he's helping keep kids captive right now.

Stone opens the pad. "I need to show you this."

My pulse races as he turns to a page full of pencil scribbles—words in circles with lines connecting them, a massive, tangled web, like a flowchart or mind map or something. "They're going to see that somebody gives a shit. Finding out about these kids has changed everything for us."

"And you're sure about…more boys being held?"

"Oh yeah. It's from somebody who wouldn't have lied."

I focus back down on the chart. It reminds me of the kind that police make when they're trying to solve a crime, but instead of photos, there are names. *Madsen* is scribbled in one circle. *Governor Dorman*. Shock squeezes my chest. "The governor was involved?"

"That's who we had a talk with," Stone says. "That's who helped to frame Grayson."

"He died recently. It was in the papers. He had a heart attack."

"Wasn't a heart attack," Stone says simply. He points to a small image. A house—*the house*. "Whoever owned the house we were kept in, that information is lost. Or more accurately, it was destroyed. We've been looking at all the big players in real estate from around that time. We've run down their information. Questioned a few…" He doesn't elaborate on *questioned*. He means tortured. Maybe killed. "It's a lot of dead ends. Nobody wants to talk. But then we were looking at who was small potatoes back then. Your father was just starting out as a real estate broker twenty years back."

My pulse races. "Was he?" I say, as if the timeline has

just occurred to me. Inside my organs have shriveled and tangled up, torn apart by guilt, but who do I feel guilty toward? Stone, for keeping information from him? Or my father, for even thinking of betraying him?

"I know it's a long shot, but maybe he could remember something from that time. Maybe somebody asking around about abandoned places." He points to a circle with *Keeper* written in it. "Or maybe he knows who this guy is."

"Twenty years ago," I say.

"It's a lot to ask, but I wanted to show this to you, so that you'd know everything I do. And maybe you could talk to him. Even if he doesn't know this guy Keeper, he could know something important. If you could get even one piece of the puzzle. Like, maybe he knew Dorman back then. Or maybe he remembers something Madsen said, or somebody else who's involved."

My heart's pounding like a jackhammer. "So you don't know who Keeper is."

"No, but see how many lines connect him to the other players?"

So many lines. Was my father really connected to that many players in this horrible underground kidnapping ring? How is it possible he had that many connections without knowing? "My father might not have known," I say, but my voice is shaky. "He didn't."

"He knew something," Stone growls, more impatient

ANNIKA MARTIN & SKYE WARREN

now. "Even if he doesn't know Keeper, he has to know something. You don't work in real estate in this city for this long without hearing something."

Oh God. "He's more on the construction side now."

"Still want to talk to him."

I nod, but there's a lump in my throat. "Because boys are out there now."

"Not for much longer."

"You're going to free them."

"Fucking right we are."

I reach up and straighten his collar. He really does seem different. It's this new focus on saving those kids. I like it. I love it. But how can I keep something from him?

But God, how can I turn over my father on a silver platter?

I've seen my father come home, exhausted to the bone from trying to keep his company afloat. And I've seen him smile at me, asking to see the poem I've written or watch my new gymnastics routine. He always found time for me, no matter how young and silly I was. He could never be involved in something that hurt children. Not knowingly.

And Stone won't ask questions. He won't care about nuance. He'll *question* my father using every method of torture he knows. Something tells me it's a lot.

"I'll talk to him," I say, my throat tight. How am I

going to ask something like that? *Hey, Dad. Do you remember anything about selling young boys on the black market?* That will be a fun family conversation, but it's better than Stone doing it.

"Thank you," he says softly. "This is important."

I reach over and take his hand. Warm and soft. Heavy on mine, years of rough living forming calluses. I squeeze. It's like holding a tiger by the paw. "Of course it's important. *You* are important."

He shakes his head. "The kids."

Doesn't he see that he's one of them? Even after all these years. But then he never thought of himself as one of them. Even when he was locked in that basement, he saw himself as the caretaker. The one responsible for the children like Grayson. *His guys,* he calls them.

"Where is Grayson?" I ask, looking around the small cabin. "If this place is safe, why doesn't he stay here?"

"Oh, we have somewhere else in the city. It's secure as hell. Completely off the grid. This is a place that only I go."

And now me. His guys are like little brothers to him. And he doesn't bring them here? My heart seems to expand, imagining him trusting me. And then *pop* like a balloon. I'm betraying that trust by not telling him everything I know.

The cabin has one main room with the sofa that we're on. Off in the corner I can see a rudimentary kitchen, a hot plate and a freestanding stainless steel sink. There's a door that I assume leads to a bathroom. I wander toward it, because I can't bear to be so close to Stone—and so far away, at the same time. It's ripping me in two.

Instead of a bathroom, I find a bedroom with an actual bed with white sheets and a navy-blue wool throw over the top. Walls of rough pine. Does Stone sleep here? He said he only comes here to think, but I realize he means for longer than an hour. Maybe even days.

"Why did you come to prom?" I ask, keeping my eyes on the bed. I'm avoiding something, not looking at him, but I don't know who it's protecting really—me or him.

I hear him come up to the door. He stops there, staying behind me. Even so, the air seems to crackle between us.

"Are you sorry I screwed up your date?" he asks, his voice neutral.

Shivers go over me. "Are you?"

"Hell no. That fucker didn't deserve to touch you."

That makes me smile, even though it feels a little sad. "Who deserves to touch me?"

"No one," he says with such stark honesty that tears prick my eyes.

I turn to look at him, then. His worn leather jacket hangs open, revealing the soft green T-shirt over faded jeans. He's fully clothed but strangely naked to me.

Because I can see him.

I can see that there is a gaping hole in his chest, a place where pride and safety and self-respect should go. It was ripped out of him a long time ago, but I only see it now. He couldn't let Liam touch me, but he can't bring himself to touch me either.

My feet move on their own, crossing the small space. And then I'm kneeling in front of him. It's a position of supplication, but one of strength.

He looks down at me. For once I can't read his expression. But I read his body. He's aching, wild with fury and loneliness, an abandoned bear cub.

Completely dangerous. Completely unused to affection.

I thought I was the innocent one. Never had sex. Barely even kissed a boy. But how many times has Stone had sex with tenderness? Maybe never.

"Have you ever been in love?" I ask softly.

There isn't jealousy inside me—not knowing what he's suffered. I want him to have found love, a hundred times over. He deserves a thousand lifetimes of it.

"Yes," he says, his voice hoarse, gazing down at me with raw pain in his eyes.

I hate the pain I see there. Is that what love means to him? Suffering?

I may be naive, but I know love doesn't have to be

about suffering. And it doesn't have to be about drunk boys in dark alleys.

There's something better in the world—I know it as sure as I know I'm kneeling in front of this strong, beautiful man who sees himself as a monster.

"Did you go to prom?" I whisper.

He laughs, uneven. "Fuck no."

"You were still…" *In the basement.* The words are etched into the air.

"Nah, we were out by then. On the run. Definitely not worried about being tardy to class."

"Did you miss it?" Maybe it was good that he came to prom night. Like some sad little replacement for what he never had, except I remember how he looked in that alley. Forlorn. It didn't replace anything. It just highlighted what he never had.

"No," he says, but I can tell he's lying. "I knew that shit wasn't for me. None of it. Tuxedos and flowers. What the fuck would I do with that? It's not for me. I can never have a normal life."

The statement rings inside me like a bell; I've been made hollow.

I reach out a hand, slide the pads of my fingers along the side of his wrist. His whole body vibrates under my touch like he's about to shatter. Like he's made of glass, even though I know he's got strong bones and hard muscles and an unbreakable spirit.

Higher. I reach his forearm. His skin feels warm, muscles hard as rock.

I can never have a normal life.

Suddenly he closes his fingers over my wrist. "What are you doing?" he rasps.

What am I doing? I'm touching him. I'm feeling him, *understanding* him, for maybe the first time ever. I turn my hand to grip him back, wrist to wrist. Our hands form links of a strange chain, joined together against everything impossible.

The air pulses with new energy. Frightening energy. I breathe in the salty, musky scent of him. There's no trace of perfumes or body spray, just pure male beast, surging with pain.

I feel drugged by his nearness. Unable to speak. I just want to touch him.

I just want him.

His fingers brand my wrist with sizzling heat. With every ragged breath, his chest rises and falls under his T-shirt. The open sides of his jacket move, too, grazing his faded blue jeans. Dull metal snaps set deep into his jacket are grayed with age and shift in the dim light that streams in from the other room.

For a moment I think I must be crazy, kneeling in front of him, holding his wrist like a lifeline, imagining he wants me the way I want him. The way he would've wanted the lucky woman he was in love with. Or maybe still is in love with.

Who does he love?

She must be older than me, I think. Worldly and beautiful. And I'm nothing but a sheltered girl who never even had a class with a boy. He would hold himself back from her; that's how well I know Stone. Whatever woman is strong enough to have taken his heart?

He wouldn't think himself worthy.

I know Stone, inside and out. I've seen him kill. I've felt his fingers dig into my flesh as he tried to drown me and couldn't. I've seen him beaten and bruised. I've held the broken little bird he made just for me. Touched myself to his rumbled commands over the phone.

God, that phone call. I've replayed those words so many times in my head, it's as familiar to me as the Girl Scout pledge.

Oh yes, sweetheart. I'm there. I'm holding your hands down to your cunt, telling you to fuck yourself. Shoving my cock in your throat until you've got tears down your cheeks. Until you've got saliva running down your chin. You're crying, but you don't dare stop touching yourself.

I pull my hand from his. Peering up at him through my lashes, I reach down and lift the hem of my skirt. I gather up all the useless fabric, pushing it around my waist to reveal pink panties.

"Holy fuck," he rasps.

My sex feels cool in the air. Soaked.

Slowly and deliberately, I push my hand between my

legs. I burrow my fingers under the hem of my panties. I reach down and stroke along the slickness I find there.

Breath shudders out of him. "Brooke."

I don't know what he means. *Brooke, don't?* Or *Brooke, more?*

But it doesn't matter. My life is full of smiles when I'm sad. Of somebody else's secondhand clothes passed off as couture. A veneer of politeness to cover survival of the fittest.

All of these things are lies.

Me kneeling before Stone is truth. The wetness between my legs is as real as the rough wood floor scratching at my knees. My desire for him is raw. Unbearable.

He's the man no boy can measure up to. He's the moon lighting the vast, dark night of my life. "You're the only one," I say. "Not Liam. Not anyone. I don't want them."

"I'm sorry," he says.

I gaze up at him from under my lashes. Meet his eyes, dark with lust. "There's nothing to be sorry about."

"I ruined you, baby," he grates, his voice thick.

"I like it." I pull my hand from my panties and start to undo his fly, unbuttoning the silver button, drawing down the zipper, clumsy with desire. "It's what I want, Stone," I plead. "I want to do it like we did on the phone call. Ruin me."

He gazes down at me—*burns* down at me.

I gather the courage to whisper the words I've said in my head so many times. "I want you to put your cock into my mouth."

"Fuck." He shoves his hands into my hair, grips my head.

"I want you to fuck my throat. I want you to," I say. "Make me cry while I touch myself. It's all I can think about." Maybe he did ruin me. Maybe if I'd never met him by the river that night, I would have had sex with Liam earlier. I would have even been satisfied with that.

But that isn't what happened. He rewired something in my brain. Or maybe I would have been like this anyway. There's no way to know. No way to separate who I could have been with who I am now. There's only lust. Only this.

Strong hands come to rest on my head.

Only that, and I sink into some strange place in my mind. He isn't even forcing me to do anything, isn't pushing me forward and back, but the strength of him is unmistakable.

My fingers are clumsy with the hard denim of his jeans. He's already thick beneath the zipper, and even without experience, I know what it means. It means he wants me.

When I get the zipper down, his cock springs out, thick and pale and ridged with veins. A gasp escapes me, which makes me sound like the untried virgin that I am. I expected there to be something constraining him. Boxers or something like that, but there's nothing. Only his cock, pulsing with expectation. Larger than I ever imagined.

The musky scent of him works its way into my lungs, into my memories, so deep I don't think it will ever really leave. He doesn't make any move to rush me, but lets me study him. The time doesn't make me any more certain. If anything, I'm intimidated by him. Maybe that's the point.

But I started this, and I'm going to finish it. Going to see if the reality of this is anywhere near as good as the fantasy. Going to see if I come as hard beneath his hands as I did beneath his words.

My hands are trembling only a little as I take hold of his smooth, marble-hard length. I press my face to his warm, slightly furred belly. I squeeze.

He groans. "Can't," he pants. His fingers are clutching my scalp.

Can, I think. *We can.* "Only you," I say.

I touch my tongue to the glistening droplet at the tip of him. He lets out a garbled cry. Strangled desire. Holding himself back from this, even as I finally, finally let myself go.

Dizziness washes over me at the salty taste. I fit my lips around his head. I can feel the tremor all the way through him. Or maybe I'm the one shaking, coming apart at my seams, not fitting back together in any order that I knew before.

My other hand moves back down between my legs. I touch myself as I take him into my mouth, just the way he said to on the phone. He feels impossibly huge. I'm riding a tidal wave of feeling, and I want him to fill me, to make him cry, to be everywhere in me. I feel like I could come in an instant. At the same time it feels like we could do this forever.

His breath gusts wild. He fits my hand around the base of him. "Squeeze, baby."

I squeeze.

A string of unintelligible words tears from his lips as I increase the pressure—swear words mixed with other words I don't understand. "Harder. Tighter. Let me feel you."

Except he doesn't wait for me to obey him.

He rocks into me, slowly, gently. The rhythm of him feels ancient. Savage. It's like he's using me, and the realization is hotter than my fingers against my clit. An imprinting so primal that it's in my DNA, the knowledge that I should open my mouth to him, that he should fill it.

"Yes," he grunts. "Fucking take it."

There's a sound I make. I think it might have been a word—*yes* or *God* or *please*. I'm too mindless to know, his cock too far inside me to let me speak. It comes out as a hum. When he moans, I realize that he can feel the vibrations on his cock. That's how close we are right now. So deep inside me that he can feel the words I can't say.

"Touch yourself," he says.

And I realize I had stopped, lost in the surrender to him. My legs are spread wide as I kneel on the wood floor. I'm shameful and unashamed. I'm needy and satiated. When I touch my forefinger to my clit, the sensation is sharp enough to bring tears to my eyes. This isn't like in my bed, when I could rub myself, again and again, in that one special spot. The need is too much, the ache almost pain, and I have to make circles instead.

I stroke myself to his rhythm, lost in him, in the surge of us together.

"You like that, little bird?" His expression is dark, knowing. He already sees everything that I feel. He wants me to nod with my mouth full of him, my eyes wide and pleading.

Something gentles in his eyes. "You can't get off, can you? Your fingers are all slippery. I can see them shining from here. You're hurting, aren't you?"

My hand clenches into a fist, slick with my juices like he said. I don't know why I can't do this. Is this because I'm a virgin? Or because there's something wrong with me?

He pushes his boot between my legs. "There," he says, like he's given me something.

I blink at him, uncomprehending, even as a spurt of salty precum coats my tongue. My throat works on its own, swallowing him down. My tongue rolls along the ridge of him, making his eyelids drop to half-mast. How does this come so naturally to me? Pleasuring him?

And why can't I do the same to myself?

It feels good, but I'm hovering on the edge of it. I'm trapped here.

"Go ahead," he says, coaxing. "Fuck yourself."

The curved toe of his boot nudges me in the most private place, gentle but still coarse, the curved toe of his boot. And I realize what he wants me to do. To press my sex against the smooth leather. To rock my hips like that while I soak his boot with my arousal.

The humiliation of it does something to my brain. It makes everything sharper, clearer. And when I position my knees around his leg, it feels a little like coming home.

Finding the exact right angle is awkward, but that just makes it better. The way I have to tilt my hips to get friction for my clit, the way he doesn't let me release his cock, the way he watches me the whole time. God. And then my clit does rub against the leather, with exactly the right amount of pleasure, and my eyes roll back.

"That's right," he says, grasping my hair tighter.

I thought he had taken control of this act before, but it's nothing compared to now. Now he holds my head steady, fucking my face with long, hard strokes. It's hard to breathe, because I can't even focus on it. Breathing doesn't feel important when my hips are rocking against his boot, when there's pressure building in my sex. When I'm one second away from exploding.

"Yeah, that's how you want it, isn't it? That's how you need it, little bird. Hard and fucking dirty. And I'm the only one who can give it to you."

I moan my agreement, feeling the climax collect above me like a tidal wave. I'm in its shadow now, in that half-second space before it crashes down, knowing nothing can stop it.

He's moving faster now too, almost jerking, his words choppy.

"The only one," he says, but it sounds a little meaner. "The only one fucking dirty enough to count. The only one wrong enough to make you feel bad."

Tears spring my eyes, because of his fists in my hair. The words in my ears. The climax doesn't care about the warning in the air. It falls and falls.

"The only one fucked up enough," he mutters, and I'm not even sure he knows he's saying it. His expression is hard as granite. "So you can stop being the good little girl."

The realization clicks with horrible certainty. He

thinks he's my rebellion. That I need a break from the prep school and the rich boys. That I only want him because he's messed up.

Then the climax crashes down on me. It rushes along my skin, lighting up every nerve ending, taking over every thought until I'm a mindless being of pleasure. My whole body shakes, wringing out the last hint of orgasm from my clit against his boot.

Dimly I'm aware of his roar loud enough to shake the cabin windows. Of the thick, salty proof of his climax flooding my mouth.

My throat moves to swallow him, taking what he gives me. Only this.

Gently he pulls himself from my mouth. He groans. He's putting his pants back together, snapping them up.

Large paws roam over my face, then up, up, up to grab hold of my hair. I'm panting. The room feels off-balance, or maybe it's me.

He gets down on his knees to face me. To kiss me. He lets go of my hair, smoothing it down. He pulls away and wipes the tears from my cheeks with the heel of his hand, rough movements, clumsy from his orgasm, maybe.

I feel happy, with him taking care of me like this. I feel…loved.

"God, little bird, look at you, so fucking hot." He kisses my cheek. "You are so fucking hot with my cock crammed in your face."

He kisses the other cheekbone.

"I liked it," I say. "I dreamed of it."

He gives me a strange look. Like I shouldn't have said that. But I have more to say than that—much more.

"Stone, I have something," I breathe.

"What is that, little bird?" He wipes another tear.

"In my clutch. I brought a…you know…" It feels wrong to say the word. Like I'm propositioning him.

He stills. Studies my face. Tilts his head. "What did you bring to the dance tonight?"

My face flashes with heat. "You know."

"Can't even say it." He slides a knuckle along my cheek. "But that's okay, because your skin is the perfect shade of pink right now, just like your pretty little cunt." He traces my swollen mouth. "And your tears are the sweetest, dirtiest things I ever tasted. I love that my cock put them there." His rough, giant knuckle pauses at the edge of my mouth. "I love this little bit of my cum still here on your lips."

My pulse races. His possessive words wash over me, heat my veins.

"So fucking hot when you're slumming it."

I frown. "I'm not slumming it."

"Shhh." He pins me with his wicked gaze. "No more talking. I'll give you what you want."

He's touching me with his whole hand now, sliding

his open palm along the side of my neck. He drags it, warm and heavy, down the front of me. Calluses scratch tender skin. Hot breath fans over my forehead. Whatever I'd been worrying about before, it turns to smoke. Any thought in my head, blown away by the soft gust of his breath.

"Stone," I whisper, enjoying the sound of his name. Amazed we're here together.

Fists close over the fragile black piping that lines the top of the bodice, over the fragile lace-covered fabric. He yanks, ripping it.

I gasp.

"Shhh," he says. "I got you. You want your junkyard dog to fuck you with the condom, don't you?"

I don't understand why he's calling himself that. My protest dies in a cry and a flurry of sensation as he pinches my nipple between rough knuckles.

"I should make you wear my cum on your face all the time," he says, voice thick. "Show the world how much you like playing at the dirty little girl."

"I'm not playing," I protest. "This isn't playing, and you're not—"

He claps his big hand over my mouth, stopping me midsentence.

…you're not a junkyard dog.

I mumble into his hand, but he just tightens it. He won't hear it.

"So polite." He kisses my forehead. He squeezes my nipple between his knuckles, rough and warm, squeezing, pinching, twisting lightning clear through my body, electrifying the place between my legs.

"No talking, I said. Got it?"

Again I shake my head, but he won't let up. I can't concentrate with his big fingers rolling my nipple, sending more zings of feeling through my body. He makes me want everything. The folds between my legs feel swollen. Achy. But tickly, too.

I mumble into his hand. I need to tell him that he's not a junkyard dog. I need to tell him he's the best man I know, loyal and good and brave.

But his fingers are between my legs now, making the feelings roll through my body. Everything he does feels like sparkles. I'm panting through my nose, mumbling frantically.

"You want me to fuck you with the condom? You want me to make you a bad girl with that condom you brought for that good boy? Because you know I can. He might have fancy shit and a fancy family for you, but he can't get you dirty like I can, can he? And that's what you want."

My hips move with his strokes, like he's fucking me already. I should be ashamed, but it feels so good.

He slides his finger harder, invading me. I cry out from behind his hand. He moves it back and forth. It reminds me of camp, rubbing sticks together to make a fire—harder and harder until the sparks come. "That what you want?"

I nod behind his hand. I'm whimpering, crying. I need him to do it.

He takes away his hand. "Yes!" I gust out. "Please!"

He watches me, and something hard comes over his face.

He stands, hoisting me up, the world a whirl. He holds me tight to his chest, breathing hard as he carries me to the bed and throws me down. "You better be out of that thing when I get back."

He stalks out of the room.

I wriggle out of my dress, pulling off all my clothes. He comes to stand over me, watching me darkly.

I lie there, naked beneath him. I want him to touch my naked skin, but not because he's dirty or he'll ruin me. Because I love everything about him. I trust him. Of all the people I've ever known, only Stone has never lied to me.

He tosses down the clutch. "Get the condom out, then. I don't have all night."

I fumble with the clutch. Something's wrong. Something's different.

He pulls off his jacket, throws it aside, then pulls his T-shirt over his head. His chest is thick with muscle, and here and there are strange white lines, like scars. Some seem to be injuries, wounds. Others make designs. I'm riveted by him, by his beauty and his pain.

"Sorry, the tattoo store was all out of yin yangs and thorny roses or whatever the fuck high school boys get. Wanna fuck the bad boy, you gotta get used to a little ugly."

"I think it's be—"

"Shut it and let's do this." He holds out his hand. "Gimme."

Beautiful, I was going to say, but he's in such a strange mood, suddenly. There's a tremor inside my chest. It's not fear, exactly, but it's uncertainty. It's being out of my depth. I put the foil wrapper on his palm. The small contact sizzles over my skin.

"Move." He pushes me back.

I curl my legs under me, waiting awkwardly on the bed below him. I feel like covering myself, but he's not even looking at me. He opens the little packet with a crinkle. "Girl like you should learn not to slum it," he grumbles, rolling it over his hardened penis with rough efficiency. Maybe he has to concentrate, maybe that's why he doesn't look me in the eyes or seem romantic anymore. "But if this is really what you want…"

"Stone," I say. "It's what I want. It always was."

"What you *think* you want."

"You don't know," I say.

He doesn't seem to be listening. He crawls onto the

bed and grabs my hair. The strange, hard look is back in his eyes. With a guttural sound, he bends me over, pushes my face into the rough wool blanket. It feels like a kitchen scrubby on my cheek.

"Ass up. Now."

"Wait…" I'd imagined it different. Us face-to-face.

He slaps my butt. "Up. You want roses and candles? Don't tell me you're chickening out already."

Slowly I raise my butt in the air, reminding myself I trust him. He's had all the reasons in the world to hurt me, and he never has.

He positions himself behind me. His hands are on me, but his movements aren't tender anymore. I don't understand what's happening. Why does he seem mad at me? His fingers are between my legs, sliding my juices around between my legs, but his touch isn't tender.

"Stone?"

"Wider. Jesus!" He pulls my thighs apart without waiting, wide enough I feel the stretch on my secret muscles. Wide enough that a blush burns my cheeks, imagining how much he can see.

I try to swallow past the thickness in my throat. My cheek itches from the abrasive fabric. I'm always doing things wrong, never measuring up. Did I do something wrong? I crane my neck around to try to see his face. Try to figure out what happened.

He's kneeling behind me, chest rippling with muscle,

every inch of him hard. But the look in his eyes is…torn. Or maybe grief. Pain.

I feel the fatness of him between my legs. He feels like a doorknob. Like something that definitely shouldn't fit into the soft private place.

"What's wrong?" I ask, a tremor in my voice.

He frowns down at me, fixes me with a glare. "Did I say you could look at me? That's not how we're doing this. You're gonna kiss that scratchy blanket and take what I give to you." He smacks my butt again—hard.

"Ow!" I say.

"Kiss the blanket! Or are you changing your mind?"

My heart hammers in my chest. *This isn't right. This isn't right.* He was rough with me before, during the blowjob, but it felt different. A little bit more like a game. A secret we both knew.

"Why are you still looking at me?"

Then I get it. The look on his face isn't grief or pain. But it's close.

It's loneliness.

What he's doing, the way he's acting—if loneliness was a sport like field hockey or badminton, he would be an Olympic gold medalist.

Looming there behind me, he's transformed into the loneliest person I ever saw. It feels like a knife twisting in me to see him so alone. Why is he so determined to keep me out? To keep me facing away from him? It isn't because he wants pleasure. There's only pain now.

"No," I say.

"Had enough?" he growls.

I turn to face him. Move nearer. I slide my palms over his chest.

"What are you doing?" he rasps out. He grabs my wrists.

"Let me go!" I hiss. I shake him off.

He lets me go—more out of surprise than anything, I think.

I run my hands over the scars and the crisscrosses that mottle his chest. Some of them old. I lean in to kiss the largest, most angry of the white lines. He called them ugly. They're anything but.

He shudders. "...the fuck?"

"I love this one," I say and kiss it again.

"Don't."

"I love this one, too." I kiss another.

"What're you..."

"I love this one very much." I press a kiss to a scar over his heart, press my face to his heart. I feel him trembling, shaking.

"Stop it." He grabs my shoulders, holds me off.

Maybe he can keep me from touching him, but he can't stop what's true. "I love you."

He seems to freeze, right there before me. "What are you doing? No."

"I love you," I say before I've even thought through the words. I've only ever said *I love you* to my parents. And not very often. They don't like to say it back. "And I want you to fuck me however you want. I'll love whatever you do because I love you."

"You can't," he says. "You don't know what you're saying."

I throw my arms around him and kiss him on the lips. Because love doesn't have to be complicated and hard. It doesn't have to hurt. This feeling inside me, something large and expanding, a lightness—it's love. As ordinary as a speck of dirt. As magical as moondust.

And something strange happens.

It's as if all the hardness melts out of him, and he pulls me to him. "Goddamn it," he snarls. "Fuck." He's holding me to his ruined chest, clutching me hard enough I can't breathe.

I make no move to stop him. I don't want to stop him.

"Why aren't you afraid of me?" he demands, but it feels a little desperate. Like I'd maybe solve everything if I just cowered from him. Like he's imagined ways he could scare me.

I let him crush me, the way I might be hugged by a wild animal. A tiger or a bear. With his claws resting against my fragile skin. He could hurt me, but when you love someone, you don't let that stop you. What's the point of fear if it keeps you from living?

He isn't going to let me go, so I turn my face, only slightly. His chest looked terrible in the moonlight. A tapestry of scars. But it's only skin pressed against my cheek. I can barely even register his scar tissue from feeling alone.

There's a message there. Something I need to understand about the man who holds me. He has been tortured and used. He has been hurt, but it doesn't change the fabric of him. He's still a man.

Only a centimeter, that's how far I can turn my face toward him.

I open my mouth and graze his skin with my teeth. He sucks in a breath. He doesn't relax, not exactly. It isn't that the pressure around me loosens, but it changes. It becomes heavy with expectation, with the knowledge of what will come next.

Not my face pressed into the blanket, with him saying crude words to distance himself. But it will be sex. And it will be rough. Maybe even rougher like this, without him holding back.

"I'm not going to use that condom," he says, his voice thick with lust.

The declaration saturates the air around us, the knowledge that he's serious, the awareness that I'm going to let him. That I like it. I want us to be skin to skin. "My mother gave it to me."

A growling sound. "She saw that fucker and gave you a condom and let you leave with him?"

Jealousy. It's weirdly mundane, even as I'm naked in a wild hideout with a criminal. Like we're an ordinary couple instead of a hostage and her captor. "Liam's nice."

It's the wrong thing to say. Or maybe exactly the right thing to say. Because when Stone pulls away from me, there's a dangerous light in his eyes. "Liam's nice," he repeats, his voice caustic. "He's fucking nice."

"He is," I protest, not sure why I'm pushing Stone.

Probably because I want him to push back.

And then he does, in a literal way. His hands on my upper arms. That's all he uses to lift me up and toss me back toward the middle of the bed, like I weigh nothing. The breath whooshes out of me as I land, and I scramble to get away from him, breathless, panting, because it's almost like a game again.

Almost. Because there aren't any rules.

Stone grabs my ankle and drags me back to the middle of the bed. Then he grabs my other ankle, spreading me wide. I have this mental picture of him having sex with me this way, my legs pressed so wide apart, him far away at the foot of the bed. It doesn't make any sense, but that's what happens when you're a virgin. Even your fantasies are a little confused.

And then he lowers his head, right there. Between my legs.

My fantasies didn't prepare me for this.

His mouth touches my stomach, and I jerk away with a high-pitched sound. "What...what are you doing? No. Wait. Not that."

He gives a low laugh. "Not that, says the girl who can still taste my cum."

And I realize that he's right. There's salt that lingers on my tongue. Oh God, that makes me think about what I must taste like.

He slips his tongue into my core, warm and thick. He's fucking me with his tongue. Invading my most secret place.

He pushes it deeper, again and again. I shudder at the sensation. I writhe and moan.

Heavy hands push my legs wider apart. He changes his motion, licking now, licking me like an ice cream cone. Except not exactly, because an ice cream cone is cold, and the heat from his tongue sizzles up through my belly.

He licks again, making wet sounds that are somehow more obscene than what he's doing to me. Then his licks get smaller, more pointed, his tongue feeling more like a finger, thick and warm.

I never felt anything like it. I grab onto his hair, stunned at the feeling. His tongue between my legs is the best thing I've ever felt. Embarrassment washes over me for a split second when I make myself think how he's licking right where I pee, but then he moans, rumbly with pleasure and approval, like he thinks it's the best thing, too, and I let go.

The rules don't apply when Stone is around, and everything is possible. I shove my hands into his hair and grab and twist. I hope I'm not hurting him.

But from his moans, he seems to like it.

He's licking faster. He's swirling good feelings through me, swirling and swirling them. It's too much, but I don't want him to stop.

There's a high noise in the room, and I realize it's me, crying out. Stone's answer is a rumble between my legs, low and dark. His tongue is a live thing, wiggling on that special spot. It's as if he knows exactly where I ache for him—even better than I do. As if he knows secrets hidden inside my body.

That's when everything explodes behind my eyes. Pulsing waves of magic flow inside my head and down to my toes. "Stone!" I cry.

His licking is different now—softer. Like he's softening with my pleasure. As if he's taking care of me, even in this.

He slows and rumbles again. I can barely think. Everything seems so wild. I tighten my grip on his hair.

He's kissing up my belly. Rumbling into the soft flesh there. He kisses between my breasts, kisses my neck.

He looms over me, cages me with massive arms.

"More, Stone."

He studies my face, muscles bulging on either side of me.

"I want all of it. All of you."

He looks down at me with a kind of wonder. "There's no going back."

"Please." I reach down to grab him like he showed me, but he's too far away. He wraps his fingers around my wrist and kisses the flat of my palm, then places it above my head. Somehow I know to keep it there. He trails rough fingers down the sensitive underside of my forearm, then down to my armpit, to the side of my breast.

I let out a gust of air. Everything with him is new and sexy.

He lowers himself. Slowly, muscles bulging. And he kisses me. He's right on top of me—not enough to crush me, but I feel him there, heavy and good.

"Please," I say into the kiss.

"I'm gonna give it to you good and slow, little bird, but you're going to feel it." *It's going to hurt*, he means.

"I want to feel it," I say, even as his thick fingers move at my entrance.

I feel the knob of him pushing into me, filling me. My breath quickens. It's bliss and pain, mingled together.

I cry out.

He stills.

"Keep going," I say.

Gentle fingers stroke the side of my forehead. "Breathe, baby." He nips my lips. "Breathe."

I take a deep breath, and he's rocking into me, rocking gently. Filling me, stretching me impossibly wide.

I feel panicky, like maybe it's too much. He's so huge inside me.

I breathe again, and something warm in me unwinds, loosens, and he's sliding deep. It feels like he's filling me down to my toes.

"Stone," I whisper.

Chapter Twenty

~STONE~

S HE FEELS LIKE heaven—warmth and goodness and the home I never had. It takes every ounce of my restraint not to pound her right into the bed, right through the fucking floor, to devour her like an animal.

I don't deserve her. But I'm taking her. It feels like I've been waiting for her forever.

She's mind-bendingly tight. I brace my arms on either side of her and press all the way in.

And nearly come, right there. Like a schoolboy.

Fuck, that was close.

I move inside her, then, slow at first. She makes this sweet little gasp every time I rock into her. I could live on just that gasp. They could lock me up and throw away the key and not even feed me, but that little gasp contains everything I need. And her tight, hot cunt and her breasts, soft pillows against my ruined chest.

Her hands roam over my back, exploring, seeking.

Take it all, I think. *Whatever you want.*

All this time I was worried about ruining her. I never

imagined she'd be the one ruining me.

Then she comes, and her little pussy squeezes me so hard I see stars.

There's been sex. There's been orgasms. There's never been *this*, the pressure that builds at the base of my spine. That explodes in a wild burst of joy. I come hard and long, rutting into her body as if I can fuck her deep enough to merge with her. We won't be two people anymore, just one fucking body.

It's the collapse of my muscles, my strength that finally puts an end to it. And I collapse on top of her.

Climax has only ever meant release for me. That I'm done with whatever woman I'm with. That whatever man has taken me upstairs is finished for the night.

This climax isn't an ending. It's a beginning. When I look at her, everything seems clearer.

I love you. She said that to me.

It seemed impossible but inevitable. Because I love her, too. It's the only thing that explains the way I take her hostage, again and again. The only thing that explains why I fucked her without a condom. *Shit.*

I push up on my elbows, looking down at her. She looks wrecked. Her eye makeup is smudged, her hair a crazy tangled halo. She's never looked more beautiful.

If I weren't already sunk, she would be a cannon blast in my side. She still is.

Even as the world is sharper to me, more colorful,

brighter, it's the opposite for her. I can tell by the hazy look in her brown eyes. By the dreamy half-smile on her face. She's blissed-out. Well-fucked. Masculine pride swells in my chest.

"You okay?" I murmur, pulling away from her reluctantly.

My dick doesn't want to leave her tight, wet clasp. It's ready for another round. To fuck her again and again until we die in agonized bliss.

But it's her first time. She might be sore.

"Better than okay," she mumbles, her eyes still soft and unfocused. Like she can't really see me, even one foot away from her. Like she can see *through* me, inside me. And for some reason, that doesn't terrify me like it should.

Her body is the very definition of welcome. A warm place to land. I want to lie beside her for a long time. A lot longer than we actually have. I'm well versed in denial, so I push out of bed and cross to the small sink. The hot water here is shit. I never cared about that. I could take a cold shower, could stand the sting of freezing spray, but I hate the thought of causing her discomfort. I find a clean washcloth and dampen it, twisting it in my hand as if I can transfer some of my body heat into it.

She hasn't moved even an inch from where I left her.

"Little bird," I say softly.

There's a small sound that might be acquiescence or denial. She doesn't want to move, so I move her myself. I pull her legs apart and use the washcloth to clean her. A gasp, the first time the cloth touches her private place. And then a soft whimper. *Fuck.* How bad did I hurt her? I hate myself a little for that, for taking her thin little hymen, even knowing I'd do it again if I could.

The washcloth comes away pink, stained with her blood. Lord knows I've seen worse injuries, especially ones that happened through sex, but none of them hit me as hard as this. It would take a thousand fucking rivets to suck the darkness out of me. I made her bleed.

She shakes her head, as if trying to rouse herself, to focus. "Stone. You okay?"

"Course," I say, but it feels like a lie. The ground beneath me trembles. Breaks apart. I'm standing at the epicenter of an earthquake. One with pale skin and pink nipples.

It fools her, my lie. She settles back into the bed like it's made of fucking velvet. That's what she deserves. Silk and lace. Everything soft and beautiful. Instead she has me.

So I force myself to clean her, thorough and careful. Even though it's hard to see her skin turned pink from my mouth, a set of fingerprints on her hips. I'm a fucking barbarian.

And then I'm done. Nowhere else to clean. Nothing

else to do but stand there, looking down at a goddess who somehow landed at my feet.

She reaches toward me, her slender arm both fragile and strong. "Come here."

My body responds before I can think it through.

I'm hers.

I curve my body around hers, protecting her from whatever real or imagined threats might be out there. "I never thought it could be like that," I say.

Maybe it makes me a coward, that I know she won't remember this. She's too lust dazed, already half in the dream world. She won't remember my confession.

The terrible truth that I didn't know sex could feel good.

For this one second, she sees how broken I am. A ribbon of worry darkens her hazy eyes, but then it's gone. "Hold me."

It's too much of a relief when I take her in my arms, when I pull her close. "You're safe here," I tell her, even though she probably isn't worried. She probably doesn't remember that her friend Liam called the police, and that they'll be desperately looking for her. There's probably a national manhunt happening right now. "You're safe."

"Good," she mumbles, nestling deeper into my chest. "I don't want to think about that."

"About what?" I ask gently, expecting her to say Liam. To say her friends, her whole life.

"About the Innkeeper," she says, with a big yawn, her eyes closed.

Then she falls asleep, leaving me cold and wide awake. The Innkeeper. Who the fuck is the Innkeeper? I have no clue, but it sounds an awful lot like the name *Keeper*.

Does she know something about Keeper? Does she know who he is? She's in that world. She's in a position to hear things, too.

She would tell me if she knew, wouldn't she?

I want to shake her awake, to demand answers. But I also want her to continue sleeping, to pretend that I'm as peaceful as I felt one minute ago.

Before I doubted the woman I love.

CHAPTER TWENTY-ONE

~BROOKE~

I WAKE UP feeling strange, as if I'm totally comfortable here, in this place I barely recognize. As if I've become someone else in the span of two hours. My cells rearranging themselves into someone who belongs in this cabin, naked and warm. A dim light streams in from the next room, keeping the darkness at bay.

There's an ache between my thighs, a musk in the air. A thousand reminders of Stone, as if I could ever forget. But not the man himself. I remember his arms wrapped around me, and then...what? It's all a haze in my mind.

My muscles protest as I stretch across the coarse blanket. I don't need to look around the small rooms to know I'm alone. The stillness in the air tells me that, but I check anyway, wrapping the blanket around me. I look into the small galley kitchen and the tiny bathroom. Empty.

I open the door. The light from the windows illuminates the white pickup truck, still where Stone left it.

I breathe a sigh of relief. Had I thought he would leave me here? No. He wouldn't do that. I may not remember exactly what happened after we had sex, but I remember the deep sense of peace I felt. Like I was finally safe after so many years of uncertainty. I think I was finally able to let go of my family's expectations.

Some sixth sense sends me around the side of the cabin, where a thin, moonlit trail separates the structure from thick brush. Twigs catch at the blanket, as if they want to pull me in. Or maybe they only want to pull the blanket. I tuck it tighter around myself.

When I reach the back, I'm struck mute for a moment.

No wonder he comes here. The cabin may be remote and modest, but God, this view. He can see the whole city from here. It stretches out in the shadow of the mountain, both large and somehow made small.

His large silhouette breaks the spread of lights. He doesn't turn or startle, even when I step on a twig with a *crack*. Because he knows I'm here. He probably sensed me getting up. He's in tune with nature in a way I never realized someone who lives in the city could be. It makes me wonder about the safe house he lives in with the other guys. Is there something elemental about it?

"Good morning," I say softly, coming to stand a foot behind him. It's two in the morning. Not really morning, I guess.

ANNIKA MARTIN & SKYE WARREN

"Morning," he says, his voice almost menacing.

It sends a lovely shiver down my spine. "I missed you beside me. Couldn't you sleep?"

"Hardly ever," he says, which strikes me as both true and terribly sad.

In the wordless moments that follow, I can hear crickets behind us and the hum of the city in front of us. We're in between them. There must be thousands of people awake right now. Some coming from work after a late shift at a restaurant. Others waking up early to work in a bakery. The city doesn't sleep; it's like Stone that way.

He turns, his eyes a glossy dark. "Are you cold?"

It's strange, this distant concern from him. Is this how he treats all his lovers? Does sex smooth some of his rough edges, make him more gentleman than criminal? "I'm okay."

"We should get back soon."

"Probably." I hate thinking about how worried my mother would be. That's what bothers me most. Not leaving Liam and my friends at prom. Not even my father. I don't know what to believe about him. "I don't want this to end."

A shadow passes over his face. "It's already over."

There's a hitch in my breath. In my heart. In the swell of hope that said somehow this could last. Of course he's right, but it's still hard to speak. So I don't. I take a step closer, standing near enough to feel his body heat in the cool night.

He wraps his arms around me, pulling me close. I can feel his heartbeat; it becomes my own. This kind of intimacy, it's almost deeper than when we had sex. Taking comfort. Giving it.

"Who was she?" I ask softly. "The woman you loved?"

Even after all this, I'm not jealous of her. Well, maybe a little bit. Mostly I want Stone to find peace in his life. I'm not sure he could find that with a secretly broke debutante, no matter how many times he takes me hostage. I don't have what he needs, but maybe someone does.

"It doesn't matter now."

I pull back, a little shocked. "Love always matters."

"Does it?" he asks, gently mocking, tracking a finger down my cheek.

"Yes. Sometimes I think it's the only thing that matters."

"I love someone who lied to me," he says with a half-smile. "Someone who betrayed me. So what does that make me, little bird? Pretty fucking stupid, but it doesn't make me stop loving her."

That explains why he's not with her, then. He might love her until he dies, but he can't be with someone who betrays him. Loyalty means everything to him.

Even if I hadn't seen that basement, I would know that about Stone. He's like some kind of rock, to have survived that. An avalanche of strength and honor when it comes to protecting his crew. He seems like he's made of something other than flesh, but I've touched him in his most private moment. I know the truth. "It makes you human," I say softly.

CHAPTER TWENTY-TWO

~STONE~

SHE'S SNUGGLED UP on the truck seat next to me, head on my shoulder, wrapped in a blanket. The headlights illuminate trees and the dirt road and the occasional startled animal, there and then gone. Soon it will be dawn and she'll be out of my car. Out of my life, because I can't trust her. I don't believe she would fuck with me this way, but I also can't ignore what I heard.

"You're gonna put on that seatbelt once we get to the road," I say.

She wiggles closer. "If you want," she whispers.

I pull her tight to my side, because I'm weak. I'm stupid, like I told her, but that doesn't stop me. I brought one of the blankets from the cottage to put around her. She said she wasn't cold, but I like it around her, like her pressed so close to me. I worry about whether she's cold or hungry. I worry about whether she wants any fucking thing that pops into her head. I'd hunt down a fucking tiger and bring it to her, if she wanted striped fur.

Which means I need to get away from her. Need to get some perspective.

That all has to end. We'll be down the trail soon. Out in the world soon. In reality.

I keep turning her words over and over in my mind. *I don't want to think about that. About the Innkeeper.*

I tell myself it could mean anything. She was half-asleep, after all. I think about pressing her on it, but I won't. I can't. Not as long as it could be meaningless. I need to get perspective, and that means returning to my roots. To my crew. They are my rock.

She fell asleep after saying the words that changed everything.

She slept hard and deep, the sleep of the innocent, curled up in my arms, unaware of the world spinning out of control. Unaware of my eyes on her lips, on her light brown eyelashes. Unaware of my attention on her every breath, or of my heart thundering in my chest.

"Really, you can drop me anywhere." Her words sound drowsy. "Some random gas station and I can call an Uber. You could drop me at Chelsea's even."

"You think I'm not going to give you a proper ride home after prom?"

She smiles at me, a little uncertain, a little sleepy. "I'm your girl?"

"Yeah." For better or for worse, and I'm thinking this might be the worst situation of all. I kiss the top of her head just as we stop at the end of the dirt trail, ready to head onto the two-lane highway heading back to Franklin City. I told her it was already over, but I don't think this is the end. It should be, for her sake, but it's not. "Buckle up, baby."

She shifts over and puts on her seatbelt.

I check my phone. Just after four in the morning.

"There'll be cops there," she protests. "Seriously."

I pull out onto the road. "It's handled."

We go over what she's going to say. I took her out of there. She was scared and went with me. We drove past Mooresville and out to Prairiefield. We stopped at the scenic overlook and talked. I asked her dumb stuff about her high school.

We go over how nobody can make her say things she doesn't want to say, or do things she doesn't want to do.

"Nobody can make you do anything. You're in control," I tell her.

She smiles over at me, sweet in the dashboard light. "I'm in control."

I frown, wondering if she's using that same logic on me, but then I put the thought aside. Nonsense mumbled by a sleeping girl. That's what I tell myself.

Fifteen minutes later I'm heading into the hilly section of Franklin City, all the mansions looming above the rest of the place.

The truck whirs into high gear. We pass a white

mansion with a gate around it. Another one that looks like a fucking fort. I pass a beat-up Jeep—wave to Cruz. He pulls out some distance after me.

Grayson and Calder are already in place up near her house, ready for showtime. There are two unmarked cars out there. Calder's going to drive all suspicious and lead them away on a chase. Calder is our best driver; he has nerves of steel. Grayson'll ride shotgun—literally. He'll shoot some shit if shooting needs to happen.

I grab her and kiss her. I don't have words.

"When will I see you again?"

"I don't know," I say.

Police lights fire up ahead. Calder. I slow in front of her place.

She jumps out. I watch her run up her fancy walk, lit like a fairy path by flowers and tiny lights. Watch her reach the huge, elaborately carved door to her mansion.

I peel out just as a cop car pulls out from the darkness. I jam on the speed, take a few quick turns. I lose him with the help of Cruz, who was lying in wait, ready to play the bumbling driver, blocking any kind of pursuit if need be.

Still, getting away clean is hard, considering they have my plates. I had the element of surprise because they didn't expect me to drop her, so they weren't really prepared. But it takes luck and help from my guys to get out of the area. I breathe a sigh of relief as I travel deeper into South Franklin City. Better still once I hit Gedney with its boarded-up buildings and ruined hotels, one of which is the Bradford.

I do a quick check of the street and then head through the slit in the chain-link fence. I hit a code on my phone, and the graffiti-splashed slab of corrugated metal and boards opens—the ugliest, most unlikely garage door on the planet.

Knox is down there, waiting in the dim garage, leaning on his Spyder, a car he never gets to drive unless he's heading out of the city.

"What the fuck?" he says before I even shut the door. "We did that whole getaway operation so you could drop a date at her front door?"

I stalk past him, into the stairwell.

He follows. "When you said make a drop, we thought it was something legit."

I keep going. "It was legit to me."

We head through the ruined lobby and into our actual living quarters.

Grayson and Cruz are on the corner couch playing video games. Calder is sitting at the table, thinking. Or maybe not thinking. That's Calder for you.

I go over to the wall of built-in cabinets and shelving. I grab a glass and set it on the long bar, scratched from years of use. I pull down a bottle of scotch and pour.

Knox stands on the other side of the bar, watching

me. "It's morning."

I down the first one and pour another. "Not for me."

"So you gonna tell us who that was?"

"A girl," I say, even though that doesn't begin to describe her.

Knox grabs a glass and shoves it over to me. I pour. He drinks the next one with me.

"A girl?"

I give him a hard stare. That's not really what he's asking. He's wondering whether she went with me willingly. Probably heard the scanners. "It's not like that. She's…" I look him in the eyes. "My girl."

"Fuck, what was that?" Grayson's in my face. "Did you just say *your* girl?"

I give him a hard look.

"You gave me how much shit for Abby?" Grayson continues. "For wanting to be with her? You fucking split us apart with your bullshit, making her think I didn't give a shit. You acted like I was betraying the group by wanting a relationship, and now it just doesn't apply to you?"

"Man has a point," Knox says.

"Look, we had a rule that *you* broke," I say. "But Abby came along and proved herself. She showed what she was made of."

"And she went on to make that turret into a pink fucking princess room," Cruz jokes.

Grayson isn't laughing.

"So maybe the rule's fucked," I say.

"Oh. Maybe it's fucked," Grayson growls.

I take another drink. "Yeah. Maybe."

Ryland wanders in. We're all here, even Nate. Nate doesn't usually come to the Bradford, but it's our ten-year anniversary from killing one of the guys who tormented us. We mark every goddamn death, because they're important. Not because we feel sorry for those fuckers, but because it's proof that we're still alive.

They're all staring at me.

"You have Abby," I say to Grayson, "and you're still upholding the vow—*one blade to protect my brothers, one blade for vengeance.* A man can do both. You proved it."

"So you're changing your mind?" Knox says.

I look around, because the five of them, they need me to be a stand-up kind of guy. "I'd be a pretty shitty leader if I made all my decisions when I was fifteen fucking years old and never updated them."

Fifteen was how old I was when I led them out of that basement. When we made the vow.

"Back then, yeah, we needed to be all about us. Survival. But, Grayson, you're still here. You'd lay down your life for your brothers. Even with that girl up there, you'd lay down your life."

"Fuck yeah," he grunts.

I stare into my glass. Given a choice, I'm not so sure

Grayson would put us over Abby. But I don't go there. No reason.

"Only an asshole refuses to let his mind be changed by new information," I say.

"So full of shit, my man," Calder says calmly. "The new information isn't Grayson and Abby. It's the girl. The girl changed your mind."

"I didn't say Grayson changed my mind. I said Grayson shows it can work. That you can meet somebody…meet a woman who is…" I stop, unsure how to describe Brooke.

Cruz laughs. "Fuck!"

"What?" I demand.

"You are whipped on this bitch," Cruz says.

My growl is low and loud. "Wouldn't call her a bitch if I was you."

I catch Grayson's eyes. My guys are looking at me like I'm an alien, suddenly, but Grayson gets it. He nods.

"It won't go anywhere, but I wanted to drop her right. That's all," I say.

"Won't go anywhere?" Grayson asks.

"Can't," I say. "Speaking of which, where are we with Keeper?"

"Still nothing," Knox says.

Calder sighs. "I have listened to a hundred hours of phone calls, and it's shit. I got a few where they mention him, but nothing we can use."

"Abby's helping us with the Franklin City archives," Knox says, looking at Grayson. "We've been finding handwritten notes on some of the margins of property transactions. We're hoping to find Keeper mentioned. We'll be back at that today."

I nod. Then, as casual as I can, I ask, "Did any of you ever hear of Keeper referred to by the name *Innkeeper*?"

"Pretty sure. Yeah," Calder says with a shrug, not realizing the seismic effect of his words on me. "A few of the phone calls reference Innkeeper, and I assume it's Keeper." My heart pounds as he continues, "Not like they sit there saying, 'Innkeeper—Keeper for short.' But it's pretty clear in context. Why?"

I turn my glass counterclockwise.

She fucking knows.

She knows who Keeper is. Something twists deep in my belly. It hurts because she knows what they did to us—men like Keeper. Keeper's at the fucking center of it. Doesn't she give a shit? Have I been an idiot all this time? Love puts a guy's head up his ass. Is that happening to me? *No way,* I think. *No fucking way.*

"Why?" Calder asks again.

"Possible lead," I say.

"Are you serious?" Knox says. "To Keeper? This is huge. What is it?"

"I need to work it out. And I will work it out." I look my guys in the eye, one after another. I let my voice go icy smooth, because I made this promise to them long before I met Brooke. "Nothing stops us from rescuing those boys. From taking our vengeance. Nothing."

Brooke is a beautiful distraction, but I don't need her. I can't need her. I only have one purpose beyond saving those boys, and that's revenge.

It's taking all the pain and fury inside myself so that the other guys have a chance at a normal life. There's no chance of that for me.

I made my peace with that long ago.

Chapter Twenty-Three
~Brooke~

I PULL THE blanket more tightly around me. It's a cashmere silk blend, soft as a cloud, but I'd give anything to be wrapped in Stone's coarse blanket instead. I felt safe in that cabin in a way I never have in this ten-thousand-square-foot home.

"I'm not calling you a liar," Detective Rivera says, voice soft.

"I know," I squeak, but he sort of is, in the way he keeps asking whether I'm holding something back. In the way his eyes seem to know that I am.

Dad sits on the arm of the easy chair, arms crossed, expression distant. I can't even meet his gaze. I haven't been able to for a long time.

Mom sits beside me, arm not around me, exactly, but on the couch back. She looks bewildered, anxious. "If there's something more, Brooke…"

"There isn't!" I say.

Detective Rivera's sitting on the coffee table, a cardinal sin in this house, but Mom allows it, which tells the story of how worried she is. He leans in, elbows on his knees. His dark slate eyes are kind, and there are faint lines to the sides of them. Laugh lines. But he's not laughing now. "Liam said you called him by name. That you called him Stone. That you seemed to know him."

"You told me that was his name," I say. "When you were last here."

"Does he like you to call him by name?"

I swallow. "How would I know?" I say coolly as I can. "If I know somebody's name, it's only polite to use it when addressing that person." I look helplessly at my mother. "There's no reason to lose my manners."

"Of course not, sweetheart," she says, her voice a little sad. Like she thinks I'm hiding something, too. "Good manners are always in style."

Usually when she says that, I roll my eyes, but now I'm so grateful I could kiss her. It's a kind of absolution from the person who's been most critical of me.

The silence goes on forever. I feel this flash of frustration at Stone. And longing. He made it sound so easy to tell them nothing, but it's not easy at all. Stone was hardened by life, but I've never felt softer or more vulnerable. And the place between my legs feels sore, raw, alive with the memory of him. If they knew about that, they would lose their minds.

Rivera watches me. I'm a bug under a microscope in front of his searching eyes. I want to grab my phone and look at something stupid, random Facebook statuses about someone's breakup at prom, but I don't want them to see how bad I need this to be over. I force myself to meet his eyes. I draw my lips together in imitation of Mom's impatient face.

"I know this is uncomfortable for you," Rivera says. "But I'm trying to work this out in my mind—why would a man kidnap you on your prom night only to ask about your life as a high school girl?"

"I don't know," I say.

After another uncomfortably long silence, he asks, "Do you think he imagines some sort of connection to you? Or that you owe him?"

I shrug.

"I think sometimes we can get scared," Rivera says, "and the easiest thing is to sweep it under the rug. But I've been in this business a long time, and trust me, that never helps. Things like this only escalate."

Too late, I think. This has escalated beyond what they can imagine. But I say nothing, reminding myself that I'm in control. Just like Stone said. I'm eighteen. An adult.

"I know this is scary," he says. "Your friends told us how violent he appeared—eyes wide, fists flying. Your friend Randall thought he had a knife. Did he show you a knife?"

"It happened so fast," I say, even though there was

no knife.

"Your friend Liam observed that he was frothing at the mouth, out of his mind. He thought drug use was involved. Did you have that impression?"

Of course Liam would make him sound like a rabid, drug-crazed monster. "No. I did not have the impression of drug use." *Or rabies, for that matter.*

"So he wasn't violent with you."

"Not at all!"

"Except to drag you away from prom."

"Right," I say, heart beating fast. "Except for that."

"He didn't sexually assault you."

"Absolutely not!"

At some point last night, I put the bodice of my dress together with two safety pins. Nobody noticed the rip, which ran neatly down the seam—luckily.

Now I'm in pink fleece yoga pants and a giant Mickey Mouse T-shirt, and the dress is tucked into my drawer. I'll sew it back up later.

"So he only asked you questions," Rivera clarifies. "For three hours."

"I don't know what more to tell you."

"It must be a heady feeling," he says, changing his tactic, making his voice smooth and almost hypnotic. "To have a man like that so focused on you. All that power and rage, except when it comes to you."

"Detective—" Mom puts a hand on my shoulder.

"What are you getting at? This is starting to sound like victim blaming. My daughter is not at fault for anything that monster did."

A shiver of gratitude washes over me.

"Of course not," he says, putting his pen in his front pocket. "I didn't mean it like that. If you come up with anything else, Brooke, I'm listening. I'm on your side, believe it or not." His eyes crinkle as he smiles. He turns to my mom, my dad. "I have some literature for you, some information about the effects of this kind of situation, if you'd…"

Dad stands. "Let me walk you to the car."

Something passes between my mother and Rivera, and suddenly she's walking him to the car, too. "Why don't you draw yourself a nice bath," she says to me, soft-like.

"Maybe I will." I say goodbye to Rivera, and I head upstairs feeling upset and like I'm in all kinds of trouble I can't understand.

When I peer out my bedroom window, I see them talking by the door of Rivera's car. I crouch down and ease the window open just a crack. I can't hear what my mom is saying, but Rivera's voice carries through on the breeze—enough of it, anyway, to get the gist. "…*develop positive feelings…reasons why she's protecting him…strong emotions like fear…feels like infatuation…*"

My pulse races. He thinks I'm on Stone's side.

And he's right.

Rivera gestures at Mom. She's holding a pamphlet. "*...some form of Stockholm syndrome...*"

My father's voice is a rumble back—he sounds impatient. I hear my name a few times. "*Why Brooke? ...why target her? ...background on this Stone Keaton...need answers...*"

Rivera's shaking his head. "*...not his real name...no record...*"

They're pointing at our neighbor's house. Why are they talking about that house? It's for sale. Our neighbors don't even live there anymore—they moved to Florida. The place is vacant. Overpriced, Dad always says.

"*Gonna come back...predictable...get this guy...*" Rivera says. He's saying things about the mall. About school. I strain to hear him, but the wind has changed directions.

I quickly duck when my parents turn to come back inside. The windows of the vacant house look down on ours. It sits above and has a good view of us, actually. It would be the perfect place for the police to hide in. Maybe that's what he was saying. That they'd hide in that house. That they'd follow me to the school and the mall.

They have a plan. They're going after Stone. Of course. Why wouldn't they?

And they're going to use me as bait, whether I want it or not.

The ding of a text makes me jump nearly out of my skin. I grab my phone. It's Kitty.

Everyone asking about U, she says. *Cops were here.*

I text back, careful to seem breezy. I already texted Chelsea, but this is the text that will get around school. *I'm fine. IDEK he drove me around and brought me home. Just a weird joy ride. Lucky I guess.*

Joy ride—that's one of the phrases I used to Rivera. Like maybe it was a joy ride and he wanted a passenger. That makes it sound more innocent, like something Liam might do if his dad didn't plan for him to run for the Senate one day.

A joy ride. So different from a grown man taking me to a secluded cabin and taking my virginity.

She texts back a surprised emoji. *Scary! So glad you're okay.*

I text her a heart emoji and she replies with a four-leaf clover. We text emojis back and forth; then I just sit there staring at the black screen of my phone.

They think Stone will come back for me.

He'll be in such danger. Doesn't he understand? Maybe he does.

Maybe he doesn't care.

A shiver of excitement slides over my skin when I think how easily he handled the cops in dropping me off.

He's coming back, and he doesn't give a crap if cops

are waiting.

I still feel him inside me. All over my skin. We had sex without a condom, and I don't even care. I should be scared, but I only feel this excitement, fine hairs on my arm on edge. Excitement and dread, because this is the worst thing I could do. The worst man I could want. A threat to everything I love.

CHAPTER TWENTY-FOUR

~BROOKE~

THERE'S THIS WEIGHT that's building inside me. When Stone first said the name *Keeper* to me, it was a tiny drop of water on a mountain of security. I know Daddy better than anyone. Maybe even better than my mom. I've seen how gentle he can be when he patches a skinned knee. He can't be involved in anything to do with Stone or hurting boys. He wouldn't.

But this terrible fear drips, drips, drips until I feel like it's a hundred pounds. A thousand. It's creating a fissure right through my middle, cutting apart everything I thought I knew.

Because it wasn't pure coincidence that had Stone at that party the night we met. He came for Mr. Madsen, who was a friend of my father's. A business friend, not a real friend, but that's enough, isn't it? Enough of a smoking gun. Enough to incriminate him in Stone's eyes.

That's how I end up in Daddy's office, my heart pounding loud enough to shake the solid wood floor, hands shaking as I pull open a file cabinet. I've been in this room a hundred times. Played Barbies under the desk. Sat on his lap in front of the fireplace. Never did I think there could be evidence of a terrible crime only a few feet away. I don't know what to believe, but I need to know, once and for all.

Because it's not just the vengeance Stone wants or the justice he deserves that's at stake. It's the boys who might be held right now. If there's even a chance I can help them, I have to try.

Daddy's at his weekly racquetball game with Uncle Bill, so now is the time.

Dang technology takes twice as long for double the cost, Daddy sometimes jokes, but this would have been before digital files and online listings. It takes a little while to look through the files and find a box in the closet from the right decade. Before I was born, but I recognize the scrawled handwriting. I've seen it on my birthday cards and permission slips. It was even on a present from Santa one year. The year I realized that Santa wasn't real, that it was Daddy all along.

"Where are you?" I whisper, my throat tight.

There are smudged yellow and pink papers slipped between white ones, copies that have faded almost to nothing. Only the hard downstrokes of pen are showing on some of them.

I'm almost afraid to see it, the street name where

Stone was held as a child.

My hands move faster, the paper thin as butterfly wings. Dust tickles my nose and blurs my vision. A dark round stain on one of the pink sheets, and I realize it isn't only dust clouding my eyes. I'm crying. How did I end up here? Snooping on my own father? Doubting him?

And then I see it, the street name in Daddy's bold writing.

A sound comes from outside the closet, a soft snick, as loud as an explosion to my grief-stricken mind. Daddy shouldn't be home for another hour. Mom's at her hair appointment. It's the maid's day off. One of the only times I'm in the house alone, which is why I took advantage.

The paper crumples in my fist. I shove it into my jeans pocket.

For a wild second, I think it might be Stone, that from across the city he realized what I'd found, that he's here to demand I give him the proof. It burns in my pocket, all the way through the denim to my skin.

Then my father's standing in the doorway to the closet, a concerned look on his weathered face.

"Brooke, what's wrong, sweetheart?"

His familiar voice makes me crack, and I run to him, press my face into his chest, feel the hard chest of him, the springy hair and the ribbed fabric of his workout shirt. Whatever aftershave he uses, a little too strong, but it only reminds me of him. Of safety. "Oh, Daddy."

"What are you doing in here?"

He doesn't sound angry. And he doesn't sound worried, even though the lid to the file box is ajar.

Has it been so long that he's forgotten? Has he done so many bad things that this one doesn't register? I don't even know what to think. Part of me wants to whip out the piece of paper in my pocket, to show it to him and make him explain it. To demand there be some innocent reason for him to own three houses on a street in an abandoned part of town.

Another part of me knows I have to be careful. I need to figure out who to trust, because right now I trust no one. And everyone. If Daddy was really one of these terrible men, then he can't know that I know. Would he hurt me? I don't want to believe that, but I don't believe he could hurt boys either.

"I'm sorry," I say desperately, wanting him to explain himself without being able to ask it of him. "I was just scared. I wanted to talk to you. I thought you were at your racquetball game, so I was waiting for you."

"Bill sprained his ankle. We had a drink instead." Familiar brown eyes darken with worry. "Maybe I should have listened to that detective. Got you in with a psychiatrist who can help you. Your mother thought—" He sighs. "She thought you didn't need it."

"I don't," I say too quickly. We both know the real reason she didn't want me to see a psychiatrist is because it would get out. People would talk.

He looks at me, unusually grave. "I always wondered, Brooke, if something happened that you didn't tell us about. That you were scared to tell us about. You know I would never be angry at you. Whatever happened, it wasn't your fault."

He means sex. He means violence. But I want to tell him, *I started to care about this man, Daddy. It's wrong, but it's also real. And he might try to kill you if he knew what I know.*

"Nothing happened," I say, my voice small.

The lie sits between us, pulsing with its own vitality.

After a long moment he nods and stands aside. I run from the office like my life depends on it. Well, maybe it does. Only that night do I smooth out the paper under a lamp and confirm my worst fears. The doubt had been a steady drip. The certainty is only a single drop more, but it's enough to break me.

Chapter Twenty-Five

~Brooke~

MR. REYES STANDS at the front of the class, talking about the Aztec culture. He shows us a chart of pictograms—little picture symbols that combine to create meaning. That's what the Aztec people used for communication instead of letters that make up words.

Somebody says they're like emojis. Reyes wants us to discuss that. From the way he says it, you can tell he doesn't agree. I can hardly bring myself to care, because I'm way too focused on what I found out last night. Only twelve hours since my world got blown apart.

Even now I want to imagine that Daddy never visited that basement, that he wasn't truly a part of that horrified business. Maybe he was just someone's contractor, without knowing what was happening. The pieces of paper with their numbers and letters—they don't tell the whole story. But I'm not sure there can be shades of guilt when children are being hurt. Maybe it's like Stone says, that everyone who looked the other way is just as guilty.

Right then my phone buzzes. A text. Discreetly I slide it out from under my notebook.

STEP OUTSIDE.

On my phone it says *BLOCKED* where his number should go. Stone.

My heart begins to pound.

He was always going to come for me, but not like this. Not at school. I may not know every last detail about him, but I know he's careful. I know he waits and watches. I know he likes to control his environment.

So why here and now?

Alarm shoots through me. Something's not right.

There's a part of me that thinks about telling Mr. Reyes that I'm afraid. What would he do? Lock down the school? We've been having drills with all the school shootings that have been happening, special procedures we're supposed to follow in order to stay safe.

But there's no drill that would keep Stone from doing whatever he wants to do. No safety when he's around. Maybe not even for him.

I shiver as I remember his words from so long ago— *I'm the winter nobody ever saw coming.*

I scroll over to the Contacts page and look through all the names. Kitty and Liam. Dad. So many people in my life who would be angry at me for what I'm about to do. I feel bad about my mom, because I think she'll worry the most. But I can't grow up to be her, even if there are some parts about her I respect. I can't smile for the cameras at society events, pretending everything's okay, now that I know there are boys kept in basements.

There's a new number on my phone, one I've never called.

It's the phone number for Detective Rivera. He's been calling me every day, leaving messages. Some of them kind. Some of them stern. "I know you're worried about what will happen to Stone," he said in the last one. "But I'm not out to hurt him, understand? I'm trying to stop him from hurting anyone else."

As arguments go, it's a persuasive one. Especially since I know the man Stone would hurt is my father.

Light streams in from the tall windows. Just a month ago the trees in the park across the street were still mostly bare, dark limbs dusted with green buds. The leaves are fully in now, vibrant green treetops shifting in the breeze.

Time moves on. The clock ticks. Stone won't wait forever.

I pull out my binder and open it a crack. There's the document I stole from my dad's office. The one that proves he owned the houses on either side of the house with the fireflies. He owned them during the time when Stone was kept in that basement.

It's damning.

So often in the hours since I found it, I imagined sending it to Stone. But then I'd hesitate, remembering what happened to Madsen. If I show it to Stone, he'll kill my father. But if I don't, what happens to those boys? I curl my trembling hands into tiny balls under my desk. I can't not save them.

Then I get an idea. A middle way.

My mom insisted that I keep Rivera's number on my phone, a kind of panic button in case something goes wrong. She means something bad like Stone coming for me, and that's bad, but nothing like what's on this sheet of paper.

My throat fills with acid as I point my phone at the paper and snap a picture.

"What's that?" Kitty hisses at me.

The last thing I need is her curiosity. "It's nothing. My notes from last period. I don't want to lose them."

She snorts. "I thought it would be something interesting. Maybe a slam book."

A slam book, something filled with nasty rumors and swear words. "What would you write about me?" I find myself asking, even though I already know.

Her eyes meet mine, at once guileless and a million years old. She is the kind of girl who will rule those society parties when she's older. I don't begrudge her that. If anything, I feel a deep sadness that I couldn't be her, for my mother's sake. "I'd say you were a good girl," she says with a little huff of laughter. "Can't stop doing the right thing even if it kills you."

My chest feels strange, like a thing that's thick and hollow, expanding, filling with air.

I start a new text. This one has the photo of the document, along with the words. *He'll need protection. That's the deal.*

Then I send the evidence convicting my father to Detective Rivera.

Those boys deserve justice, but not vengeance. There's a difference. Maybe my father was part of the people who hurt him, even if that makes me want to throw up. Or maybe he knows something that can help nail them. Either way I have faith in Detective Rivera's insane determination, if nothing else in this world.

And I won't let Stone kill my father.

I can do the right thing, but that's where I draw the line.

There are boys being held against their will out there, I text at the end. *Make my father lead you to them.*

I'm up and running to the door even as I ask to go to the bathroom. My phone and the evidence are still sitting on my desk, hidden in plain sight.

Mr. Reyes says something that sounds like *yes*, so I grab the hall pass from its hook on the door.

I'm barely in the hallway when a hand closes around my wrist.

I look up to meet Stone's green eyes, more cold than blazing today. Features harder, somehow. Everything about him feels more distant. Maybe even suspicious.

Wherever we're going, it isn't going to be a cuddle session in a remote cabin.

Chapter Twenty-Six

~Stone~

T HE COPS HAVE been sticking close to her. So close it would be impossible to miss them. Do they think I'm blind? Once I let them glimpse me outside a pep rally and took a couple of uniforms for a two-hour chase only to lead them back, finally losing them right outside the school where we started.

Hey, I have to get my amusement somewhere.

Because nothing else about this situation is funny.

I have taken Brooke hostage many times, but none of them like this. None where I know I love her. None where I know I have to break her.

Her fancy private school puts serious limitations on how far the cops can encroach on the property, though.

The school has its own security, of course. Lots of cameras, alarms, and locks. There's exactly one entrance, and it involves two doors and a watchful woman in an office who decides whether you get buzzed in.

It would've been easy enough to grab her using the crew, but I needed to do it myself. She's mine.

I watched the place for a long time until I found the weak link in the security—the custodian taking out trash after lunch. He's alone, vulnerable. Easy prey for somebody who might want to tie him up and take his keys and uniform.

I blended in easily enough with a beige janitor's uniform and a cartful of supplies, pushing slowly through the sea of plaid skirts and starched, button-down shirts. A few of the girls straightened up and touched their hair when they saw my face, their cheeks turning flushed, their bodies alive with hormones I could smell from where I stood.

I kept my head down. Not interested. Never been interested in anyone beyond my crew.

Until Brooke.

I've had her schedule and the school layout for some time now, courtesy of Knox's hacking skills; I knew she was in social studies fifth hour. Room 501. I headed down the corridor with my cart and slipped into the supply closet, the next door down. I texted her from a burner phone, perfectly untraceable.

I knew the cops would be pulling records on everything incoming, but it takes a while to run numbers, separate the horny teenage boys from the dangerous predators.

At first I wasn't sure if she was going to bite. All I heard was the teacher, droning on. Finally her sweet voice rang out, asking to go to the bathroom.

A male voice. "Take the hall pass." Harried. Distracted.

I cracked the closet door, listening to her squeaky patent leather shoes broadcast her slow and uncertain progress down the hall. Quick as a flash, I reached out and clapped a hand over her mouth, capturing her sound of surprise in my palm. Looked into her frightened eyes for just a second before dragging her inside.

And now I have her. "Quiet."

Her breath feels warm against my hand. She nods. Reluctantly I pull away, knowing she won't scream.

"How did you get in here?" she asks.

"Walked in the door," I tell her, because no one fucking knows what to look for. I can only imagine what ridiculous description they have circulating. Violent criminal. A maniac. Deranged. No one expects a man with a regular haircut and a polite fucking smile.

"They're looking for you," she says, almost breathless with it. "They've been following me. Watching from the house next door. You have to be careful."

So concerned and worried. I almost want to laugh, considering how bad I'll have to scare her before the day is done. "I'm careful."

There's something hanging from her hand. I take it from her, this laminated piece of plastic with a piece of string tied to the end. *St. Mary's Hall Pass*, it says. So official-looking. So goddamn adorable. Jesus.

"What's social studies?" I ask her.

She looks bewildered in the dim light from a single bulb. "What?"

"Social studies. What's it for? I know about math. Reading." None of us had a regular education, and definitely not any high school. I don't remember much beyond adding numbers and writing letters. Grayson went on to get his GED. Knox is a fucking genius, knows more than they could teach in school. Nate graduated from college and now he's a bona fide vet. All my guys have made themselves smarter, but not me. I've just made myself harder.

"Oh," she says, like it's a normal question. Like it's a normal thing not to understand how school works. "It's about society. A little bit of history, a little bit of geography. But also government."

That all sounds useless to me, but I guess that's because I'm not smart like her. I squeeze the little zip pouch around her shoulder, feeling the contents. "Where's your phone? It's not in here."

She shakes her head. "I left it there. I didn't want them to find you."

Protecting a guy like me. I suppose she'll regret it soon enough.

"Let's get out of here," I say, tossing the fancy little hall pass into the trash bin.

✧ ✧ ✧

SHE'S QUIET MOST of the way over, aside from updating me on her conversations with the detective. Does she know she's in trouble? Sometimes people act calm and try to have normal conversations when they know they're in trouble. I pretend to be interested. Like that's my main concern in all this and not the fact that she knows the identity of Keeper.

And that I have to get it out of her.

I think she senses something off with me. We're in tune with each other in a way I never have been with my brothers. In tune in a way I can't think about too hard.

She stiffens as the modern apartment buildings and boutique shops give way to trashed apartment complexes and payday loan places, and finally the vacant lots and boarded-up buildings deep in South Franklin City.

"Where are we going?" she asks, eyes wide.

"Home."

"Wow. You take Gedney Drive," she marvels.

I suppress a smile. She thinks I'm using the notorious Gedney Drive to cross the city, to get to the other side, something her kind would never do, even though it's the shortest route to the lake suburbs.

Her lips part as I take a turn around the hulking behemoth that is the Bradford, as I pass its windows, long since covered over with graffiti-sprayed boards.

"Where are we..." The question dies on her lips as I

nose the car through the slit in the chain-link fence, as the yawning gap appears in front of us.

I flip on the headlights and navigate down into the basement garage.

"What is this place?"

"Never seen a garage before?" I get this twinge of guilt, giving her a surly answer.

But I need to stay remote. I need it for me. And she needs to understand that things are different now. Serious.

"I never saw a place like this. I mean, down here...I never imagined..." She can't understand how there could be such expensive rides down below an abandoned hotel—way nicer than even what her daddy can afford. "Are these..."

"Stolen?" I pull in next to Calder's vintage Mustang, supplying the word she's too polite to voice. Knox isn't the only one with nice-ass cars. "Nah. They're bought. Cash. Don't let anybody tell you crime doesn't pay, little bird."

I let her open her own door and get out on her own, but I stay nice and near in case she tries to run. Not that she'd have anywhere to go.

"Come on." I lead her past the row of vehicles and into the stairwell. Up we go. I feel her behind me as I hit the code on the door up top, resisting the urge to take her hand, to touch her back, to let her know I give a shit.

I push into the ruined lobby. Leaves and rubble litter the broken tile floor. Sunlight streams through the shattered dome-shaped roof, once a grand atrium.

"This is where you *live*?" she asks, voice full of dread and wonder.

I find myself wishing I had something nicer to show her. But that's not what this little jaunt is about. "You like it?" I ask. "I could give you the name of our designer if you want."

"Don't," she says.

I kick a broken crate, feeling like everything's gone to shit. Dust flies up as the thing knocks into a scrub tree. A few pigeons flap up from a corner, all the way up through a jagged hole and into the blue sky beyond.

She puts a hand over her chest. The pigeons startled her. Fuck.

"You're okay." I sling an arm around her. Just an arm. It means nothing. I punch in a code on the far door, and we're in the cavernous main room, the place where we actually do live.

Knox and Grayson are playing a video game in the corner seating area, but she doesn't see them right off.

She's gawking at how fucking tricked out it is.

The floor and walls may be rough old brick and concrete, but the rugs and couches are total uptown shit. The bar area opposite us was imported from Ireland— the wooden contents of an entire old pub they were tearing down. Calder made it happen. He likes the old things.

She may be oblivious to Knox and Grayson kicked back on the couch in front of a massive screen, but they're not oblivious to her, standing there in her little schoolgirl uniform—the short plaid skirt. The white shirt with some logo that looks like it was designed by the fucking queen of England. And don't get me started on the knee socks. Or the question of what kind of panties she has underneath there.

Yeah, they stopped playing the moment we walked in. They rise as a unit. The game rolls on without them. Fake shit exploding. The world ending because of this one girl.

She still doesn't see them, even as they stalk around the long group table, past the nook where Calder likes to read.

Knox's brows knit in confusion. Grayson looks pissed.

I pull her closer. I don't like them looking at her in her uniform. It's too fucking sexy. The only women they've ever seen in schoolgirl clothes like this have been strippers.

Never the real thing.

She is the most real thing.

I can feel when she sees them, because she squeezes in closer to me, like she thinks I'll protect her from them.

332

Yeah, right.

It's me she needs protection from.

Still she squeezes closer. I try to not let it make me feel good. I tell myself she'd cower into the side of Godzilla himself if that's who was beside her, because Grayson and Knox, they're definitely a scary pair.

It's not true, though. She loves me. She fucking loves me, and I love her.

But that can't matter.

I try to imagine them through her eyes. The way Grayson looks like a goddamn avenging angel. No woman can resist him, but they're afraid of him too. The violence in him runs too deep not to feel it. And Knox, wearing an emerald-green button-down today. So sharp. Like a goddamn blade.

I can't put this girl above my guys. I've struggled too long for vengeance. And now there are those kids to think about. I need her to give me the answers. Will she understand that?

Grayson's huge. Seriously built—prison'll do that to a guy. He's a looker for sure, but he radiates threat, and that's the first thing you ever notice. Yeah, time inside definitely hardened him.

Knox has blond hair and blue eyes, but he looks the opposite of wholesome, somehow. He's sharp as a razor. Bright, cold edges like the tech he loves so much.

"Who's this?" Grayson asks tightly.

ANNIKA MARTIN & SKYE WARREN

"This is Brooke," I say, though that's not at all what the fuck he's asking.

"Hey there," Knox says to her in that smooth way of his.

"Brooke, this here's Knox." I don't have to tell her who they are to me. Brothers from the basement. I see in her eyes that she gets it.

She steels her spine, chest rising and falling. "How do you do?" she says, holding out her hand.

They both kind of stare. Because, *how do you do?* Who the fuck says that?

Knox takes her hand and shakes it. "You two on a date here or something?" he asks gruffly. Neither of them will directly challenge me.

"Or *something*." I pull her away and up the stairs that lead to the rooms—luxury suites back before this place went to hell.

There are still a few broken chandeliers hanging in the hallway. Weathered carpet still in parts, but it's clean and dry. The Bradford catered to the elite of the elite before Franklin City went from land of the wealthy to rust-belt hellhole.

Grayson catches up. "Something?"

I give him a look over her head, like, *what do you think?* "Yeah, *something*," I growl.

I see when he gets it. There's only one thing I care about right now, as far as he's concerned, and that's finding and freeing those boys. This is about Keeper.

She's the lead.

"Okay, then," he says, still walking alongside of us.

"Got any more questions?" I ask.

"Yeah, you gonna introduce me? I'm Grayson," he says to her. "Pleased to meet you."

She smiles up at him, even gives him her hand as we walk. "Hi," she says, voice hushed. Is she getting that she's in trouble right about now? Could be. And God, the schoolgirl uniform.

I force my gaze to Grayson. "Later," I say.

Grayson stops. I guide her onward. Even from this light touch, I can feel the tension in Brooke's body. Every instinct inside me is screaming to soothe her, to pull her up into my arms and carry her, to whisper that she's okay. To kiss her soft cheek and let her know I love her. Fucking love her.

Yeah, things couldn't be more messed up right about now.

"They don't like guests," she observes.

"We don't do guests much."

We come to my door. You can still see the faint outline of the number five on the polished wood, even though the brass plate is long gone.

I push it open and guide her in, touching the small of her back. She doesn't need me to show her the way in. But her shirt is soft as heaven under my fingers.

And also, she's mine.

I remove my hand and let her get her fill of the place, even though it feels wrong not to be touching her when she's feeling uncertain like she is now. To reassure her.

My suite is simple like the cottage. Things are sturdy and wooden.

The other guys' places, not so much.

Knox has his suite decked out with massive screens and shiny tech. Cruz has a collection of vintage rock guitars and oil paintings that don't look too different than the graffiti outside if you ask me.

Grayson's suite is comfortable and welcoming, thanks to Abby. The nicest to be in, though maybe a little girly. We all teased her when she hung bright curtains over the windows, which are covered with double-thick sheet metal. All the windows here are. No good if people on the street see light coming from the Bradford.

Me, I don't need much. I flip on the bedside lamp, a little wood and metal thing. "Not much of a view, I'm afraid."

She moves around the space. "It's…nice."

I grunt like my heart isn't jackhammering out of my chest. Like I don't give a shit whether she likes it. This is a girl raised in a goddamn palace, and here she is in my half-empty room.

"How do you get electricity in here?"

I close the door. "Is that what you really want to

ask?"

She turns around, uncertain. What happens now? That's what she wants to know. The mood isn't romantic like it was at the cottage, much as I want to flip up that skirt and devour her sweet pussy. Much as I want to make her moan and scream in ecstasy. We have a darker purpose here.

It probably would've been better to bring her to the cottage, but I don't know how this turns out. If it's anything like everything else in my life, it'll go to hell, and I want one place to go where all the memories are good. Like a time capsule of something I can never have. That time in the cottage when Brooke looked at me like I was worth something.

She's wary. "What do I want to ask?"

I go to the bureau and grab a bottle of Macallan. The good shit—older than she is. I pour two glasses. I hand one to her. "Drink."

"What is it?"

"Scotch."

"It's…kind of early." The sentence tilts up at the end. Almost a question.

I lower my voice. "Drink it."

She takes a tiny sip. Miserably, I throw mine back. I need it more than she ever will. I pour another. There's no amount of liquor that can make me hurt her.

"They're going to be wondering what happened to me," she says. "They'll be looking for me."

"No doubt." I tip my head at her glass. "Finish it."

"What if I don't want to?"

"You should," I say softly.

Wariness shines in her eyes. *Finally.*

I should feel relieved that she's starting to get what's happening, but I just feel a deep, nauseating dread. I've had to do a lot of bad things in my life, but I've never felt this level of reluctance. Anytime we needed to kill someone, torture someone for information, I would do it. Even when you know that the guy's a scumbag, it chips off a piece of your soul. I did it so the other guys in my crew wouldn't have to, because I don't really have a soul. At least I thought I didn't. Now there's Brooke standing in front of me, looking so strong and so vulnerable that I want to kneel at her feet.

"Why do I have to drink it?" she asks.

"Because that's how this is going to go."

She peers into the glass. "What if I don't want to?"

"You want to."

She raises her gaze to me. The trust still there kills me. "Okay," she says. God, that trust. I'd take a haughty sneer a million times before this last dying glimmer of trust. Keeping her eyes on me, she swallows it down, then gives me back the glass.

"Good girl." I pour another.

"I think you should take me back," she says.

"I will. As soon as you tell me who Keeper is."

Chapter Twenty-Seven
~Brooke~

THERE'S A FEELING when lights are flashing in your face. When people you barely know call out your name like you're best friends. Where it starts to feel like a dream. It makes things easier to handle. Going through a party with a cool half-smile on my lips.

It's the same thing I do now, when I realize why Stone has come for me, why he brought me here.

"What makes you think I know anything?" My voice comes out weirdly calm. There's a panic inside me. A full-scale Big Bang explosion, ending everything that came before. On the outside I must look the same, but on the inside everything has changed.

"Because you told me yourself," he says, nearly growling. "I called him Keeper, but you called him Innkeeper."

Fear whooshes in my ears. "When?"

"When you were fuck-drunk."

I flinch at the harshness of his words. At least I know how much I revealed to him. When we were in that cottage, when he touched me. How had I let something so important slip? But I was so impossibly relaxed. I learned early on to never let down my guard, with anyone. Not for the cameras or the society mavens. Not even for my mother. But the one time I slip, it could ruin everything.

"I never used the name Innkeeper," he says. "That told me you know the man. And it's not a fucking surprise, is it? Not in the circles that you run in."

I swallow past the dryness in my mouth.

The cabin was beautiful but rustic. Raw. He used that to seduce me. This hotel room with its old-world grandeur and strange intimacy? He'll use this to hurt me. Make me tell.

I wrap my arms around myself.

Daddy came to every ballet recital. He worked late every day to afford my private school tuition. We might not have a normal happy family, but it's mine.

Stone will protect his crew, even if they did something wrong. That's the way I have to protect my father. He deserves justice, nothing more. Not revenge.

"He's somebody to you. That's why you're keeping it from me. Family or friend. One of your girlfriends' daddies." He gives me a hard look. "Maybe even yours."

I try not to react, but some things I can't control, like the way my heart bangs against my ribs. There's movement on my face, like a flinch. But it feels far away, like my muscles belong to someone else.

"You should just tell me," he says simply. "You're going to, in the end."

The threat is ten times worse because of the calm way he delivers it. If he were beating his chest, it would seem like an exaggeration. But I know the calm, cold reality here. He's going to hurt me. "Why? Because you'll make me?"

He watches my face, seeing everything, saying nothing.

I stand my ground, senses humming from his nearness. Or maybe that's the scotch. "I can't."

Still he says nothing.

I swallow. Stone can't trust anyone, but I can. I trust Detective Rivera. I trust the system, even knowing it failed Stone. I trust my father, even if I shouldn't. "I won't."

Threat runs thick in the air between us. "I'm not fooling around, Brooke."

"You don't want to hurt me." I gaze into his eyes, looking for the man who couldn't drown me. The man who carved that tiny bird. The one who made up a fairy tale about a rivet.

"No, I *don't* want to hurt you." His tone is soft, but there's darkness underneath—the darkness of hundreds of hopeless nights. "But I do lots of things I don't want to do."

He does those things for the men in his crew. For the boys who were down there in the basement with him. For the ones who might be held now. That's part of why I respect him, why I *love* him, but there's also something broken in it. The way he acts like killing people doesn't matter. Like it doesn't break his heart again and again.

My pulse races. "I don't know anything—not for sure." It's the last words that change everything for the worst. The confession I didn't mean to make. He knows I have something specific. Even his gaze is colder. More resigned. Like he knows this is going to get messy.

Fear arrows through me. Instinct takes over. I whirl around. I bolt past the bathroom, to the door, fling it open.

A large hand smashes it back closed.

I turn around, shoulder blades flush against the door. He stands in front of me, half caging me, dark stubble gleaming under high-cut cheekbones. The door is hard on my back, but my knees are jelly. "Please."

He shakes his head. "We've been on this collision course for two years, me and this Keeper. Longer. There's only one way out—my bullet in his brain."

Fear threatens to overwhelm me, but I force it back. I force myself to focus on the handsome, furious face in front of me. "Think about it, Stone. You once said you can't have a regular life like other people, but you can. You can start now with this one step, seeing that justice is done instead of poisoning your soul with more violence."

"Poisoning my soul? It's a little late for that. It's a black well in there."

"No," I whisper.

"There are boys out there being kept like animals. Worse than animals, and what you know could help me find them. Do you not give a shit about that?"

"Of course I do! I want those boys to be rescued. I want justice for them, and for what happened to you. That's why I forwarded my information about Innkeeper to the police."

He straightens. "You did what?"

"It's what the police are there for." I'm pleading with him, praying he'll understand even though I know he won't. "They have resources you don't. Resources to find the boys, and to help them recover once they do."

"You think the police aren't in on it? God! That'll just tip them all off." He scrubs his face. He seems angry. But tired, too. So tired.

"Not everybody is corrupt. Detective Rivera—"

"Is one of the good guys? Really? You sure about that?"

"I am."

"Fuck." Frustration radiates from his broad shoulders. "You don't know. You can't know that for sure."

"You have to trust somebody sometime." The words

come softly, but they land like bombs. Obvious, because I mean me. I want him to trust me, even though he won't. Maybe he can't.

Green eyes blaze under inky lashes just inches from my face. My skin tingles, as if his gaze has weight. Mass. Force. "I have to trust somebody? That's what you think? Who should I trust? Who?"

My belly twists. It was a stupid thing to say—to Stone, anyway. He was thrown to predators when he was most vulnerable. Failed by every system imaginable. Forgotten. Left for dead. The ultimate lost boy, leading his band of lost boys out of hell.

But he never really escaped. He's still trapped in hell, or more like the hell's inside him now. He seems almost to vibrate with it, a furious dark-haired god, tormented and torn.

He trusts nobody. Why should he?

"You need to tell me who Keeper is before they all get tipped off and move those poor kids somewhere we can't find them—*now*," he gusts out, breath warm on my forehead. His hand slides up from my waist in a deliberate threat. Higher, higher. To my throat, his hand hot against my skin.

"You're scaring me," I whisper.

"About time." Soft, heavy fingers bracket my chin. His touch is achingly gentle, even as it threatens. "Don't make me choose."

I close my eyes, bracing for the worst. He won't choose me.

Heavy fingertips tremble along my jaw, tracing a path toward my ear, shifting my hair in a way that tickles.

I steel my spine, replaying Madsen's grunts like a tape loop in my mind. Is that what he's going to do to me? It hurt Stone to do that; I know that now. He isn't some cold-blooded psychopath, even though he probably wishes he were. It hurt him to do that to a bad man; what will it cost him to hurt me?

"Tell me," he mutters, almost an incantation. "Fucking tell me."

I want to tell him, to spare him the pain, but I have my own broken heart. Doesn't he understand that it would kill me? It would kill me to see my father tortured and killed, knowing I could have stopped it. Maybe Stone does know what it would do to me. Maybe it's worth the sacrifice. I'm collateral damage. "Swear you won't kill him. Swear you won't hurt him."

A laugh, cruel and sharp. "I'm going to rip his balls off his body and feed them to him."

I shake my head. "Then I won't tell you who he is."

A knuckle brushes my neck. Will he choke me? Lock me up? Pretend to drown me? "Do you really want to play this game?"

"This isn't a game," I say.

"No," he growls. "This is a basement of boys, some-where in this city."

"Then let Detective Rivera find them. He'll save them. He'll bring Keeper to justice. If you only care about saving them, you'll take the deal. I'll tell you as long as you promise not to kill him, not to hurt him. This is how you save those boys, Stone."

He studies me, his eyelids low. It's a line in the sand. I'm offering him justice. He wants vengeance. Maybe that's always what would have broken us. The single and brutally important fracture point.

Stone's hand settles around my throat. He doesn't squeeze, but it's clear he could. There's enough strength in that hand to cut off my air. To break my neck. My breath comes shorter. "No deal," he says finally, and it sounds like regret. Maybe he does regret what he's going to do to me. How he'll hurt me. Torture me. Kill me?

There's a hitch in my chest. A crack in a foundation that should never have formed.

"Because you have to choose those boys," I say in a burst of clarity. "Because it's who you are."

"Yes."

"Except you're wrong. You think you have to give up your humanity to save them, but you don't."

"Give up my humanity? You know who you're talk-ing to here? Other men, they might dream about that soft cunt you let me have. They might want to fuck your pretty little mouth again, but all I want is blood. My humanity is long gone, baby."

"You're wrong. It's too late—I've seen you. You're a good person. You have a good heart."

He snorts, jaw set, gaze distant.

"I saw it in the river the first night," I continue. "Every time we were together, I saw it. In the tiny bird you carved."

"A broken piece of shit."

"Not to me. I love it." There's pain in his gaze, but I don't shut up. I won't shut up. "I love you."

"Stop it."

I reach up for his hand, still snug and warm around my neck. Instead of pulling it away, I squeeze harder. First with one hand, then with two. I press his hand so tight around my throat that I see black spots behind my eyelids. He's right; this isn't a game. Lives are at stake. And I'll give up mine before I give up my father's.

Darkness closes around the edges of my vision.

"Fuck," I hear him say. "Fuck."

I suck in breath without thinking, my body reacting on its own, air like fire in my lungs, the pressure on my neck gone.

"Fuck, baby." Gentle fingertips alight on my face. Soft, warm lips come down on my cheeks, my chin, my forehead. He's raining kisses on me. "Fuck," he says between kisses. "Fuck." Then he takes my lips, devouring my mouth like a starving man.

My body ignites. I grab fistfuls of his soft flannel shirt, knuckles against the hard planes of his chest. Pulling myself against him even as I push him away. I'm clinging to him on a stormy sea, wanting his comfort even as I know I'm going to drown.

The tears don't go away, even when he's holding me, kissing me. They come faster. A flood. They spill onto my lips, and when his tongue touches mine, I can taste them. Salt. Fear. Grief tastes like the ocean.

"I never could've hurt you," he mutters, moving his lips over my eyelids, sipping my grief. "Not for anything. I would have ripped off my own arm, but you knew that, didn't you, little bird?"

A sound behind me. The knob turning.

Stone grabs me, pulls me to him, one arm slung around my chest, bracketing me to him. The other around my neck. If he pulled any tighter, he'd be choking me.

But that's not what this is.

A large form darkens the door before emerging into the soft light of the room.

The big one from before—Grayson. He glowers at us. He's the one who just got out of prison. He wasn't released or anything official like that. He broke out. Escaped.

Another man comes in, fists balled at his sides. Knox.

The blond one. Sharp as a blade.

They both have that hard look of someone who's given their share of violence. Taken it, too. My heart breaks for them even as I know what they're here to do.

"You're done," Grayson says, nice and soft.

Stone pulls me against him. "Out."

Grayson's voice stays low and calm. "It's done. You didn't break her. I don't think you can, which is interesting, but it doesn't matter. We can do it."

"I got this," Stone says.

A sudden silence firms up around us, cold and hard as ice.

"You don't," Knox says, incredulous. "Not at *all*."

"Told ya," Grayson mutters.

"No one touches her," Stone says.

Another guy crowds into the room, long blond hair nearly white. Stone swears under his breath and shoves me behind him. There's a snick and a flash. A blade appears in Stone's hand.

I suck in a breath.

"What the fuck, Stone!" Grayson says, looking harder than ever before. Like every gilded edge in him turns to steel. "You're gonna fight me?"

"You fought me," Stone says, sounding just as hard. There aren't any people left in this room. Only metal and rock. Only me, light as a feather. "When I went after Abby, you stopped me."

"That was different. You just didn't want her here. Your own fucking rules. But this girl? She's holding secrets, secrets that protect *them*. Since when do you pick their side?"

"I'm not on their side," Stone says, soft with menace. "I'm on hers."

"So that's the way it is," Knox bites out.

"That's right."

"Fuck that," Grayson says. He picks up a chair like it's a toy and swings at Stone. With a roar, Stone absorbs the hit. Something cracks—wood? Bone? I scream and melt into the corner.

Stone has hold of the chair. He shoves back. Grayson falls.

Knox grabs Stone from behind. The one with long pale hair goes for his arm.

Stone hits the blond one in the face.

Knox grunts, struggling with Stone. There are more punches. More grunts.

A deep voice—"Fuck!" Stone fights harder than I've ever seen, but he's outnumbered.

I squeeze more deeply into the corner, horrified. The knife flies into the corner opposite me. More punches, more grunts. Fists and *thwaps* and swear words fill the room.

Stone's protecting me. From his brothers.

"Stop it!" I yell. "No more!"

It's a whisper in the wind.

I make myself small, unused to so much fury and violence. A table crashes over, and I jerk deeper into myself. The most vicious fights I see happen with words and cutting glances. Except that night of my sixteenth birthday. This is like that. Only Stone is the one losing.

Somebody else comes in, shorter, smaller. I can barely see this new one behind the blur of fighting men. Only that the room fills up even more.

Will this one attack Stone, too? How many men can he defend himself against?

A blast rips the air—loud and sudden. Massive as dynamite. Instinctively, I tuck my head into my chest, clapping my hands over my ringing ears.

Something exploded.

No—a gunshot! There's a shooter!

My blood races. *Did somebody shoot Stone?*

But no, there he is, lip bloody, crowded on one side of the room with his arms protectively over his guys, as if he can ward off bullets. They're all together, panting, side by side like they weren't just fighting a moment ago.

"What the fuck!" Grayson says.

A woman with brown hair and glasses comes into the room. She has fine features like a bird. She's wearing red yoga pants and a long T-shirt with a bright pink and gray flower design. But the most remarkable thing about her is the shiny gun in her delicate hand.

She gestures at the group of them. "Not a move. Don't even."

Who is this girl in this place? Is she one of them? Stone only mentioned brothers in the basement.

"You are in so much trouble," Grayson growls.

A mischievous glint appears in her eyes, but the way she holds the gun says she isn't playing.

The guys stay back as she moves toward me.

"Gimme the gun, Abby," Grayson says. There's an intimacy to his tone. Are they together? Is this the girl Stone threatened? There are undercurrents in this room strong enough to drag me under, but right now it looks like she's on my side. Our side?

Stone and I have a side.

"This isn't your fight, Abby," Stone growls.

"You okay?" It takes me a while to realize this woman—Abby—is talking to me.

"I'm okay," I say, but my voice comes out shaky.

She turns back to the guys.

"Not cool," Grayson growls.

"Oh, I'm sorry, you guys killing each other is cool?" Abby asks. "*That's* cool?"

"She knows where the boys are," Grayson says.

Abby stills. "Oh." She looks thoughtful. Her chest rises and falls. She turns to me. "You know where the boys are?"

"No! I don't know where they are!" I say.

Abby frowns at them. "She says she doesn't."

"She knows who Keeper is," Knox says.

Abby turns back to me. "You do?"

"I think so, but the police are handling it," I say. "I gave them evidence."

"You should tell them who it is," Abby says.

I shake my head.

"Is it somebody close to you?" she asks, voice gentle. "Brother? Father?"

I look over at Stone. See the gears turning in his head.

"Vigilante justice is never right," I plead. "Killing is never right. Let the police handle it."

Abby groans.

The blond one seems to still, like he's alerted to some faraway signal. Or maybe there's an actual sound—I can't hear anything with the way my ears are ringing. Then Stone turns toward the open doorway.

Somebody's there.

I gasp in horror.

It's my father, eyes wild, head tipped back, arm twisted back. He's being held from behind by somebody bigger and stronger.

"Look who I found skulking around out there," the man says. His dark hair is shaven to a sheen of black against his scalp.

"Daddy," I whisper.

"Let her go. It's me you want," my father says.

"Don't hurt him," I say.

I see when Stone gets it, or maybe he already figured it out thanks to Abby's question. Father or brother. Someone close enough I'd die to protect him. This is Keeper.

"You have me," my father says. "You can let her go."

Stone steps out from the group. "Keeper." If you didn't know him, the word might sound casual. But I hear the ice. It's formed into daggers, that ice. Made for slicing skin apart.

"I'm Keeper."

A thunderous silence falls over the room. The world takes on hard edges. Fear vibrates in my chest.

Daddy looks over at me. "You okay?"

"I'm fine." I turn a pleading gaze to Stone. "Don't hurt him. You promised."

"I said I wouldn't hurt *you*," Stone snarls, eyes on my father. "You bring the cops?"

"No," Dad says.

"He's alone," the man who brought him says. "Perimeter is secure. Scanners are clean."

"How'd you find us?" Stone barks.

Dad nods at my shoulder bag. "Her bag. Chipped."

It's not that surprising that they had a tracker put in my bag. I should have expected that. But I thought it would be Detective Rivera who did that. Not Daddy.

Not Daddy coming alone.

"Well. We've been waiting a long time to meet you," Stone says. "Years we were down there. But then that's not a surprise. You knew that."

"I didn't know," Dad says, pale but determined. "Not while it was happening—I swear. I found out later."

The blond holds out his hands like he wants to hug my dad. The guy holding Dad shoves him at the blond one, who grabs his shirt front with one hand and smashes his fist into Dad's jaw with the other.

Dad crashes backward into the wall.

I scream.

Grayson is on him, hitting him. The sound sickens me. Knox piles on. Stone hangs back, expression furious. He feels far away.

I look helplessly over at Stone, at Abby. "Do something!"

"I—" She shakes her head, seeming bewildered. She could stop them from hurting each other, but not from this. Not from hurting my father.

"He said he didn't know! Stone!" I beg tearfully. "He's my father!"

He sucks in a breath. "Fuck!" He grabs the gun from Abby. He raises it and shoots the cracked ceiling.

The explosion splits my eardrums just like the last one. Drywall falls like snow, settling on everyone's shoulders. But through the haze of the chaos, the guys pause.

"Enough," Stone says.

Knox gets right into Stone's face. It's like he doesn't even care about the gun. "It's Keeper. He needs to die."

Dad is half lying on the floor, eyes peering at me through his bloody face. He mouths something to me over and over. Words. *I'm sorry.*

"Please," I say. "It's my dad. *Please.*"

"He says he didn't know," Stone says.

"Since when do you give a shit about that?" the buzz-cut guy who brought Dad in demands. "He looked the other way. He admitted he knew eventually, so why didn't all these fuckers end up in prison? Oh right, because they're all fucking in bed together. This guy needs to pay."

"If he wants us to kill him quick, he'll tell us what we need to know about the boys," another one says.

Stone steps in front of Dad. "Try it and I'll cut your fucking throat." Certainty vibrates in his every word.

The room goes silent. The guys look shocked. Outraged.

Stone's outnumbered, but he's the one with the gun. Who would win that fight? I have a feeling no one would. Every single person in this room would lose as soon as one brother killed another.

"What the fuck are you doing?" Knox asks him.

Stone looks at me, his features arranged like a sculpture. Like they've always been this visage of fury and determination. Like he never came apart in my body.

But then I see it. Something new. Something different. "Those scumbags treated us like animals," he says. "But we're not animals. Fuck that."

"Like hell we're not," Cruz growls.

Stone gives him a hard look. "We're gonna hear what he has to say, and then we're gonna think of how we fucking make some justice happen."

"Are you fucking kidding me?" Knox says.

"We'll hear what he has to say," Stone says again. "And see what we can do together."

The guys just stare. Violence rolls off their bodies like they're heat lamps set to a thousand degrees. Suns that landed on Earth.

I have to pass between Grayson and Knox, and I half expect them to reach for me. To rip me apart with their bare hands. They look capable of it.

I make it to my dad, who's still slumped against the wall.

I take his hand. It feels cool to the touch. God, did they hurt him? Of course they did. But it could be worse.

"Daddy," I whisper.

"Princess, I'm sorry. So sorry. I never wanted you to know. You or your mother. Never wanted any of this to touch you."

"Didn't mind it touching the rest of us," Grayson drawls, but I squeeze Daddy's hand, keeping his attention focused on me. Stone's giving us this window. We have to do what's right.

"How did you find out?" I ask, bracing myself.

Even though I'm expecting the answer, it still hurts to hear it. "When it burned down. The fire caught onto the house next door. They told me about the accident—that's what they called it, an accident."

Someone snorts from behind me. Probably Grayson.

"Dorman—the late governor—he was involved. Just an executive back then. He said they'd pay me for the loss of the houses, but they'd need some time. I said don't worry about it, I have insurance. But he said no way, no one goes there."

There's a hand on the back of my neck, both exerting pressure and providing comfort. I know exactly who it is, even without looking. Know by the sense of rightness that slides through my body.

"What happened next?" Stone asks.

"I was curious." Dad looks away, and it takes me a second to recognize his expression. I've never seen it on his face before. Embarrassment. "I should have been curious sooner. I know that now. But they were important men. Pillars of the community...I never imagined..." He coughs, wipes his mouth. "I drove down myself one night, expecting some kind of gambling ring. Maybe a full-service massage parlor."

"You weren't wrong," Knox mutters, cutting. That blade, it's sharp on both ends, and I see my father flinch. I see something dark flicker in Stone's eyes.

"Keep going," I murmur, helping Daddy sit up a little.

"I thought, the fire must not be that bad if they wanted to keep things running. But the place was abandoned. And really just ruined. The fire had burned through that old structure. It would be a teardown, if anyone ever bothered, but I knew they wouldn't. As soon as I went downstairs, I knew."

"How did you know?" Stone asks in this hard voice that doesn't imply curiosity. It's the leading kind of question that says he already knows the answers.

My dad's silent a moment, and I have the feeling he's far away, seeing it for the first time again. Experiencing it all over again. "My family owned a farm," he says finally, looking at me. "You know that, right? It was my grandfather who started it, when he came here from Poland."

"You don't talk about it much," I say softly. It's part of our family history that doesn't fit into the society pages. That doesn't fit into my mother's story about our lives.

"We kept cattle, you know. That was the primary source of income, but my dad, he had a thing for horses.

Not the regular kind, for riding or for work. He liked the wild ones. The ones who weren't quite broken. The ones who hadn't been trained right."

"Where is this going?" Grayson demands.

I hold up my hand. "Let him finish."

And somehow they listen to me.

"But there was this one horse. Domino. That was his name. It was more than bad training. He'd been abused. He had marks all over his hide. He was beyond saving, you know?"

"I hope this isn't going where I think it is," Knox mutters.

Abby is the one who steps forward. "Stone asked him a question. He's answering it."

"No one could go in the stall," Daddy said, shaking his head. "I still have this scar on my shoulder from the last time I tried to go in and muck it out. And my father wouldn't put him down. We ended up just throwing feed over the gate. It was terrible. The smell. I'll never forget the smell. When you even got close, you could smell what happens when an animal is left to rot. That's what the basement smelled like. Even over the ashes and cinder, I could smell it. And I knew something horrible had happened there."

A growl from Stone. "And then you turned yourself in to the police, I'm sure."

"No," Daddy says, sounding half repentant, half

defiant. "What good would it have done? There wasn't anyone left in that basement. Everyone dead. Evidence burned. You can't arrest somebody because of a smell. And Brooke was a baby, her mother still in the hospital from complications. I had to do what was right for the family."

"And fuck everyone else," Grayson says, sounding more resigned than angry now.

"I talked to Dorman," Daddy says with an uneven laugh. Then he winces, those injuries they gave him running deep. "I told him I wouldn't be part of anything like that again. He told me I was imagining things, that it was a massage business with a little extra. I think he knew I didn't buy it."

I shake my head, more heartbroken than I want to admit. Even though I'd suspected Daddy, there was still a part of me that wanted him to be absolved completely. "Then why did he come to my sweet sixteen?"

"Because he was the governor by then," Daddy says, sounding tired. He closes his eyes, pale.

And because my mother wanted a new wing on the house. "Did Mom know?"

He meets my gaze, mournful. "It would kill her."

It's at least some relief to realize one of my parents has their hands clean. "Stone thinks there are boys being held right now. Today. Do you know where they could be?"

"I never did a deal with the governor after that."

Stone swears behind me. In a perverse way, my father's attempt to do the right thing has made this harder.

"Any kind of clue can help, Daddy. This is important."

He looks up at the ceiling with its spider web of cracks, its missing pieces.

Does he feel the angry eyes on him? Does he feel the pent-up rage in the room? I do.

"I never did that, where I kept a house empty for him. But I did construction work for him. Legit work. I made sure to check out every property he dealt with me on, and he knew that I did. Mostly commercial stuff."

Dad clears his throat. Impatience wells up in the room.

"There was this one project he really wanted me in on," he continues, "but something didn't feel right. He had these contracts with businesses who were going to rent storefronts in this old strip mall, but I knew the area was suffering. I'm thinking, who's paying this much for class C property? So I run some inquiries about the businesses."

"They're fronts?" Stone grits out. He's keeping himself locked tight—for me. It's costing him—I can tell. He has a lot of rage that needs to blast out of him.

All the guys do.

"Yes, they exist on paper, but there's no people. Only

this umbrella corporation. An LLC with another LLC on top of them. Layers on layers. I told the governor we were too booked to take the job, even though we were struggling."

Part of me is proud that Daddy made the right choice, refusing work when it seemed shady. Then again, the right thing to do would have been to turn in the governor years ago, to alert the police to that basement. In Stone's book that would make him guilty. Just as guilty as the men who hurt him.

Daddy looks at me, his eyes haunted. "The last umbrella I found? Good Shepherd, Inc."

I suck in a breath, because I know who that is. "Uncle Bill?" I say.

My father nods grimly.

"An uncle?" Stone barks.

"Family friend," Dad says. "That pregnant woman story was bullshit, but your mother overheard us using those names, and Bill thought it up."

No wonder he hated Mom repeating it. A perverse and twisted version of the original one.

Stone grunts. "Bottom line, you didn't cut off contact with all the bad guys."

A few of the men exchange looks. The air seems to quiver with barely restrained violence. That beating was just the start. But they're willing to follow Stone.

For now.

"I was pretty sure Bill didn't know," my father continues. "I couldn't imagine he did. And at the time, he was going for the judgeship. I warned him off Dorman, but I didn't tell him what I suspected. Knowing about the crime, whatever it was, would've made him an accomplice after the fact. I didn't want to do that to him."

Grayson growls, a dog, ready to attack. "Judge William Fossey?"

Dad nods, his expression grave.

"Uncle Bill," Stone spits, angry. "He fucking ran that whole operation. Didn't you know?"

"No," Dad says.

"God!" Stone's enraged. He has every right to be. They suffered down there thanks to powerful men giving each other the benefit of the doubt. "He was the puppet master. We never saw him, but he destroyed our fucking lives."

"I'm sorry," Dad says, and it sounds like he means it. I also know how little that helps these men who suffered in the basement. This is what they're fighting. Not only the evil that kidnaps them, that uses them, but the silent danger of men who look the other way.

"Too little, too late," Cruz snarls, fists balled. He's a hurricane, trapped in a bottle, his tattoos like a warning sign. "Let's have that address."

"Wait," my father says. "I didn't help you then, but

let me help you now. If I give you that address and you storm that place, these guys who did this to you will go free. I could even see them finding a way to implicate you. But if I go to Bill Fossey and his cronies wearing a wire, warn them about you guys or something, get them to talk, that's the one thing that can't be explained away."

I watch Stone's eyes, the hard line of his lips. He gave up his bloodbath. He gave up instant vengeance for him and his guys. Instant freedom for the boys. But this is something, right? A way to get proof.

The guys are exchanging glances, seeming to communicate with just that. I suppose being trapped together for years will give you that.

Do they realize what my father is giving up? If he turns on his own kind, his livelihood is gone. It's not much compared to what Stone and his guys lost, of course. But it's a sacrifice from a man who's poured everything into his work.

"How do you know that'll even work?" Stone asks. "The man's a judge. A friend and ally to every officer on the FCPD. You think they'll want to bring him down?"

"The honest ones will," Dad says. "Rivera will."

"How do we know Rivera's honest?"

Dad watches him, eyes bleak. "You've got to give me some credit here…" He trails off. "I'm more careful now. You're gonna have to trust me. And…they're children."

Stone stills, seems to contain himself with great effort.

He and his guys were children, too.

Everyone watches him.

Stone turns his gaze to me. It's a silent question—do I believe my father? Do I think Rivera's one of the good guys? I told him he has to trust somebody sometime. He's trusting me.

"I think Rivera's a good cop," I say. "He'll want to do the right thing."

Stone's still not convinced. "So what? We wait for you to meet with these assholes? For Rivera to get a search warrant? And who does he get it from? One of Fossey's bench buddies?"

"You want them put away?" my dad asks. "This is how it happens."

"I don't like those boys in there one second longer than they have to be," Knox growls. "You seriously considering leaving it up to rich white guys to punish each other?"

Stone looks around at the guys. "How many people went through that place when we were there? Hundreds?"

I feel sick. I can't look at my father now. I won't.

Stone's next words are low and hard. "We could get them all. All their names. All the names of the men visiting that strip mall. So they can't victimize anyone again."

My heart swells. Justice instead of vengeance. Preventing future crimes instead of retaliating. It feels huge.

"What about when Fossey makes his plea bargain?" Grayson barks. "What if he gets away with it? What if he builds up a new fucking organization and does it again?"

"We'll kill him ourselves, then," Stone says. Like that's obvious. "Slow."

Okay, but it's still a step. A big one.

Knox doesn't look convinced. "What did the system ever do for us?"

"Nothing," Stone says, getting in his face. "Will a killing spree fix it?"

Knox looks away.

"We could bring down half of the city," Abby says. "Half the elites, anyway. I agree. This is important. This is better."

Better than killing my father. Better than vengeance.

There's a tense silence. Knox is the first to nod.

Cruz nods. The others agree in grunts and head gestures.

Stone goes over and nudges my father with his foot. "The address."

"No reason you can't get something for yourselves," my dad says. "I understand you're all in some degree of trouble." He's looking at Stone and Grayson, but it's all of them. He must know that. "I want to see you get some kind of immunity for helping to put these guys away. I'll go to bat for you. Rivera, too."

They just stare at him, wary. Has anybody ever gone to bat for them?

"The address," Stone says. "Give it up. Now."

Dad doesn't have the address memorized, but he gives Stone the name and the cross streets.

Stone sends Grayson and a few other guys to watch it, to make sure the boys don't get moved. "And you see anyone driving up to visit? You got my permission to abduct them and beat the shit out of them. Just don't tip anyone off. Good chance to practice those stealth skills."

The guys move out.

He makes my father call Rivera after that—on speaker—to set up a meet. Dad insists they meet tonight. As soon as possible.

Tonight. It seems like forever since I got that text message in class, but it's only just past dinnertime.

Mom'll be there, waiting, probably sitting alone at the dining room table. It'll be perfectly set, salad forks exactly one-eighth of an inch to the left of the dinner forks. The roast in a covered pan, ready for serving on the elaborately carved warmer that I bought her last Christmas.

The salad will be tossed, a bright green against the festive blue tablecloth she bought in town. She'll be wondering where we are, why we're not answering our phones. Staring at hers. Worried out of her mind.

I swallow hard. What will she do when she learns the truth about Innkeeper?

Rivera agrees to a meet at the Old Steer Steakhouse.

Stone orders the blond—Calder—to go along with Dad. Apparently Calder isn't known to the authorities like the rest of Stone's guys are. Calder grabs my father's arm and practically drags my father out, allowing him to slow just long enough to give me one last backward glance. Grief. Worry.

"I'll be fine," I say.

"Get him the fuck out," Stone grates.

They disappear, leaving the two of us alone.

Without warning, Stone spins around and punches the wall.

I jolt to attention. The speed and violence of the act shocks me. Was that what he was bottling up? Is that what he had in store for my father?

Dust suffuses the air. When it clears, there are exposed beams where drywall had been.

He stares at the ruined wall, trembling with fury, not looking at me. "I wanted to kill him," he whispers.

The barely leashed violence. Both power and terrible pain.

"But you didn't kill him."

He says nothing. I can't see his face, but I feel him like I never felt anybody. I go to him. I wrap my arms around him from the back and hold him.

His breath is ragged, and I think I've never met any-body stronger. This beautiful, brave, desperately wounded man struggling to do the right thing—and succeeding.

Men with every opportunity in the world did the wrong things to him over and over. Men who should have been helping a kid like him.

And here, he did the right thing.

Putting this situation in the hands of the law. More or less. My heart swells with so much love, I don't think my body can contain it.

CHAPTER TWENTY-EIGHT
~STONE~

MY HAND BLAZES with pain. Did I fracture it? I kind of hope I did. I need something to balance out the churning hell in my mind.

I can't believe I let him go. But with Brooke's hopeful eyes on me, it's all I could do. It's more than just the fact that he's her father. She watched me kill someone the first night we met. I can't do that to her again.

I feel her behind me. She shouldn't even be near me right now. There's too much violence inside me still. All of it unspent. I may have spared his life, but that doesn't make me a good man.

She moves nearer. I'm not fit for her right now.

And my mind is still reeling with doubt. What if they get away with it? They've gotten away with it for years; why should things change now? What if the dirty cops just kill her old man? What if they send in a SWAT team and move the boys?

"You did it."

"I should've gone with the guys. To sit on that

place."

"Having an army there will alert somebody. You're here. Ready to make decisions. Thinking things through. Being the leader they need."

I know she's right.

"My father wants to help—whatever you say about him, he's tenacious when he sets his mind to something. Rivera is one of the good guys. This will work, Stone."

I think about what she said, how I need to trust somebody sometime. It's hard.

"You and your guys aren't alone."

Something strange happens. There's heat in my eyes. Pinpricks. What's happening? Then I realize the pinpricks are tears. Am I crying? I'm more shocked than ashamed. When's the last time I cried? Not ever. Not even in that basement. It's because she's right. So right I'm fucked up over it. So right I'm shaking like a motherfucker deep down inside.

Maybe I just don't know how to feel okay. Maybe that's what they took away from me.

Her cool hand settles onto my shoulder. "You blow me away," she whispers.

I shut my eyes, not sure what she means. Not sure I want to know.

"You blow me away, Stone." Her fingers close around my shoulder. Her touch is sweet. Cool beyond imagining. "I love you so much."

A breath I didn't know I was holding gusts out of me. She's the rain, soothing the fire in me, washing the rage.

Before I can stop myself, I spin around and grab her small frame. I push her up against the wall and devour her mouth—mercilessly, hungrily.

I'm a starving man, and Brooke is the only food for me. The only nourishment in all of time, in all the universe.

I can feel her hands pulling at my shirt, busy and frantic, like she needs this as much as I do. It makes my heart swell up as huge as my cock.

She's a wild thing against me, but small enough that I can hold her in both hands. I cup her face, tasting her lips. She's trying for my fly and not really getting it. I don't care. The feel of her fingertips grazing my steely dick is pure madness.

Her breath is soft and rhythmic in my ear. I kiss her cheek. I pin her to the wall and glide my teeth along her jaw line. I taste her neck, giving her a hard suck, marking her as mine. She cries out, but I keep on. I suck and pull at her neck as I yank up her schoolgirl skirt.

My hands rip at her panties. Find her soaked. I groan and release her neck. "You're so fucking wet for me."

She's panting, watching my eyes.

Just that.

I love the way she watches my eyes. The sweetness of

her trust. The bravery of her love. I grip her hair. I tilt her head back so she has to look at me. "I only ever want you to look at me."

"Only you," she says, panting. "Don't stop."

"I can't be sweet like last time," I say. "I can't be gentle. I need you too much."

"Fuck me," she says. "That's all you need to know. Fuck me. Now. *Please*," she adds.

It's the *please* that kills me. My perfect little bird, panting against the wall with her schoolgirl skirt around her waist, asking me please.

Like a madman, I'm tearing off my pants. They end up across the room with my shirt.

I grip her bare thigh and pull up her leg. I open her to me like a flower.

I press my chest against hers, heart pounding right into her tits through that schoolgirl shirt. The way her eyes are, I know she feels it. Then I guide myself into her and drive home. The tight silken warmth surrounds me.

She's so tight and so ready, I nearly lose it. I begin to thrust, fucking her deep and hard.

"Yes, Stone," she says, fingers squeezing my ass to pull me closer.

"Omigod omigod," she moans.

I come out of my haze enough to slow. "You need me to stop?"

"It feels so good," she says.

"So good," I say, sliding a knuckle over her cheek, just hanging out inside her, feeling the way her muscles move and clench around me.

"What are you doing?"

"Looking at how beautiful you are. I can't believe I'm inside you right now."

"You'll always be inside me."

I kiss her again. Gently this time. I slide my hands under her hips, urge her up. "Wrap your legs around me, baby."

She complies. I lift her and walk her to the bed, kissing the fuck out of her pretty face, staying hard as rock inside her. I yank away the blanket and settle us down on the soft sheets.

"Stone," she says, looking up at me. Her dark hair is splayed out over my pillow, calm waves on either side of her.

"I'm here, little bird."

I climb over her. I fuck her slow and sweet and easy. Not like she's a piece of food about to be taken away, but like the woman I love. The woman who loves me.

I can't trust a lot, but I can trust that. I can start with that.

CHAPTER TWENTY-NINE

~STONE~

Two days later

THE DECISION TO keep Brooke's old man alive and work with a cop and all that might've been easy for a better man than me. A no-brainer. Kids rescued. Faith in the system. No more violence. Brooke happy.

I'm not that man.

It took every ounce of restraint I had not to let loose on her father. It took everything in me not to drive over to that strip mall at top speed, get those kids out, and drive my fist into the men's faces over and over and over again—enough so that there would be no faces left to pound. It would've felt amazing. I'd promised my guys vengeance. I wanted it, too.

I'm their leader, though. I got them out of that shithole, and somewhere deep down in my miserable self, I knew this was the way forward. So I held off. Buttoned down all my darkness.

Wasn't easy, but I didn't let my guys know that. They needed to see one hundred percent confidence.

They needed to believe. And they did. They followed me, even in this.

It took almost twenty-four hours for Brooke's dad to get that meeting with Uncle Bill Fossey. He called him up, told him there was trouble, and Fossey couldn't get away until the next day.

Whatever Fossey said on that wire that Brooke's dad wore, it was enough to get a search warrant…three hours later. So that was twenty-seven long hours of my guys looking at me sideways, all of us knowing those kids were down there, miserable. And we weren't doing a damn thing to help them, aside from making sure visitors weren't arriving.

Rivera actually helped with that—he had a utility crew and a police cruiser set up at the place across the alley, making it look like an issue with that warehouse there. The official presence scared the lowlifes off and served as an excuse for why the ones my guys intercepted never showed.

Those were long fucking hours, though. But sometimes when I really got silent and clear inside myself, I could feel it was right, deep down. And when I'd look into Brooke's eyes, I could find it there, too. I could be better for her.

We cooked pasta while we waited. Knox and Cruz tried to get her into playing *Destiny 2*, their latest video game addiction, but mostly we stayed in bed, Brooke and

I.

I thought about Nate a lot. When we were first out of that basement, I didn't understand why he went the way he did, working toward his vet degree and healing animals instead of making guys pay. We'd give him so much shit for playing the game. But now when I look at him, I think he got himself free in a way we didn't.

Brooke once said I was still down in that basement, that I never left. Maybe she was onto something.

Not that I plan on strapping on a necktie anytime soon—or ever—but maybe I don't need to go killing everyone I hate. Baby steps.

Brooke's dad managed to persuade Fossey to reconvene the old gang at some club in East Franklin they all belong to. A place where they all feel safe and in control.

Brooke's dad gave Fossey some bullshit story Rivera cooked up that there's some guy peddling information on Grayson and the prison break—shit that could get us all locked up.

So that's where the takedown will happen. Rivera wanted us to steer clear of that entire part of the city.

Yeah right.

We really wanted to be there when those kids got pulled out, but Rivera talked us out of it. He promised we could see them, but the social workers have some special protocol that's best for the boys. Something better than a bloodbath and a blazing inferno. Who knew.

We arrive on the street where the fancy club is well before showtime. We might not be pounding their faces in, but this takedown is ours.

"It'll be that door," Cruz says, pointing out the unmarked cars up and down the street. Because he knows how cops arrange things.

We hang back in the shadows, in the service entrance to a grand event center across the oak-lined street from the ornate stone and marble historic landmark.

The seven of us waiting together, just like old times, along with Brooke and Abby. This is their day, too.

Brooke is right by my side, like the strong ally that she is.

Calder is on my other side, stoic and silent, bright hair concealed in a dark cap, unmoving as a statue, eyeing the entrance to the exclusive club. Knox has his phone out, checking it over and over like it's part of his brain, which it is. Nate leans against the wall, hands shoved deep into his pockets, eyes on the pigeons jockeying for perches at the top of the three-story building. Grayson and Ryland sit on the stoop, the least happy about this wait-and-see shit. Abby is right next to Grayson. She pulls out a paper bag.

"That better not be popcorn," Grayson says.

"It's fresh-baked chocolate chip cookies," Abby says. "You gonna tell me you don't want cookies for this?"

We all do, it turns out. Leave it to Abby to lighten

the mood, but there are things to celebrate beyond the guys getting caught.

Rivera got a lead on the real cop killer from whatever Fossey told Brooke's dad—he's all but promised Grayson's conviction will be overturned and charges from the escape vacated. We're all getting clean slates. That'll be the deal for our testimony.

Things get tense when the cars start rolling up, when familiar guys start getting out. And by tense, I mean belly-twisting, fist-balling, jaw-clenching tense.

They're all fifteen years older, but we recognize them like it was yesterday. We gave them all nicknames back in the day, and we murmur them now, remembering together.

A few step out of cabs. Familiar faces, every one of them. Brooke's dad arrives, still with the wire, according to Rivera. Eventually all the big players are there.

I put a hand on Grayson's shoulder. "This is them going down," I say, more for myself than anything.

"Gotcha, motherfuckers," Cruz whispers into the air between us.

Once they're all in there, we wait some more. Rivera warned us that the cops would keep back until they felt like they had everything they could get off the wire. Cruz thinks they'll come in the back and flush them out the front if they run.

Suddenly a white van rolls up. "What the fuck?"

Cruz says.

"TV news," Knox grumbles.

Another news van arrives. Reporters are getting out, staking out sight lines to capture the arrests live.

Nate gives me a look. "Somebody called the news." The way he says it, he thinks it was me.

He's right. "That's terrible," I say. "Awfully embarrassing to be arrested on live TV."

A couple of the guys snort.

"Love it," Grayson growls.

And then it's happening. Police cruisers zoom up, as if out of nowhere, stopping right up on the sidewalk, one, two, three, four, five. A police van turns the corner, lights flashing. There are more flashing lights from cop cars on the other side.

The windows of the place are thick with stained glass, but I'm betting they're seeing this. People are gathering. It's a circus. The cops put up tape to create a perimeter.

"It's time," I say. I don't mean anything specific by that. Just everything. It's time for everything. I grab Brooke's hand. Our gazes meet. Hope swells in my heart. "Come on."

We step out of the shadows, all of us together—my brothers. Brooke and Abby. We edge up between news vans, hanging together as a group.

The ornately carved doors burst open. Detective

Rivera appears with Judge William Fossey at the top of the marble steps. Fossey's hands are cuffed behind his back. His jaw is set, his face pale, and his eyes bright with horror as he surveys the crowd and news cameras, but then he seems to collect himself, and he smiles as the reporters rush up and ask for comment.

"Fake news," he says. "Nothing but lies."

Then he sees me. He sees Grayson. He sees the group of us, strong together. A force for right.

It's then that I think he knows he's well and truly fucked. I swear, some of the life visibly drains out of him. He seems smaller, even. Rivera drags him the rest of the way down the steps and toward the waiting police van.

Other men get dragged out in the same way, there in full view of the world, the beginning of a long walk of shame and misery. And each and every one of them sees us. We make sure of it.

Something stirs in my chest each time, like I want to shout and swear and throw shit and I don't know what else. It's fucking overwhelming.

In a good way.

We stay until the last of the guys are out. We stay there long after the news crews race down to the police station to do more interviews. Long after the crowds disperse and the sun is setting over the buildings.

We're a little shell-shocked, I think.

Grayson is the one to break the spell. "Let's go home."

Chapter Thirty

~Stone~

One month later

THEY LOVE VIDEO games and pasta.

Nate looks over at me from the other side of the couch and just rolls his eyes. We're out at his farm. We had this whole outdoor trek and meet-the-animals thing set up for the four boys who were stuck in that strip-mall basement, but they haven't gotten past the sweet setup in the living room.

Cruz shovels spaghetti and meatballs into his face like he's never eaten before in his life. Knox groans. "You're getting tomato sauce on the controllers."

"Got you!" One of the kids—Harley—blows up Grayson's guy. Grayson's laughing, working the controls, vowing to get them all back. Being the baby of the group, Grayson connects with the kids best.

Miles—he's maybe thirteen—plays with sullen determination. He reminds me a lot of me. Angry. Hard-eyed. Zero trust. He was the oldest one, too.

The four of them know we were inside like they

were. Years longer. They know we got them out, but we're not here for a thank you or some big fucking emo moment. We're giving them what we wanted when we got out. A place to be kids. To be their own kids.

Child protective services almost didn't let us take them out of the group home for this day-on-the-farm thing, but Rivera and Brooke's dad intervened. They got a child psychologist on the case who told the authorities how healing it would be for them to hang out with guys who came out the other side of what they'd been through.

And the boys, they weren't talking. I mean, even more than they aren't talking here. They were clammed up hard, not trusting any adults. It didn't take a genius to realize we could reach them.

They sent a social worker along. He's reading in the corner.

"That's the first time I've seen them smile," he told me fifteen minutes after they got here.

The room explodes in laughter when Grayson goes down. I clap a hand on his shoulder. "Too slow, old man."

The kids laugh at him. They sound like…kids.

They're looking for homes for them. Two of these boys were orphans; two were runaways. Throwaway boys, all four of them. Just like us. Except they'll get lots of therapy and hopefully a stable place to grow up, unlike us.

I thought about taking them for like two seconds, but we don't have the life for raising kids. Not yet, anyway. I don't know whether we ever will. For now they deserve a stable life, not an abandoned hotel or a hidden cabin in the woods.

Nate wanders over to Miles, sitting beside him on the sofa, all nonchalant like he's not observant as fuck. He's got something in his hand. A book. I can't read its title from this far away, but there are enough glossy pictures as he flips through the pages to show me it's about animals.

The animals gave him a purpose.

Miles passes the controller to one of the other boys, then scowls down at his hands. But even from here, I can see his gaze shifting to that book with every turn of the page.

Nate's a gentle man, something most of us can't really claim to be. Maybe he could end up adopting one of them.

In a few minutes the book is half in Miles's lap. He's silent as they turn the pages, but it's something. God, it's something.

Knox takes over for Grayson, running the games. He's talking trash.

I have to hand it to Detective Rivera—he took point on the investigation. Dozens of guys have been arrested beyond what we saw that day at the club. City leaders. Business luminaries. Dirty cops. Wealthy heads of Franklin City's oldest families.

The arrests have torn the city apart. *Good.* Most of the men have been denied bail. They tried to get special treatment. No-go. They'll be heading into the general population of a prison with child-predator signs on their backs.

I won't be losing any sleep over it.

Ryland comes in and collects the plates, offering fourth servings to anyone, but we're full. Beyond full. The pasta, it was a little overcooked; the sauce, a little too salty, but that's not the point. The point is that it was cooked with love by someone who gives a shit about these kids. That's what made it fucking perfect.

There's a hole in my chest, like there always is when Brooke isn't near me. She offered to skip class for this, but I don't want to be a bad influence. Well, not too bad. She has important shit to learn. About government and fucking society.

The kids are going to have a lot more meals like this, wherever they end up. No more stale pizza. No more crumbs.

The gaming winds down. Nate manages to get the group of us outside to kick around the farm.

It's a nice evening, with one of those sunsets where the light feels glowy and soft. There are different fenced-in pastures here, and rolling hills beyond. We stop at the goat pen. I suppose we're quite a sight, the seven of us older guys like battered Vikings watching four boys feed the goats.

I put my hands over the length of the wooden fence. Watch them laugh. Watch them forget themselves for a while. Nate's laughing, keeping the goats in check.

The oldest one—Miles—comes out and stands next to me.

"That brown one almost took your thumb," I say.

He shrugs. He's so like me, it kind of hurts. He doesn't even want to say that much. He doesn't think anyone gives a shit. It's cool. I get it.

He's staring at my arm. He looks away when he thinks I'm noticing. I'm not sure what the fuck is up with that until I realize it's the scarification he's eyeing. "It's axes," I say.

"I thought it was just an *X*," he says.

I hold it out. He's curious to touch the thing with its raised white lines, but I won't invite him to. It's not what he needs. "Double-sided axes. We all have them."

"You did it…"

"Yup." *In the basement.* That's what he's asking. "With a sharpened nail we pulled out of the wall. Scratched the hell out of each other."

"They musta been mad," he says.

Nobody likes marks on the merchandise. "They were

mad, but it was too late because we had a plan to get out. Got out a few days later."

"And you killed the fuck out of them," he growls.

I nod, glad the social worker isn't nearby. We promised we'd be positive role models. I trace the *X* that the axes make. "Old-style battle-axes. We found the design in some moldy book down there."

"And you scratched it in. Like war paint or some shit," he says.

"It goes with our vow to each other," I say. "'One blade to protect my brothers, one blade for vengeance.'"

"That's your vow?"

"That's our vow," I say.

"You have a vow." He stares at my arm a long time. I let him. "I wish we'd got to kill them."

"Nah, it's better this way," I say. "Way worse for them, too."

"You think?"

"I know," I say.

"I wish we at least had a vow," he finally says.

"You do have one." I wait until he's looking up at me, and I repeat it. "This vow of ours? It covers all four of you. You're my brother same as Nate or Knox over there. *One blade to protect my brothers* means you. It means you're not alone out there. It means you have somebody to reach out to. Okay?"

He touches his own arm. I don't know whether he

believes it. "I want one, too. I want you to make it on me."

Grayson catches my eye from the other side of Miles. How long was he listening? A glimmer in his eyes tells me he must've heard that last part, anyway. "Let's all think about it for later," he says. "Okay? Don't go doing it yourselves."

Pretty sure the caseworkers would be mad, too.

Somebody finds a Frisbee, and we throw it around awhile. And then the farm dogs get involved and it's a party. It feels good. I don't know who's helping each other more—are they healing us or are we healing them?

But the answer doesn't matter. With brothers it goes both ways.

EPILOGUE

~BROOKE~

Five months later

MY CRIMINAL JUSTICE class is in one of the oldest buildings on campus, with seats so small and so packed it's hard to squeeze out of them. There's an old bell that still rings, from when colleges still had those. It runs a little early, and the professor always tries to keep talking.

Normally I like to be respectful, to take excellent notes, to be a model student. That's something I did for myself, not for my parents, so I keep doing it now. Except when it comes to my last class of the day. Then I use my arm to sweep my books and notebooks into my messenger bag and dart into the horde of other impatient students. There's chatter all around me. A frat party tonight. Some kind of protest happening in the quad. I'm sure it's interesting, but I have my own kind of party to attend. My own kind of protest.

I skip down the old rubber-lined steps, keeping a light handle on the scarred wood railing. When I reach the bottom, I push out of heavy metal doors with the rest of the crowd. The sun makes everything glow—the concrete sidewalks, the flagpole. The cars lined up in the parking lot.

Tucking my bag close to my body, I dart along the sidewalk.

It takes me an extra second to find this car, because it's parked behind a big delivery van. Then I see it, the white truck that's distinctly Stone. There are way too many fancy cars in the garage, new ones, expensive ones. This is the one he drives.

I dash to the driver's-side door, holding my breath. The door opens.

Then I'm sliding into the seat, tossing my bag into the back. The man in the passenger seat doesn't say a word. At least until I start the engine with the remote key sitting in the cupholder.

"Five o'clock," he says.

I glance in the rearview mirror. Sure enough there's a suspicious-looking black Toyota sitting in the corner of the lot. Suspicious because the dust around the front bumper doesn't match the license plate. It's been switched. Recently. Probably from some poor car stuck in impound.

"No problem," I say, easing out of the lot.

We'll go west, which is also the direction that the Bradford Hotel is located. Of course we'll probably go all four directions before this is over. That's the fun part.

"What's the plan?" I ask. "Anything I need to know? If Knox is cooking again, I vote we stop for takeout."

Stone reaches over and slides a strand of my hair between two fingers. "Cruz on the grill."

I smile. "That works." Cruz on the grill means burgers. He gets creative, mixing in mushrooms and cheeses and crazy spices. He makes veggie versions for Calder. The guys make fun of that, but Calder's impervious to any and all teasing. We'll eat at the giant table, all nine of us. Sometimes Ryland noodles around on his guitar, taking requests.

I've never loved a place more than the Bradford Hotel. The guys are like a big, unruly family, but the love between them runs strong as steel. They yell a lot and argue and laugh too loud and even throw things when somebody's being annoying or incredibly hilarious.

There are no rules. No stern glances when you take a second helping of dessert. No lectures on manners…unless they're coming from me.

Not that I do it a lot—just the basics. For example, I've got the guys holding their dinner knives in their right hands while cutting food; then they put the knives down and switch their forks to their right hands to eat. They groaned a lot when I first taught it to them. Stone thought I was joking the whole time, but now they're doing it. Maybe they do it just for me, but it's a good thing to know.

Nate adopted the oldest of the boys—Miles—and he sometimes brings him around when things are quiet on the farm. He seemed happy to have Miles learn this stuff.

My parents still keep my stuff in my bedroom, and I visit them for Sunday dinner now and then, but I'm living at the Bradford full-time while I go to the local college. The guys are fascinated by my criminal justice books—I sometimes catch them reading them—and you can tell they don't know what to think about my plans to be a lawyer, but Stone is one hundred percent with me.

He still leads that group with the wild strength and passion that I love him for. I know that he comes off like he doesn't need anybody in the world, but I also know a different part of him. I get a part of him that nobody else gets—the strong, passionate man who's also tender, curious. Vulnerable, sometimes.

I took over one of the rooms for my study space and painted it yellow and decorated it with pictures and posters and a bookshelf full of my favorite novels.

Sometimes if I'm in there too long or late, Stone comes pounding at the door, blazing with raw heat, kissing me like a madman, shoving me up against the wall like we haven't seen each other for a year.

The Toyota waits for a minute and a half before following.

"Are you sure?" He's baiting me. "I can take over if

you can't lose him."

Working with the authorities had one very nice bonus. Those arrest warrants for Stone? They're gone. Which means he's a free man. That doesn't mean he's off the hook for anything illegal he does now. That's why Detective Rivera can't let it go. He's a good cop, down to the bone. He worked with Stone and his crew to free the boys, but he can't leave us alone either.

And he's desperate to figure out where their headquarters are.

It would put a wrinkle in the crew's activities if they had to hide their comings and goings from Detective Rivera. The secrecy of the Bradford Hotel is a real advantage, but mostly the men just like it.

And maybe the women, too. Abby and I don't really love the cops sniffing around, even if we like law and order. The men are a bad influence on us, maybe. But we're a good influence on them. We complement each other. We help each other. …

"Give me ten minutes," I say, pulling to a stop at a red light.

And most of all, we challenge each other.

Stone reclines in the passenger seat, watching the rearview mirror. He's in a dusky green shirt that matches his eyes.

He gives me a quick grin. I can't believe he's mine, sometimes. I want to kiss him, to feel his hands on me, to feel his heat on me, but not yet.

The black Toyota changes lanes, oh so casually, the next lane over. "Ten? I don't know. It took you almost twenty yesterday."

The light turns green, and I grin. "Ten."

"Prove it, little bird."

I press the pedal to the floor, and we fly.

~THE END~

THANK YOU for reading HOSTAGE! We hope you love Stone and Brooke's story. If you haven't read Grayson and Abby's book yet, read *PRISONER* now.

Want more dangerous romance from Skye Warren? SIGN UP for her newsletter at www.skyewarren.com/newsletter

Want more sexy romance from Annika Martin? SIGN UP for her newsletter at www.annikamartinbooks.com/newsletter

The price of survival... Don't miss Skye Warren's bestselling Endgame series, starting with the critically acclaimed THE PAWN! Gabriel Miller swept into my life like a storm.

"Edgy, provocative and deeply erotic, The Pawn is one of my top reads of the year! Skye Warren brings you a sensual battle of wills guaranteed to leave you gasping by the end."

– New York Times bestselling author
Elle Kennedy

He's a devil in Armani...and he'll do what it takes to reunite his long-lost brothers—even kidnap his enemy's daughter. Grab DARK MAFIA PRINCE.

"Twisted, sexy and dark—Dark Mafia Prince is everything I love in a stay-up-all-night-can't-put-it-down read!"

~author M. O'Keefe

✧   ✧   ✧

You are warmly invited to join our Facebook groups, Skye Warren's Dark Room and the Annika Martin Fabulous Gang, for exclusive giveaways and sneak peeks of future books.

✧   ✧   ✧

Turn the page for a sneak peek of PRISONER, Grayson & Abby's story....

Sneak peek of Prisoner
by Skye Warren & Annika Martin
~Abigail~

H EAVY BARS CLOSE behind me with a clang. I feel the sound in my bones. A series of mechanical clicks hint at an elaborate security mechanism beneath the black iron plating. I knew this would happen—had anticipated and dreaded it—but my breathing quickens with the knowledge that I am well and truly trapped.

"Can I help you?"

I whirl to face the administrative window where a heavyset woman in a security guard uniform stares at her screen.

"Hi," I say, pasting on a smile. "My name is Abigail Winslow, and I'm here to—"

"Two forms of identification."

"Oh, well, I already filled out the paperwork at the front desk. And showed them my IDs."

"This isn't the front desk, Ms. Winslow. This is the east-wing desk, and I need to see two forms of identification."

"Right." I dig through my bag for my driver's license and passport.

She accepts them without looking up, then hands me a clipboard with a stack of papers just like the ones I already filled out.

I've been dreading this day for weeks, wishing I'd been assigned any other project but this one. You'd think I was being sent here for a crime. My professor—the one who'd forced me into this—warned me that prisoners were not always receptive to outsiders. Apparently nobody here is.

I complete each form, arrange the pages neatly on the clipboard, and bring them back up to the window. The guard accepts them and gives back my IDs…still without looking at me.

My hands clench and unclench, clench and unclench while the guard eyes my paperwork.

Seconds pass. Or are they minutes? The damp chill of the place seeps in through my cardigan and leaves me shivering.

Leaning forward, I read the name tag of the guard. "Ms. Breck. Do you know what the next steps are?"

"You can have a seat. I have work to do now, and then I'll escort you back."

"Oh, okay." I glance at the bars I just came through, then the open hallway opposite. "Actually, if you just point me in the direction of the library, I'm sure I can—"

Thunk. The woman's hand hits the desk. I jump. Her dark eyes are faintly accusing, and I wish we could go back to no eye contact. How did I manage to make an enemy in two minutes?

"Ms. Winslow," she says, her voice patronizing.

"You can call me Abby," I whisper.

A slight smile. Not a nice one. "Ms. Winslow, what do you think we do here?"

The question is clearly rhetorical. I press my lips together to keep from making things worse.

"The Kingman Correctional Facility houses over five thousand convicted criminals. My job is to keep it that way. Do we understand each other?"

Heat floods my cheeks. The last thing I want to do is make her job harder. "Right. Of course." I shamble back, landing hard on the metal folding chair. It wobbles a little before the rubber feet stop my slide.

I understand the woman's point. She has to keep the prisoners in and everyone else out, and keep people like me safe.

I reach down and pull a book from my bag. I never leave home without one, even when I go to classes or run errands. Even when I was young and my mother used to take me on her rounds.

Especially then.

I would hide in the backseat with my nose in the book, pretending I didn't see the shady people who came to her window when we stopped.

A little green light above the barred doors flashes on and there's an ominous buzz. Somebody's coming through, and I doubt it will be a library volunteer. I slide down.

Pretend to be invisible.

It's no use. I peer over the top edge as a prisoner saunters through the door, and my pulse slams in my throat double time.

He's flanked by two guards—escorted by them, I guess you'd say. But they seem more like an entourage than anything. Power vibrates around him like a threat.

Read, read, read. Don't look.

The prisoner is half a foot taller than the guards, but he seems to tower over them by more than that. Maybe it's his broad shoulders or just something about the way he stands, or his imperiously high cheekbones. The dark stubble across his cheeks looks so rough and unforgiving I can feel it against my palm; it contrasts wildly with the plushness of his lips. His short brown hair is mussed. There's one scar through his eyebrow that somehow adds to his perfection.

The little group approaches the window. I can barely breathe.

"ID number 85359," one of the guards says, and I understand that he's referring to the prisoner. That's who he is. Not John Smith or William Brown or whatever his name is. He's been reduced to a number. The woman at the desk runs through a series of questions. It's a procedure for checking him out of solitary.

The prisoner faces sideways, spine straight, the corner of his mouth tilted up as if he's slightly amused. Then it clicks, what else is so different about him: no visible tattoos. Tough guys like this, they're always inked up—it's a kind of armor, a kind of *fuck you*. This guy has none of it, though he's far from pristine; white scars mar the rough skin of his hands and especially his forearms, a latticework of pain and violence, a flag proclaiming the kind of underworld he came from.

The feel of brutality that hangs about him is compelling and...somehow beautiful.

I drink him in from behind my book—it's my mask, my protective shield. But then the strangest thing happens: he cocks his head. It's just a slight shift, but I feel his attention on me deep in my belly. I've been discovered. Caught by searchlights. Exposed.

My heart beats frantically.

I want him to look away. He fills up too much space. It's as if he breathes enough oxygen for twelve men, leaving no air for me at all. Maybe if we were in the library and he needed help finding a book or looking something up, then I wouldn't mind the weight of his attention.

No. Not even there. He's too much.

Two sets of bars on the gate. Handcuffs. Two guards.

What do they think he would do if there were only one set of bars, one guard?

My blood races as the guards draw him away from the window and toward the inner door, toward where I sit. His heat pierces the chill around me as he nears. His deep brown eyes never once meet mine, but I have the sense of him looming over me as he passes, like a tree with a massive canopy. He continues on, two hundred pounds of masculine danger wrapped in all that beauty.

Even in chains, he seems vibrant, wild and free, a force of nature—it makes me feel like I'm the one in prison. Safe. Small. Carefully locked down.

How would it feel to be that free?

"Ms. Winslow. *Ms. Winslow.*"

I jump, surprised to hear that the woman has been calling my name. "I'm sorry," I say as a strange sensation tickles the back of my neck.

The woman stands and begins pulling on her jacket. "I'll take you to the library now."

"Oh, that's great."

That shivery sensation gets stronger. Against my better judgment, I look down the hallway where the guards and the prisoner are walking off as one—a column of orange flanked by two thinner, shorter posts.

The prisoner glances over his shoulder. His mocking brown gaze searches me out, pins me with a subtle threat.

Though it isn't his eyes that scare me. It's his lips—those beautiful, generous lips forming words that make my blood race.

Ms. Winslow.

No sound comes out, but I feel as though he's whispered my name right into my ear. Then he turns and strolls off.

Want to read more? PRISONER is available at Amazon.com, BarnesAndNoble.com, iBooks, and other book retailers.

Turn the page for a sneak peek of THE PAWN, the USA Today bestselling full-length dark contemporary novel about revenge and seduction in the game of love...

SNEAK PEEK OF THE PAWN
BY SKYE WARREN...

WIND WHIPS AROUND my ankles, flapping the bottom of my black trench coat. Beads of moisture form on my eyelashes. In the short walk from the cab to the stoop, my skin has slicked with humidity left by the rain.

Carved vines and ivy leaves decorate the ornate wooden door.

I have some knowledge of antique pieces, but I can't imagine the price tag on this one—especially exposed to the elements and the whims of vandals. I suppose even criminals know enough to leave the Den alone.

Officially the Den is a gentlemen's club, the old-world kind with cigars and private invitations. Unofficially it's a collection of the most powerful men in Tanglewood. Dangerous men. Criminals, even if they wear a suit while breaking the law.

A heavy brass knocker in the shape of a fierce lion warns away any visitors. I'm desperate enough to ignore that warning. My heart thuds in my chest and expands out, pulsing in my fingers, my toes. Blood rushes through my ears, drowning out the whoosh of traffic behind me.

I grasp the thick ring and knock—once, twice.

Part of me fears what will happen to me behind that door. A bigger part of me is afraid the door won't open at all. I can't see any cameras set into the concrete enclave, but they have to be watching. Will they recognize me? I'm not sure it would help if they did. Probably best that they see only a desperate girl, because that's all I am now.

The softest scrape comes from the door. Then it opens.

I'm struck by his eyes, a deep amber color—like expensive brandy and almost translucent. My breath catches in my throat, lips frozen against words like *please* and *help*. Instinctively I know they won't work; this isn't a man given to mercy. The tailored cut of his shirt, its sleeves carelessly rolled up, tells me he'll extract a price. One I can't afford to pay.

There should have been a servant, I thought. A butler. Isn't that what fancy gentlemen's clubs have? Or maybe some kind of a security guard. Even our house had a housekeeper answer the door—at least, before. Before we fell from grace.

Before my world fell apart.

The man makes no move to speak, to invite me in or

turn me away. Instead he stares at me with vague curiosity, with a trace of pity, the way one might watch an animal in the zoo. That might be how the whole world looks to these men, who have more money than God, more power than the president.

That might be how I looked at the world, before.

My throat feels tight, as if my body fights this move, even while my mind knows it's the only option. "I need to speak with Damon Scott."

Scott is the most notorious loan shark in the city. He deals with large sums of money, and nothing less will get me through this. We have been introduced, and he left polite society by the time I was old enough to attend events regularly. There were whispers, even then, about the young man with ambition. Back then he had ties to the underworld—and now he's its king.

One thick eyebrow rises. "What do you want with him?"

A sense of familiarity fills the space between us even though I know we haven't met. This man is a stranger, but he looks at me as if he wants to know me. He looks at me as if he already does. There's an intensity to his eyes when they sweep over my face, as firm and as telling as a touch.

"I need..." My heart thuds as I think about all the things I need—a rewind button. One person in the city who doesn't hate me by name alone. "I need a loan."

He gives me a slow perusal, from the nervous slide of my tongue along my lips to the high neckline of my clothes. I tried to dress professionally—a black cowl-necked sweater and pencil skirt. His strange amber gaze unbuttons my coat, pulls away the expensive cotton, tears off the fabric of my bra and panties. He sees right through me, and I shiver as a ripple of awareness runs over my skin.

I've met a million men in my life. Shaken hands. Smiled. I've never felt as seen through as I do right now. Never felt like someone has turned me inside out, every dark secret exposed to the harsh light. He sees my weaknesses, and from the cruel set of his mouth, he likes them.

His lids lower. "And what do you have for collateral?"

Nothing except my word. That wouldn't be worth anything if he knew my name. I swallow past the lump in my throat. "I don't know."

Nothing.

He takes a step forward, and suddenly I'm crowded against the brick wall beside the door, his large body blocking out the warm light from inside. He feels like a furnace in front of me, the heat of him in sharp contrast to the cold brick at my back. "What's your name, girl?"

The word *girl* is a slap in the face. I force myself not to flinch, but it's hard. Everything about him overwhelms me—his size, his low voice. "I'll tell Mr. Scott my name."

In the shadowed space between us, his smile spreads, white and taunting. The pleasure that lights his strange yellow eyes is almost sensual, as if I caressed him. "You'll have to get past me."

My heart thuds. He likes that I'm challenging him, and God, that's even worse. What if I've already failed? I'm free-falling, tumbling, turning over without a single hope to anchor me. Where will I go if he turns me away? What will happen to my father?

"Let me go," I whisper, but my hope fades fast.

His eyes flash with warning. "Little Avery James, all grown up."

A small gasp resounds in the space between us. He already knows my name. That means he knows who my father is. He knows what he's done. Denials rush to my throat, pleas for understanding. The hard set of his eyes, the broad strength of his shoulders tells me I won't find any mercy here.

I square my shoulders. I'm desperate but not broken. "If you know my name, you know I have friends in high places. Connections. A history in this city. That has to be worth something. That's my collateral."

Those connections might not even take my call, but I have to try something. I don't know if it will be enough for a loan or even to get me through the door. Even so, a faint feeling of family pride rushes over my skin. Even if he turns me away, I'll hold my head high.

Golden eyes study me. Something about the way he said *little Avery James* felt familiar, but I've never seen this man. At least I don't think we've met. Something about the otherworldly glow of those eyes whispers to me, like a melody I've heard before.

On his driver's license it probably says something mundane, like brown. But that word can never encompass the way his eyes seem almost luminous, orbs of amber that hold the secrets of the universe. *Brown* can never describe the deep golden hue of them, the indelible opulence in his fierce gaze.

"Follow me," he says.

Relief courses through me, flooding numb limbs, waking me up enough that I wonder what I'm doing here. These aren't men, they're animals. They're predators, and I'm prey. Why would I willingly walk inside?

What other choice do I have?

I step over the veined marble threshold.

The man closes the door behind me, shutting out the rain and the traffic, the entire city disappeared in one soft turn of the lock. Without another word he walks down the hall, deeper into the shadows. I hurry to follow him, my chin held high, shoulders back, for all the world as if I were an invited guest. Is this how the gazelle feels when she runs over the plains, a study in grace, poised for her slaughter?

The entire world goes black behind the staircase, only breath, only bodies in the dark. Then he opens another thick wooden door, revealing a dimly lit room of cherrywood and cut crystal, of leather and smoke. Barely I see dark eyes, dark suits. Dark men.

I have the sudden urge to hide behind the man with the golden eyes. He's wide and tall, with hands that could wrap around my waist. He's a giant of a man, rough-hewn and hard as stone.

Except he's not here to protect me.

He could be the most dangerous of all.

Want to read more? THE PAWN is available at Amazon.com, BarnesAndNoble.com, iBooks, and other book retailers.

And turn the page for a sneak peek of Dark Mafia Prince…

Sneak peek of Dark Mafia Prince
by Annika Martin

I PLEAD REPEATEDLY for news of my father, if only to know he's still alive. My captor just texts.

A crash from inside our mansion. They're wrecking the place.

"This is pointless." When he doesn't acknowledge me, I grab his wrist. "What does this get you? Come on!"

He looks at my hand and then looks up at me. For a moment I think he, too, senses the weird familiarity between us. Like we know each other from another life. He drops his phone in his pocket and takes my wrists. "You need to stop focusing on your beautiful life in there and start praying that Daddy decides to come through."

"Ow," I breathe.

"Good. That's you getting with the program. I'll do whatever I have to do to get my brother back. Do I want to hurt you? No. I don't. Will I?"

My heart races.

"Will I?"

"I get it," I whisper.

His grip is too tight, his gaze too intense, like he sees

everything inside me. People rarely look too hard at me. When they look at me at all, they accept the version of me I serve up to them. The shopaholic Mafia princess. The dedicated lawyer in glasses.

"Dad's innocent. He'd tell you if he knew anything else."

"Wrong, Kitten. *Dad's* playing the odds."

A ping sounds. He lets me go and pulls his phone out of his pocket. A twenty-first century general waging battle.

Whatever the person on the other ends has texted him, it troubles him.

That's my chance—I take off running, tearing for the main road.

I get maybe ten feet when guys seem to materialize around me, taking me by the shoulders. I twist and fight. They lift me right off the ground, practically carry me back.

The strangely familiar intruder is still on the phone, eyeing me with that intensity, watching me struggle. A model between photo shoots if you didn't know any better.

They put me back in front of him. He lowers the phone and addresses me quietly. "Do it. Go ahead, Mimi, do it again. See what happens."

Mimi.

He blinks, waiting. "Do it, go for it."

Mimi. Only one person ever called me Mimi—Aleksio Dragusha. My childhood friend. But Aleksio and his family were slaughtered by a rival clan back when we were kids. I was wild with grief. They had to sedate me.

Five caskets lowered into the ground. Three small, two large.

I focus on the familiar freckle on his cheekbone. This man is so much bigger. So much harder and meaner. But his freckle…his eyes… "Aleksio?" I say in a small voice.

"Ding ding ding, we have a winner." He says it off-handedly, keeping his eyes fixed on the mansion with its majestic stone wings. The house where he once lived. Prince of a mafia empire.

"Oh my God. Aleksio!"

Still he won't look at me.

"We thought you were dead. We buried you."

"You buried a few rocks. Maybe some boiled cabbages, who knows."

I can't believe he's being so…flip. "Aleksio! We buried you." I'm repeating myself. "I thought they killed you…" If my life were postcards on a bulletin board, the image of Aleksio Dragusha's casket being covered up with dirt would be central, affecting everything around it. He was my best friend. I doubt I was his. Aleksio had lots of friends. Everybody loved Aleksio. Back when he was a boy, anyway.

He focuses on his phone, running his soldiers.

"We went to your funeral. It was so, so…" *Sad* isn't the word. *Sad* barely touches it. We were adventurers together, bonded together, carving out a sunny niche inside a world of darkness and secrets we sensed but didn't understand. I think that's what made us friends— the feeling of being refugees at the edges of something evil.

"Aleksio, you're being crazy!"

"You need to stop thinking you know me." He lowers his voice to a threatening tone. "You knew me once, but I promise, you don't know me anymore."

Want to read more? DARK MAFIA PRINCE is available at Amazon.com, BarnesAndNoble.com, iBooks, and other book retailers.

Also by
Skye Warren

Endgame Trilogy & Masterpiece Duet
The Pawn
The Knight
The Castle
The King
The Queen

Underground Series
Rough Hard Fierce
Wild Dirty Secret
Sweet
Deep

Stripped Series
Tough Love
Love the Way You Lie
Better When It Hurts
Even Better
Pretty When You Cry
Caught for Christmas
Hold You Against Me
To the Ends of the Earth

Criminals and Captives standalones
Prisoner
Hostage

Standalone Dark Romance
Wanderlust
On the Way Home
His for Christmas
Hear Me
Take the Heat

Find a complete Skye Warren book list, along with
boxed sets, audiobooks, and print listings at
www.skyewarren.com/books

Also by Annika Martin
(aka Carolyn Crane)

Dangerous Royals
Dark Mafia Prince
Wicked Mafia Prince
Savage Mafia Prince

Criminals & Captives standalones
Prisoner
Hostage

Romantic Suspense
Against the Dark
Off the Edge
Into the Shadows
Behind the Mask

MM Spies
Enemies like You

Romantic Comedy
Most Eligible Bastard

Ultra dirty romantic comedy
The Hostage Bargain
The Wrong Turn
The Deeper Game
The Most Wanted
The Hard Way

About Skye Warren

Skye Warren is the New York Times bestselling author of contemporary romance such as the Chicago Underground and Stripped series. Her books have been featured in Jezebel, Buzzfeed, USA Today Happily Ever After, Glamour, and Elle Magazine. She makes her home in Texas with her loving family, two sweet dogs, and one evil cat.

Sign up for Skye's newsletter:
www.skyewarren.com/newsletter

Like Skye Warren on Facebook:
facebook.com/skyewarren

Join Skye Warren's Dark Room reader group:
skyewarren.com/darkroom

Follow Skye Warren on Instagram:
instagram.com/skyewarrenbooks

Visit Skye's website for her current booklist:
www.skyewarren.com

ABOUT ANNIKA MARTIN

Annika Martin (aka Carolyn Crane) loves dirty stories, hot heroes, and wild, dramatic everything. She enjoys hanging out in Minneapolis coffee shops with her writer husband and can sometimes be found birdwatching at her birdfeeder alongside her two stunningly photogenic cats. A NYT bestselling author, she has also written as RITA award-winning author Carolyn Crane.

Sign up for Annika's newsletter:
annikamartinbooks.com/newletter

Like Annika on Facebook:
www.facebook.com/AnnikaMartinBooks

Join the Annika Martin Fabulous Gang:
www.facebook.com/groups/AnnikaMartinFabulousGang
/

Follow Annika Martin on Instagram:
instagram.com/annikamartinauthor

Visit Annika's website:
www.annikamartinbooks.com

CPSIA information can be obtained
at www.ICGtesting.com
Printed in the USA
LVOW12s2323200318
570605LV00001B/141/P